"Every time I leave you I think…"

"What?" Nadya asked.

"That it's the right thing to do. The honorable thing. And then…"

"We both know all the arguments against it."

"And seem to have rejected them," Rhys said softly. "So that we're back to this."

"And what is *this?*"

"I don't know. All I know is that I've never felt about another woman the way I feel about you."

At one time hearing him make that confession would have meant everything to Nadya. Now she wondered if it were enough.

"What do you want from me, Rhys?"

"Whatever you're willing to give."

* * *

Claiming the Forbidden Bride
Harlequin® Historical #1008—September 2010

London, 1814

A season of secrets, scandal and seduction!

A darkly dangerous stranger is out for revenge, delivering a silken rope as his calling card. Through him, a long-forgotten scandal is reawakened. The notorious events of 1794, which saw one man murdered and another hanged for the crime, are ripe gossip in the ton. Was the right culprit brought to justice or is there a treacherous murderer still at large?

As the murky waters of the past are disturbed, so servants find love with roguish lords, and proper ladies fall for rebellious outcasts until, finally, the true murderer and spy is revealed.

· Regency Silk & Scandal

From glittering ballrooms to a Cornish smuggler's cove; from the wilds of Scotland to a Romany camp—join the highest and lowest in society as they find love in this thrilling new eight-book miniseries!

Gayle Wilson

CLAIMING THE FORBIDDEN BRIDE

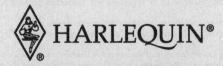

HARLEQUIN®

TORONTO • NEW YORK • LONDON
AMSTERDAM • PARIS • SYDNEY • HAMBURG
STOCKHOLM • ATHENS • TOKYO • MILAN • MADRID
PRAGUE • WARSAW • BUDAPEST • AUCKLAND

Recycling programs
for this product may
not exist in your area.

ISBN-13: 978-0-373-29608-8

CLAIMING THE FORBIDDEN BRIDE

Copyright © 2010 by Mona Gay Thomas

Printed in U.S.A.

Dear Reader,

I can't tell you how delighted I am to be a part of the Regency miniseries SILK & SCANDAL. Although I began my career writing Regency historicals, I have spent the past several years writing rather dark romantic suspense for HQN Books and MIRA Books. When I was asked to participate in this continuity series, I jumped at the chance to get back into Regency mode.

Little did I know, however, what a true joy it would be to work on this project. The other authors were so knowledgeable and always willing to offer advice and suggestions to someone who was a bit rusty on the period details. It was also great fun to toss ideas around while plotting the continuity elements together and to figure out how to make eight individual stories flow into a smooth and ever more exciting narrative. I could not have asked for a better experience in which to revisit my writing roots.

I hope you'll enjoy Rhys and Nadya's story as much as I enjoyed writing it. For a well-born English gentleman to fall in love with a beautiful Romany healer was certainly scandalous in society's view, but we all know that, despite Gypsy curses, murderous family secrets and vindictive brothers, true love will not be denied. I hope you find *Claiming the Forbidden Bride* a worthy addition to the books that came before it and an enticement to read those that follow. Look for *The Viscount and the Virgin* from Annie Burrows in SILK & SCANDAL. Coming October 2010.

Gayle

To grandmothers everywhere in honor and recognition of
their love and guidance and dedication.

And to my newest, very beloved grandbaby, Aidan

Prologue

In an unthinking response to the image in the cheval glass, Major the Honourable Rhys Morgan, late of His Majesty's 13th Light Dragoons, lifted his left hand to help the right in the adjustment of the intricately tied cravat at his throat. Pain seared along its damaged muscles and nerves, reminding him that, although he was finally home, the effects of the years he had spent campaigning on the Iberian Peninsula were still with him.

Incredibly, given the severity of his injuries—caused by a burst of grapeshot—the surgeons had managed to save his left arm. It was not the same, of course, and he had gradually become reconciled to the reality that it never would be.

A minor consideration, he reminded himself. He was glad to be alive. And infinitely grateful to be back in England.

This time, he used only his right hand to smooth over a persistent wrinkle that disturbed the line of his jacket. There had initially been some discussion of attempting alterations, but the scope of the required changes had proved those impractical. His chest was broader, for one thing; the muscles in his thighs and calves still hardened from long hours spent in the saddle. In addition to the debilitating effects of his wound, he had, since he'd been home, suffered another bout of the recurring fever he'd picked up on the Continent. As a result, his body was far leaner than it had been before his departure. In short, almost nothing he had left behind in England almost four years ago could be remade—not with the preciseness of fit that fashion demanded.

The local tailor had been called in to produce the coat of navy superfine he was wearing, as well as his striped waistcoat and close-fitting pantaloons. The tasselled Hessians that completed the ensemble were the only item that had been salvaged from his pre-service attire.

The garments were neither in the most current style nor constructed of the finest materials, but they would do for travel. Rhys had promised his brother that as soon as he arrived in London he would be properly outfitted from heel to crown by one of the capital's premier tailors.

A prospect he wasn't looking forward to, he acknowledged. Other than his surgeons, no one had yet been forced to view the carnage that had been inflicted on his body.

Determinedly putting that from his mind, he met his brother's eyes in the mirror. 'Shall I do?'

'Very nicely,' Edward said. 'At least until you have time to visit my man in London.'

Rhys smiled. 'If Keddinton doesn't turn me away from his door, the credit shall be yours.'

'He won't turn you away. You're his godson.'

'A godson he hasn't seen in more than five years.'

'That doesn't matter. Keddinton knows his duty.'

The word seemed to hang in the air between them, the crux of all the arguments that had marred the last few days. To break the suddenly awkward silence, Rhys returned his gaze to the reflection in the glass, tugging down his waistcoat.

'A few more days can't hurt,' Edward said after a moment.

'Unless the weather changes. Autumn can be unpredictable.'

'All the more reason—'

Laughing, Rhys turned to face his brother. 'One more day of sitting by the fire, Edward, and I promise you I shall go stark raving mad. You wouldn't want that on your conscience.'

'You *are* mad. Surely, you've done enough for King and country. *More* than enough.'

'I'm alive. Relatively sound of mind and body. And I've explored a great deal of geography during that service. Most of which, I remind you, is about to be carved up and redistributed in Vienna.'

'You can't expect Keddinton—'

'You'd be surprised how little I expect,' Rhys interrupted. 'I simply believe that my experiences during the last few years might prove valuable to *someone*. That's my hope, at least.'

It was a discussion they'd had several times during the previous month. One which had never satisfactorily been resolved on either side.

'You can be useful here.'

Rhys laughed again, putting his hand on his brother's shoulder. 'If I thought you really needed me, you know I'd stay. I owe you that and more. The truth of the matter is I should only get in the way of your very competent estate manager, and you know it.'

'You owe me nothing, Rhys. I hope *you* know *that*.'

Rhys pulled his brother close, embracing him for perhaps the first time in their lives. Older by a decade,

Edward had always seemed almost as distant as their father. Rhys had no doubt they both cared for him, but demonstrations of their affection had been few and far between.

'You'll forgive me if I disagree,' he said. 'You and Abigail have not only made me welcome, you have cared for me as if…' Rhys hesitated, searching for an analogy that would express his gratitude, without making the other man uncomfortable.

'As if you were my brother?' Edward's rare smile faded as quickly as it had appeared. 'My *only* brother, might I remind you. And having spent more than one night convinced you wouldn't live to see the sunrise, I confess a reluctance to let you out of my sight.'

'I managed to survive Boney's best efforts to eradicate me. I believe I may be trusted to make it all the way to London without incident.'

'Alone. *And* ridiculously on horseback,' Edward added, shaking his head.

'The saddest indictment of my boredom is that I'm looking forward to that journey immensely.'

He was. Despite the deep gratitude he felt toward his family, they had been determined to wrap him in cotton wool since his arrival at Balford Manor almost six months ago.

He'd endured his sister-in-law's potions and his brother's strictures until he'd wanted to throw the former at their collective heads. The thought of finally being free of their solicitous, if loving, supervision had done more for his spirits than had even the prospect of once more feeling his life had some meaning.

'Take care,' Edward urged. 'Promise me that you won't do anything foolish.'

'If there are highwaymen about, I shall toss them your

money with abandon. Believe me, Edward, I am *not* looking for adventure.'

Simply a little fresh air and anonymity. Both to be enjoyed with no one hovering over him.

He knew very well what the next argument advanced against this journey would be. It was one he had heard *ad infinitum* during the tedious days of his recuperation.

He didn't intend to listen to another injunction that he must guard his fragile health. Not today. Today was an opportunity to escape the confines of that familial concern.

'If I don't start now, however, I shall not make Buxton by nightfall. I don't fancy spending a night in the open. The dampness, you know.' Unable to resist, Rhys closed his right hand into a fist, which he tapped lightly against the centre of his chest.

Edward's eyes widened. He opened his mouth, but at the last second he came to his senses or perhaps he glimpsed the teasing light in his brother's eyes. In any case, Edward clamped his lips shut before he nodded.

'Off to adventure then,' Rhys said, gesturing his brother out of the chamber door ahead of him.

'Dear God, I hope not,' Edward muttered as he passed.

Rhys grinned again, but somewhere in the back of his mind was an acknowledgement that a small adventure would not come amiss. Perhaps he was not quite so ready for that promised boredom as he had imagined.

Chapter One

Rhys had kept the promise he'd given his brother about the leisurely pace of his journey. In actuality, the first day he'd spent in the saddle had reminded him of exactly how long it had been since he'd ridden any distance at all.

He had reached the inn at Buxton in the early afternoon, more than willing to continue the longer portion of his trip on the following day. His godfather's invitation, issued some weeks ago, had been open-ended, and despite Rhys's outward show of confidence, he had been concerned enough about his stamina to phrase his acceptance in like terms.

He was pleased that, despite the protest of sore muscles, he'd been up and on his way fairly early the next morning. The crisp autumn air had been an elixir for the ennui of the last few months. As had the beauty of the downs, still green despite the turning leaves.

A shout brought his mount's head up and Rhys's wandering attention back to the present. A young girl, screaming something unintelligible, ran across the meadow below him.

Instinctively his eyes swept the countryside behind her. There was no sign of pursuit.

Rhys's gaze then tracked across the area in front of the running girl, where he quickly discovered the object of her concern. A child, her long pale hair streaming behind her like a banner, flew across the rough ground.

His lips lifted in response, remembering his own childhood. A day such as this had too often lured him from his studies. He had been older than this little girl, and he had usually paid the price for his escapades with a hiding from his tutor, but he had always considered those rare tastes of freedom to have been well worth the pain.

Almost idly, he considered the landscape that stretched in front of the child. As he did, the reminiscent smile faded.

From his vantage point, it was apparent that the field she flew across ended abruptly at a steep escarpment, one of many scattered throughout the area. The land rose slightly just before its edge and then fell away as if sliced by a giant's knife. Below the drop-off, the shining surface of the rain-swollen stream glinted in the morning sun.

His eyes flicked back to the child, who was now toiling up the rise that led to the cliff. There was no way she could see what lay beyond. And no way, he realized, his gaze tracking backward, that the bigger girl running behind could intercept her before she reached the precipice.

As soon as he reached that conclusion, Rhys dug his heels into his mount's flanks. Startled, his brother's bay leaped forward, taking the slope at a dangerous pace. As soon as they reached the meadow, Rhys crouched low over the gelding's neck, urging him to an even greater speed. They raced diagonally across the expanse of flat ground, Rhys's eyes focused on that distant gleam of blonde hair.

Despite the best efforts of the horse, they seemed to move as slowly as in a dream. *Or a nightmare.*

The child came closer and closer to the edge as Rhys's

heart hammered in his ears, drowning out the pounding hooves of the beast that strained beneath him. He was aware almost subliminally that the older girl continued to scream, which had no more effect than before.

Rhys pressed his mount on, feeling its muscles begin to tremble beneath him. As he closed the distance between them, the object of his frantic chase evinced no awareness of his pursuit. She ignored horse and rider as completely as she ignored the importuning cries of her caregiver.

As the little girl neared the lip of the rise, Rhys balanced his weight to the left, preparing to lean down and pick her up on the run. He had no other choice. She would be over the edge before he had time to dismount. And despite the noise they were making, she still seemed oblivious to their approach.

Guiding his horse on a course parallel to the treacherous edge of the cliff, he leaned to the side as he drew near, stretching out his left arm.

Despite the pain of that movement, he was determined to grasp the child's clothing and snatch her away from danger. He added his own warning shouts to those of the nursemaid, but she continued to ignore both.

His heart lodged in his throat, Rhys knew it would be a matter of inches. One chance to catch hair or fabric before the child's headlong rush carried her over the cliff.

As he prepared for the attempt, the little girl turned, finally reacting to his presence. He watched her blue eyes stretch impossibly wide when she caught sight of the horse.

In that split second, Rhys's straining fingers touched the back of her dress. As she dodged away from his reaching hand, the ground beneath her seemed to give way, sending her tumbling over the edge.

The gelding was close enough to the precipice that

Rhys could feel the crumbling earth shift under its weight. Frantically, he turned his mount aside. As soon as they were back on solid ground, he pulled the horse up. He had dismounted before their forward motion stopped. Running back to the place where the child had disappeared, he peered over.

The height was not so great as he'd feared. Below him, caught in the slowly moving current, a foam of white petticoat was clearly visible. The girl's long hair, darkened by its immersion, floated behind.

He examined the bank, desperately searching for a way down. There was none. Other than that which the child had just taken.

His searching gaze found her again in time to see her disappear beneath the surface. Without another second's hesitation, Rhys jumped, following her into the water.

It was far colder than he had expected, even for September. He fought his way to the surface, the weight of his boots pulling against him.

As soon as his head broke free, he began to scan the surface. Kicking, stroking with both arms, unconscious now of the pain and the limited range of motion of the left, he kept himself afloat as he waited for the child's re-emergence.

As soon as he'd spotted her, he began to swim. He had always been a strong swimmer, but as during that frantic race across the meadow, he felt as if he were making little progress.

The little girl was being carried downstream by the current more swiftly than his one-sided stroke could propel him. If she went under again...

Frantic at that thought, he urged his tiring body to a greater effort, one he would not have believed possible only seconds before. There was no time to look for her. He swam by instinct, or by faith, and finally was rewarded.

The fingers of his right hand, extended to the limit of his arm's reach, touched something, only to have it slip away from his grasp. In some diminishing corner of rationality, he knew that what he'd felt might have been anything. A broken limb or some other piece of flotsam.

If it were, then all was lost. The only chance he had to rescue the child was if she were indeed the object his hand encountered. He knew she would not surface again.

Trusting once more to his instincts, Rhys dove beneath the surface, kicking with the last of his strength to force his body deeper. He opened his eyes, straining to see through the silt, and caught a glimpse of something that glittered before him like threads of gold.

He reached for them, strands of her hair gliding through his fingers as she continued to sink. Desperately he closed his fist around a handful.

Once his hold was secure, he began the laborious process of dragging himself and the drowning child to the surface. Sunlight beckoned from above. The same glint that had warned him before of danger now offered the promise of safety. If only he could reach it and then fight the current to shore.

His head finally broke the surface, his mouth open to draw in a gasping, shuddering lungful of air. At the same time, he awkwardly manoeuvered the child's body so that her face, too, was above the water.

She had appeared so small when viewed from above. Now her weight seemed more than his numbed arms and fading strength could manage.

He had come too far to turn back, he told himself, calling on the same determination that had seen him through every danger and deprivation the French could throw at him. He would get her out or die trying.

And he well might, he conceded, when his eyes found the nearer bank. The distance seemed overwhelming, as did the child's weight.

He glanced down at her face. Translucent eyelids, through which he could see a delicate cobweb of veins, hid the blue eyes. The water spiked colourless lashes, which lay like fans against the paleness of her cheeks. Her lips, blue with cold, were open, but no breath stirred between them.

Rhys had seen death more times than he could bear to remember, but never that of a child. And despite the damning evidence before him, he was unwilling to concede this one.

If he hadn't startled her, perhaps she wouldn't have taken that final step toward the edge. Her death would be on his hands, something he was unwilling to live with for the rest of his life.

There was nothing he could do for her here. Her only chance—his only chance—was if he could get her to shore.

Lungs aching with cold and fatigue, he forced his damaged arm around the child's midriff. Then he leaned to his right, almost lying on his side in the water. Using his good arm, he laboriously began to swim toward the bank.

The girl lay practically atop his body, but his hold on her was precarious. Several times he had to stop and grasp her more firmly around the waist. The second time he did, she stirred, coughing a little.

That small sign of life gave him a renewed burst of courage, and he continued to pull himself and his burden across the deadly swiftness of the current. He refused to look at the shore, afraid that the distance remaining would defeat the thread of determination, all that sustained him now. That and the thought that if he let this little girl die, her blood would be eternally on his hands.

He was almost too exhausted to realize what had

happened when his hand made contact with the bottom. He turned his head and saw that only a few feet separated him from his goal.

He allowed his feet to drift downward, feeling the silt shift beneath them. Holding the girl now in both arms, he dragged himself from the water. Staggering under the weight of his burden and his own exhaustion, he had taken only a couple of steps onto the verge before his knees gave way.

He attempted to break his fall, but his left hand slid across the slick rocks, throwing him forward. Unable to use his right arm, which was still wrapped around the child, to cushion his landing, his temple struck one of the stones.

The girl he had carried from the water rolled out of his arm to lie beside him. Wide blue eyes, opened now and staring into his, were the last thing he saw before the world faded into oblivion.

Nadya Argentari watched her grandmother sort through the goods in the peddler's wagon. The quick movements of her gnarled fingers expressed contempt for their quality, but the three of them understood that was part of the timeless ritual in which they were engaged. Items would be selected, bartered for and finally accepted with the same lack of enthusiasm the old woman displayed while assessing them.

Having watched this process a hundred times, Nadya lifted her eyes to survey the somnolent encampment. She realized only now that, while she'd been helping her grandmother, the sun had slipped very low in the sky.

Anis should have brought Angel home long before now. Almost before the knot of anxiety had time to form in her chest, Nadya saw the fair hair of her daughter catch the dappled light under the beech trees as she and the girl who had been instructed to take her for a walk moved toward the centre of the Romany camp.

Nadya raised her hand to wave. Angel broke away from her caretaker, running toward her mother and great-grand-mother. She threw herself against Nadya's legs, burying her face in her skirts. Laughing, Nadya put her hand on the little girl's head, running her fingers through the colour-less silk of her hair.

'Did you have a good walk?' she asked, raising her eyes to the twelve-year-old who trailed behind her charge.

The older girl nodded, her eyes shifting quickly to the old woman, who was still occupied with her examination of the goods in the cart. 'I need to help my mother now. If that's all right, *drabarni*,' she added deferentially.

Nadya was accustomed to such deference. After all, the Argentari were one of the *kumpania's* most prominent families, and her own reputation as a healer was unsur-passed among their people.

Nadya had almost nodded permission before she began to wonder why the girl was in such a hurry to be away. Her earlier anxiety resurfaced, causing her to pry her daughter's fingers from her skirt so that she could get a good look at the little girl's face.

The smudges on Angeline's dress and her disordered hair didn't concern her. Released from the confines of the camp, her daughter tended to run wild through the fields that lay just beyond the great forest. Perhaps she'd fallen, and Anis was afraid she would be blamed for the accident.

'Did something happen during your walk?'

The older girl's downcast eyes flew upward. Her mouth opened and then closed, but eventually she shook her head.

'Then why are you lying to the *drabarni*?'

Until her grandmother's question, Nadya hadn't realized

Magda was listening to this. She knew the old woman would be angry to have her bargaining interrupted. Still, Magda had grown to love her great-granddaughter with a fervour that almost matched Nadya's own.

'You think she's lying?' Alerted by her grandmother's observation, Nadya examined the girl's face.

Anis's gaze darted from one to the other, but it was Magda she answered, as befitted the old woman's esteemed position in the tribe. 'Nothing happened. I swear it, *chivani*.'

'Be careful what you swear to, little one. Tell the truth, and I'll see to it that no blame comes to you.'

'Don't make promises you can't keep,' Nadya warned, kneeling to examine her daughter more carefully.

By now she had recognized that her grandmother was right. For some reason the girl who'd been instructed to look after Angeline was lying.

As Nadya put her hands on her daughter's shoulders, what she had failed to notice earlier became apparent. The child's clothing was damp.

'Why is this wet?' she demanded.

Anis licked her lips. Her eyes moved again to Magda. Whatever warning or promise of succour she saw there convinced her to tell the truth. 'Because she fell into the water.'

For a moment, the words made no sense. The only stream within walking distance ran through the small gorge it had cut into the chalk cliffs.

'Fell? How could she possibly fall into the water?' Even as she posed the question, Nadya's hands were busy feeling along her daughter's small, delicate body, searching for injuries.

When she raised her gaze again, reassured that the child was apparently undamaged, despite her misadventure, the older girl had begun to cry, tears coursing down her reddened cheeks.

'I asked how she fell.'

'She started running, *drabarni*. Across the meadow. I couldn't catch her. I tried, *chivani*,' she added, pleading her case now to Magda. 'I didn't think about the stream. I didn't think she could run that far.'

'And she just ran to the cliff edge and fell off?'

The girl hesitated, but her eyes had returned to Nadya's face. Finally she nodded.

Relieved that what could have been a terrible tragedy seemed to have ended with no ill effects, Nadya pulled her daughter close, once more made aware of the state of her garments. She rose, intending to carry the little girl to her caravan to get her into something dry.

'And you pulled her out?' Magda's tone was of interest only and not the least accusatory. 'How very brave of you. Perhaps I should give you a reward for taking such good care of my *chaveske chei*.'

The older girl's head moved slowly from side to side. Her eyes never left Magda's, mesmerized by the old woman's tone as the cobra is fascinated by the music of the snake charmer.

'No?' Magda asked kindly. 'You don't deserve a reward?'

The side-to-side motion was repeated.

'Because someone else pulled her from the water,' Magda suggested softly. 'Isn't that the truth of this?'

The answer was clear in the girl's eyes even before she nodded. Although she was celebrated for her fortune-telling abilities, Nadya knew that whatever gift Magda had been born with was augmented by a keen understanding of human nature. She had read the truth behind the girl's lies as if it had been written in a book.

'Who?' Nadya demanded.

As if she had been following the conversation, Angeline took her mother's hand and pulled, urging her to go with her. The wide blue eyes shifted from Nadya's face to the line of beeches from which the two girls had emerged.

Then, with her free hand, the child made the first sign Nadya had ever taught her. The one that carried the strongest possible warning she could ever have given her daughter.

Gadje. The word used to indicate anyone not Romany.

Nadya's eyes met her grandmother's. The old woman lifted her brows as if to ask, 'What will you do now?'

'Did you see him? The *gaujo*?' Even as Nadya questioned the older girl, Angeline tugged at her hand, trying to draw her toward the woods.

'She didn't want to leave him. She made us stay by him all afternoon,' Anis said, 'but he was too heavy to move.'

As Nadya struggled to make sense of the words, she realized that she was dealing with someone who was little more than a child herself. Someone into whose care she had foolishly trusted her daughter.

'Are you saying that the man who saved Angel was injured? And you left him there?'

'I tried to wake him, *drabarni*.' The girl scrubbed at her tear-stained cheeks with grubby knuckles. 'But it was late. I knew we should get back or you'd be angry.'

'So you left him.'

'He's *gadje*,' the child said dismissively. 'Let them look after him.'

'What if he'd said that about Angel?'

'But *drabarni*, she's…' The words the girl had been about to offer in her own defence died unspoken.

'Can you take me to him?'

Looking after this *gaujo* wasn't a responsibility Nadya

wanted. Nor was it one she would ever have sought, despite her skills.

Whatever else the injured man was, however, he was apparently Angeline's saviour. Seeing to his safety was an obligation she couldn't refuse. Not according to tribal law.

Or, she acknowledged, her own sense of right and wrong.

Chapter Two

Darkness had fallen before they reached the escarpment where Angeline had fallen. Under Nadya's direction, the men of the tribe had come prepared for that eventuality. Their hand-held torches led the way for the small procession that followed them down the steep slope to the stream.

The light, horse-drawn cart they had brought to carry the *gaujo*, living or dead, back to camp had been left at the top. Under Nadya's watchful eye, they searched the bank of the stream, softly calling directions to one another in the stillness of the sleeping countryside.

Angeline had refused to be left behind. She'd screamed uncontrollably, seemingly inconsolable, until Nadya had relented. Now she huddled against her mother's skirts, eyes wide as she watched the searchers.

Anis, who had been brought to give directions, stood off to one side. She seemed reluctant to get near enough to Nadya to chance the punishment the girl still feared would be inflicted.

Although she had been angry at first, by now Nadya had acknowledged that what happened wasn't Anis's fault. The responsibility for this near disaster lay squarely on her shoulders for trusting someone else to look after her daughter. That was her job—her joy—and the thought of what might have happened…

'We found him, *drabarni*.'

The shout prevented her from having to acknowledge that terrible what-might-have-been. Taking Angel's hand, she hurried to the place where the men were gathered around something on the ground. Sparks from their torches swirled in the wind.

'Is he alive?' Her voice sounded tremulous in her own ears.

'For now. Whether he'll stay that way…' The shrug that accompanied Andrash's comment seemed as heartless as the flash of his white teeth revealed by the torchlight. What did he care about a *gaujo*, even one who'd saved the life of a little girl?

'What do you want us to do with him?' Nicolaus asked as four of them hefted the man's limp body between them, carrying it as they would have a boar they'd killed in the forest.

Although her grandmother would disapprove, Nadya knew there was only one answer. 'Take him to my caravan.'

Her instructions didn't cause even a raised brow among the men. After all, that's where she had cared for Nicolaus when he'd broken his arm and where she had stitched up the knife wound in Michael's shoulder.

The *vardo* was also where she kept all of her remedies. At least until she knew what she was dealing with, it was the only possible place for the injured *gaujo*.

As the men passed by, Panuel leading the way with two of the torches, Nadya caught a glimpse of the face of the man they carried. The flickering firelight seemed to emphasize his features: high cheekbones, reddened now with the cold; an almost roman nose; and an equally strong chin. She found herself wondering about the colour of his eyes and his hair, darkened now by the water.

As the small cavalcade began to struggle up the slope, a tug on her skirt brought Nadya's gaze down to her daughter, who was standing at her knee. The tear tracks beneath her eyes were exposed by the same torchlight that had illuminated the injured man's countenance.

Nadya smiled at the little girl as she nodded reassurance. Then, unable to resist the impulse, despite the child's disobedience to Anis and the tantrum she'd thrown at the threat of being left behind, Nadya bent and put one arm around the small shoulders, pulling Angel close.

'It's all right,' she said aloud. With the thumb of her other hand she made a soothing gesture along the child's cheek. 'We'll fix him.' Leaning back, Nadya added another smile to the words her daughter couldn't hear.

With the reassurance of her mother's touch, the concern in the blue eyes melted away. Their focus shifted to the older girl. Seeing the direction of her daughter's gaze, Nadya tilted her chin upward, giving permission.

The child ran to where Anis stood, her arms wrapped tightly around her thin body. Angeline tugged at the older girl's hand until she bent down. Then the child drew her tiny thumb along Anis's cheek, repeating the gesture her mother had made.

As she watched the scene, a reluctant smile tugged at Nadya's lips. Whatever heartache this little one had known, it was clear all was now right in her world.

And thanks to the actions of the unknown *gaujo*, in Nadya's as well.

She owed her daughter's life to the man being carried up the slope to the waiting cart. Whatever she had to do in order to satisfy that debt, she vowed it would be paid.

* * *

When the men had deposited the *gaujo* on the bed at the front of the caravan, they stood in its narrow aisle, awaiting Nadya's instructions. If she asked them, they would remove his wet clothing, but she found that, despite the shivers that now occasionally racked his body, she would rather do all that herself.

There was little room in her profession for prudishness. Not when lives were at stake. That was the first thing her paternal grandmother, who had been *drabarni* before her, had taught her. The mysteries of the human body. *All of them.*

'Thank you,' she said to the men without looking up.

'You want us to help you undress him, *drabarni*?'

'I'm not sure how badly he's injured. Maybe it would be better if I determine that first.'

'As you wish, *drabarni*. Call us when you need us.'

She had asked Anis to take Angeline to Magda for the night, so that, as the last of her helpers exited her caravan, she found herself alone with the Englishman. She bent over the platform bed she had converted for her patients' use from what had once been her father's workbench.

Thom Argentari had been a silversmith of great renown, even in the world of the *gadje*. He had bought this caravan from a travelling showman in order to have a safe place to keep his tools and the precious gemstones and metals with which he worked. At his death, the *vardo* had passed to Nadya.

As soon as she'd entered tonight, she had lit the lamp that provided light for the front of the caravan. Now, as she moved it to the table at the head of the bed, her initial impression of the injured man's features was verified.

The *gaujo* would be considered handsome by any standards. Even, she acknowledged, her too exacting ones.

Dismissing that evaluation from her mind, she gently turned his face into the lamplight, examining it for injuries. She found what she had expected, given his prolonged unconsciousness, above his left temple. The gash no longer bled, but with a blow to the head, she knew that whatever was going on beneath the skin was often more serious than what was visible.

Carefully, using only the sensitive tips of her fingers, she felt the area around the cut. Then, using the same method, she traced over the rest of his skull, searching for the telltale signs of fracture as her grandmother had taught her.

When she straightened, this part of her examination complete, it was with a sense of relief. She had felt no breaks in the bone that protected the brain. As for his continuing unconsciousness…

She shook her head, still puzzled by that. Then she directed the same careful attention she'd given his head to the rest of his body. She felt along his torso and then down each extremity, looking for damage, which her experienced fingers would quickly identify. Once more she discovered nothing.

Now she sat down on the edge of the bed beside her patient. She struggled a moment to understand the intricate folds of the knotted cloth at his neck, but was soon able to pull it free. When she had, she pushed aside the edges of his shirt to expose his throat.

She placed her fingers against the pulse in his neck, reassured by its strong and steady beat. After a moment, she raised her hand to put the back of it against his forehead.

The heat she found there confirmed her suspicions. Since she had found no other injury that would explain his condition, the *gaujo* was obviously developing a fever, undoubtedly the result of exposure after his immersion in the icy water.

As she began to take off the rest of his garments, she tamped down a renewed sense of outrage at the girl who had left him, injured and alone, on its banks. Quickly discovering the impossibility of removing his coat, given the fashionable snugness of its fit, she briefly considered sending for her helpers. Instead, in the interest of efficiency, she used the tip of a knife to slit the seams, removing it in pieces and then the waistcoat.

She decided that, with its looser fit, she should be able to take off his shirt by slitting it from the deep neck opening to the hem. Once that was done, she eased his right arm from its sleeve by the simple expedient of rolling his body slightly toward the front of the bed as she'd worked the material off.

That accomplished, she slipped her arm under his left shoulder in order to push his torso in the opposite direction, which would then allow her to remove the other sleeve. As soon as she applied pressure, he moaned, the sound low and anguished, as inarticulate as an animal in pain.

Startled, Nadya glanced up to find his eyes were still closed. Perhaps this shoulder had been dislocated when he'd jumped into the water. That could be remedied easily enough, although she would have to call the men back in to hold him while she manipulated the joint into place.

She eased him down against the bed and then pushed aside his shirt. As soon as she did, she realized the injury that had caused him to cry out in pain had been inflicted long before his rescue of Angeline. Hardened by years of dealing with the variety of wounds and accidents suffered by members of the tribe, she was still shocked by the extent of the scarring. Was it possible he still had the use of his arm after such damage?

She pushed his sleeve upward, revealing that the muscle

in both the lower and upper arm appeared almost normal. Despite whatever had happened to him, the limb hadn't atrophied. Manipulating his shoulder more carefully now, she managed to remove the shirt without provoking any other outcry.

As she tucked a dry blanket around her patient, she bent to take another look at the cut on his head. There was still no swelling, and the clot seemed to be holding.

Other than that, she had found no evidence of new injuries. In an older person, she might suspect an inflammation of the lungs. In someone his age, who seemed to be in relatively good physical condition, that seemed unlikely.

All she could do tonight was watch over him. If his fever increased, there were remedies for that, even if she was unsure of its cause.

In her very limited experience with prolonged unconsciousness, there were only two possible outcomes. He would wake up on his own, his faculties intact. If he didn't, eventually he would die. And despite all her grandmother's careful teaching, Nadya knew of nothing that could tip the scales toward the more favourable outcome.

As she had expected, due to the rapid onset of symptoms, her patient's fever began to climb during the night. She knew that her English colleagues, with the advantage of their medical degrees, would at this point begin a very rigidly proscribed course of treatment. The patient would be bled and then blistered. If the fever did not abate, both remedies would be repeated until it did. Or until he died.

Nadya instituted instead a regimen she had learned from her grandmother. She'd had the men remove the rest of his clothing, and then, despite the night chill, she pulled the blankets they had put over the Englishman down to his waist. Using a cloth dipped into a basin of water drawn from the barrel that served as the camp's cistern, she bathed his face, neck and torso.

At first, his shivering had increased, so strongly that at one point his teeth rattled with the strength of the tremors. He tossed and turned, as if trying to escape the discomfort of what she was doing, but she persisted.

On the morning of the third day, when the congestion of the lungs she feared had not materialized, she added another of her grandmother's remedies to the treatment. With endless patience she dribbled tea brewed from her small supply of a dried bark, supposedly acquired from some medicinal tree in Peru, between his parched lips.

At some point during her vigil, the Englishman's inarticulate noises had become words. Uttered in the throes of delirium, they made no sense to Nadya, but she listened as he called names and issued directives to the phantoms he seemed to believe had gathered around his bed.

Finally, near dawn on the sixth day, her efforts were rewarded by the formation of a dew of perspiration along his upper lip. Exhausted, unable to remember the last time she had eaten a complete meal or slept for more than a few restless hours, Nadya discarded her basin and cloth as the rays of the sun crept steadily into the caravan.

She sat down on the low stool beside her patient's bed and laid the back of her hand against the *gaujo's* brow, which was as cool as her own. Now that the fever was broken, his body would attempt to heal itself through sleep. Not the restless, fever-induced unconsciousness of the last few days, but a restorative rest that would almost certainly last for several hours.

Since it was safe to leave him, she would ask Magda or one of the other women to sit with him. She needed something to eat. And after she'd seen Angel, a few blessed hours of uninterrupted sleep for herself.

Rhys opened his eyes and then quickly closed them against the light that had seemed to stab through them, like a knife thrust into his brain. On some level, he realized that he had been aware of the agony in his head for a long time. Finally, its persistence had dragged him from sleep.

He had a vague memory of being carried from the field, but he couldn't think what battle they'd been engaged in. As adjutant, he should certainly know, but in spite of his struggle to remember, there was nothing about any of that left in his consciousness.

Perhaps that was because there was room there for nothing but pain. And a thirst so profound it was almost worse than the other.

He tried to swallow, but his mouth was too dry. Even in the makeshift field hospitals set up near the lines, someone always brought water to those awaiting treatment. If he could only make them aware of his need…

He dragged leaden eyelids upward again, but more cautiously this time. Through the slits he allowed, he saw that what he had avoided before was a single candle. And that its light was not bright at all.

He turned his head, trying to locate one of the orderlies or even a surgeon. A shard of the previous agony sliced through his skull.

He clenched his lips against the resultant wave of nausea, one so severe it threatened his determination never to move again. Hardly daring to breathe, he willed himself not to be sick.

He tried to think of something—anything—other than the overwhelming urge to vomit. And finally, in his travail, realized that in the split second his eyes had been open, some still-functioning part of his brain had recognized that, wherever he was, it was like no hospital he'd ever seen.

And like nowhere else he'd ever been.

Curiosity engendered by that realization was almost enough to quell his roiling stomach. His eyelids again opened a slit, and for the third time, he peered out between his lashes.

The light was definitely a candle. It had been pushed into a twisted holder made of some unidentifiable metal, blackened with age or use.

Beyond was a blur of colour, reds and golds predominating. He turned his head another fraction of an inch in an attempt to bring his surroundings into better focus.

The wall opposite where he lay was so close that, if he had had the strength, he could probably have stretched out his arm and touched it. And every inch of it, from floor to ceiling, was crowded with objects.

He allowed his gaze to follow their upward climb, trying to identify what was there. Baskets, woven of vine and stacked full of what appeared to be dried roots. Earthenware crocks, their tops sealed with wax. Glass jars whose contents were indistinguishable, dark and strangely shaped. And sitting incongruously in the middle of what he had now realized were a series of shelves was a rag doll, exactly like those sold in every penny shop in England.

England.

He was no longer in Spain, he knew with a flash of clarity. He hadn't been for months.

If that were true...

He raised his right hand to touch his face. Clean-shaven. Which must mean he'd been here—wherever here was—only a short time.

His gaze came back to the table. A measuring cup and a small medicine bottle stood near its edge.

A memory swam to the surface of his consciousness. A pair of long, slender fingers had poured out a measure of the liquid the bottle contained. Then a hand had slipped behind his head, raising it enough to allow him to swallow the dose. He tried desperately to retrieve the image of the face of the person who had administered the medication, but the only thing he could remember after that was the same searing pain he had experienced a few minutes ago.

He closed his eyes, releasing the breath he'd been holding in a long, slow sigh. Something moved against his leg. He opened his eyes to see what and realized gratefully that the pain in his head was less than before.

A little girl, perhaps four or five, stood beside his bed. Her eyes, the exact colour of the hyacinths that bloomed in his sister-in-law's garden, were surrounded by long, nearly colourless lashes. In contrast, the unbound hair that framed her face seemed almost golden in the candlelight.

When she saw that his eyes were open, the child's mouth rounded into an O of surprise. Clearly his visitor hadn't expected him to be awake. Which made him wonder how many times she'd stood at his bedside as he slept.

''Lo.' His voice was little more than a croak, which made him remember his thirst.

The Cupid's bow lips rounded even more. Then the child whirled and disappeared from his sight.

Rhys resisted the urge to follow her movement, remembering what that curiosity might cost him. Instead, he allowed his eyelids to fall once more.

Although there had been no physical activity during this brief period of wakefulness, he was aware of an almost terrifying sense of fatigue. Maybe he'd been wrong about the fever. Maybe someone had shaved him. Or maybe…

Suddenly, trying to piece together what might have happened became too difficult. And far less important than the sleep that again claimed him.

Chapter Three

'Wake up, *chavi.*'

At the childhood term of endearment her grandmother still used for her, Nadya opened her eyes to find the old woman bending over the bed. Her first thought was that something had happened to her patient.

'Is his fever up?'

'No, no. That one's fine.'

'Then why aren't you with the *gaujo*? You promised you'd watch him.'

'Angel is watching him.'

'Angel?' Nadya struggled to clear the cobwebs from her brain as she sat up. She had no idea how long she'd been asleep. All she knew with any certainty was that it hadn't been nearly long enough. 'I don't understand.'

'Stephano's back. I thought you would want to know.'

Although he was the *Rom Baro*, titular head of their *kumpania*, her half-brother had spent most of this year away from camp. And since Nadya had no doubt what his feelings would be about the Englishman she was caring for, to have Stephano unexpectedly show up now, with her patient on the verge of recovery, seemed the height of irony.

'Have you told him about the *gaujo*?'

Nadya knew that if Magda hadn't, she soon would. The old woman shared a bond with her grandson stronger even than that between the two of them.

'He's just arrived. I came to let you know while the others are welcoming him home.'

'Someone's bound to tell him.'

'Of course they will, *chavi*. It's his right to be told what has gone on here in his absence.'

'That should take a while,' Nadya said bitterly.

She flung her covers off and then ran her fingers through her hair as she tried to think. Her reasons for succouring her daughter's rescuer were valid, but Stephano harboured a deep-seated hatred of all *gadje*, especially those belonging to the same social class as his English father.

To Nadya, that made the fact that Stephano chose to live among them rather than with his mother's people more incomprehensible. Of course, her half-brother had been reared as a privileged member of that world for most of his childhood. In her opinion, the bitterness he felt for the *gadje* had far more to do with the interruption of that idyllic existence than did his Romany blood.

'What are you going to do?' Magda asked as Nadya threw her shawl around her shoulders.

'See to my patient, who has apparently been left in the charge of a four-year-old.'

Nadya had hoped to return to her own caravan before her half-brother came looking for her, but as she descended the high steps of her grandmother's *vardo*, she saw Stephano coming across the compound. His long stride checked when he spotted her.

'We need to talk,' he called.

'Later. I have something important to see to.' Pretending to believe that would satisfy him, she wrapped her shawl more tightly around her shoulders and continued on her path.

She had no doubt Stephano would follow, but at least this way their confrontation wouldn't be witnessed by the entire camp. As she hurried toward her wagon, head lowered against the bite of the evening wind, she almost ran into her daughter.

Angel grabbed a handful of her skirt, tugging at it imperiously. With one finger she pointed in the direction of the caravan they shared. Then, looking back up to make sure she had her mother's attention, the little girl closed her eyes very tightly and before opening them wide again.

Apparently the Englishman was awake. Just in time to be introduced to her arrogant half-brother, Nadya thought resignedly.

A hand on her shoulder, as demanding as her daughter's had been on her skirts, turned her. The sight of Stephano's furious face drove any other consideration from her mind. Clearly, it hadn't taken as long as she'd hoped for someone to share with him all that had happened while he was away.

Stephano opened his mouth, but Angel's headlong rush toward him postponed whatever invective he'd been prepared to spew. His dark eyes flashed a warning to Nadya that this wasn't the end of it before he bent to pick the little girl up and toss her high into the air. When he caught her, Angel wrapped both arms around his neck, hugging her uncle with delight.

'Someone's glad to see me.' He looked pointedly at Nadya over her daughter's shoulder.

'I'm glad to see you. Actually, it's been so long since you've graced us with your presence, I'd almost forgotten what you look like.'

'Or perhaps you were too busy with other, more pressing concerns to think about me,' he suggested with a mocking smile.

'We all must be busy with something, I suppose.'

After her lightly veiled reference to Stephano's mysterious affairs, she turned to continue walking toward her caravan, knowing he would follow. And every step he took lessened the odds that the others would overhear his tirade.

Of course, their grandmother had been correct. Stephano had every right to question her actions. Or those of any member of the *kumpania*.

Thus far, however, none of the others had seemed to find anything strange about what she'd been doing. And until the Englishman was well enough to leave, she had wished for nothing more devoutly than to keep it that way.

'Why in God's name would you do this?'

That demanding voice dragged Rhys reluctantly from sleep. He opened his eyes, instinctively searching for whoever had asked that question. Although it seemed he was now able to turn his head without setting off a cataclysm of pain, he couldn't locate the speaker.

'Because he saved Angel's life,' a woman said. 'What would you have done?'

The answering shout of laughter was harsh. Full of derision. And clearly male.

Two voices. The feminine one low, almost musical. The other, the derisive one, was different somehow. A difference not only in tone and volume.

Rhys tried to piece together the clues that had led him to that conclusion. Only when he realized the argument he was eavesdropping on concerned him, did he give up that frustrating process.

'What would I have done? I should have wondered briefly at his motives,' the masculine voice mocked, 'and then forgotten him.'

'I don't believe even you are that cynical.'

'Cynical enough to know that no *gadje* means us well.'

'He saved my daughter's life.'

'Angel isn't your daughter.'

'In every way that matters. Don't judge me by their standards.'

The masculine laughter this time was softer. No longer derisive. 'You're right. You aren't one of them. But he is. The sooner he's gone, the better for all of us.'

'What if I tell you he's my guest?' In their culture guests were treated with great courtesy, given the finest food and drink, even if that might be a hardship for the host.

'I'd say that he's been your guest long enough. I want him away from here.'

'He isn't well enough—'

'Then let his own care for him. Get rid of him, Nadya. I mean it.'

'Yes, *my lord*. Of course, *my lord*.' The feminine voice had now adopted the ripe sarcasm of the other. Her assumed humility dripped with it. 'What else can I, a poor Gypsy girl, do to please his lordship?'

'Stop it.' Anger this time, rather than mockery.

'I don't tell you what you should do, Stephano. You do what you feel you must. I understand that. So remember, please, that I'm not yours to command.'

'Get rid of him.' The man's voice was deadly quiet. Whatever raillery had been between the two had faded into animosity. 'Or had you rather I arrange that myself before I leave?' he asked silkily.

'If you do,' the woman said, 'you'll be sorry.'

'Is that a threat, *jel'enedra*?'

'I don't make threats. *You* of all people should know *that*.'

The silence that followed lasted long enough that Rhys had time to wonder if the quarrelling pair had moved out of earshot.

'Get rid of him, Nadya,' the man said. 'Or I'll do it when I return. I don't want that *gaujo* here. And I still have the authority here to see to it that what I want happens. *You* of all people should know *that*.'

A slight movement of the surface on which Rhys rested awakened him. Somewhere a door creaked open—a sound he knew he'd heard before. No light came into the room, but a whiff of wood smoke drifted inside before it closed.

Rhys's eyes strained against the darkness, trying to get a glimpse of the person who'd entered. The sound of a flint being struck across the room preceded the faint glow of a candle.

He lay perfectly still, waiting for the person who'd lit it to move into his field of vision. As the light came closer, his heart rate increased slightly, driven by curiosity about the owner of the feminine voice he'd heard outside.

Her back to the bed, the woman set the candlestick down on the table where it had rested earlier. Curling black hair, held back by a kerchief, cascaded down her spine. The shawl around her shoulders was intricately patterned, its rich colours glowing faintly in the candlelight.

Finally she turned, reaching out to touch his forehead. Her hand hesitated in mid-air when she realized his eyes were open. As the long seconds ticked by, silently they regarded one another.

The mocking phrase 'poor Gypsy girl' had prepared

Rhys for much of what he now saw. Nothing, however, could have prepared him for the effect of the rest.

A few dusky curls escaped the restraining kerchief to cluster around the perfect oval of her face. Her skin, like the colours of the shawl, was almost luminous in the candle's glow. Only the almond-shaped eyes, as black as her hair, hinted at the ethnic claim she had made during the argument he'd overheard.

Finally she swallowed, the candlelight tracing the movement down the slender column of her throat. 'You're awake.'

'I don't know. I think so.'

His meaning was ambiguous, even to him, but the corners of her lips curved upward. Coal-black lashes quickly fell to hide the laughter in her eyes, which she controlled before she looked up at him again.

'Good.' The hand she had begun to extend completed its journey, resting cool and light against his brow.

Something peculiar happened to Rhys's breathing. The normal functioning of his heart and lungs seemed to hesitate for the first time in the thirty-two years of his existence. After a moment, the Gypsy removed her hand, allowing both to resume their normal rhythm.

'No fever.' Her pronouncement held a trace of satisfaction, as if she were somehow responsible for that.

He nodded agreement, and then realized he still had no idea why he was here—or even where here was. A dozen questions formed in his brain, but she turned away from the bed before his befuddled mind could frame them.

When she came back, the slim fingers he'd remembered held the medicine cup again. As she had before, she slipped her hand under the back of his head, lifting it enough to allow him to sip the liquid it contained.

The taste was bitter, almost numbing his tongue with its astringency. At least this time that, rather than the agony in his head, was his primary sensation. Relieved, he swallowed the remainder of the potion, realizing only after the fact that she might have been giving him anything.

'Water?' he requested hoarsely.

'Of course.'

Again she moved out of his line of sight, giving him a brief respite from emotions that had been running rampant since the moment she'd appeared in front of him. Too long without a woman, his friends would have jeered. Time to think about settling down, his brother would have advised. Smitten, Abigail would have proclaimed smugly, just as she had when he'd obediently fetched punch at a country dance for the prospective bride she'd chosen for him.

Perhaps all of those things were true. Or perhaps his brain was merely addled by the pain in his head or by another attack of fever. Still, whatever had happened in the last few moments had been quite beyond his experience.

Smitten. He had never been completely sure what that term meant. Other than that someone was about to become an object of ridicule to his fellows.

The strange thing was he didn't feel ridiculous at all. What he felt was as alien as his surroundings. Territory as unexplored as any he'd encountered during the long years he'd spent in Iberia.

'Here.'

He lifted his eyes to find the girl leaning over his bed again. Once more she slipped her hand beneath his head, raising it as she placed a horn cup against his lips. He swallowed gratefully, the coolness of the water relieving the seemingly constant dryness of his throat.

As he drank, he was aware of her closeness. A strand of midnight hair had fallen over her shoulder to rest against his pillow. It smelled of sunshine.

She lowered the rim of the cup when he'd finished all it contained. 'Enough?'

He nodded. 'Thank you.'

'How are you feeling?'

'Disoriented,' he answered truthfully. 'Where are we?'

There was a moment's hesitation. 'You're in my home. Which at the moment happens to be in the middle of Harpsden Wood.'

'At the moment?'

'I fear you've fallen among the Rom, my lord. My home is on wheels.'

Fallen among the Rom...

Which made it sound as if he'd come here through some misadventure. Try as he might, he couldn't remember what that could have been.

'Had I been overcome by fever?'

'And a blow to the head.' With her thumb she touched a place on his temple, causing him to flinch.

The movement was too sudden, setting off the now-familiar peal of anvils against his skull. He closed his eyes, knowing that all he could do was endure until the pain and the nausea had faded.

'I'm sorry. I should have known better. I can give you something for the pain.'

She began to turn, but before she could complete the motion, his fingers fastened around her wrist. 'No.'

He'd had experience with the drugs the doctors gave to deaden pain. And far more memorable experiences with learning to do without them. He could better endure the ache in his head than endure that again.

Her eyes had widened at his command, but she didn't argue. Nor did she pull her arm away.

'As you wish,' she said simply and then waited.

After a moment Rhys found the presence of mind to release her. Even after she'd gone, however, taking the candle with her, it seemed he could still feel beneath his fingertips the cool, smooth skin that covered the slender wrist he'd grasped.

And despite his exhaustion and the Gypsy's potions, it was a long time before he could sleep.

Nadya blew out the candle she carried and set it down on the floor beside the bed in her grandmother's caravan. Angeline was already asleep there, snuggled under the covers like a tired puppy.

Nadya lifted the piled quilts and slipped under them. She pulled the little girl to her, relishing the warmth of her body. Her chin settled atop the child's head, but she didn't close her eyes for a long time. Instead, she stared into the darkness, thinking about the Englishman.

Stephano's ultimatum didn't worry her. After all, he would be away for the next few days—as he had been for most of the spring and summer. Although her half-brother certainly had the authority he'd bragged about tonight, his own concerns had kept him from exercising the kind of control on the *kumpania*'s activities that her father had enforced. Besides, given the fact the *gaujo* was coherent tonight, his recovery would, in her experience, occur very quickly now.

It wasn't the possibility that she couldn't get him out of the encampment fast enough to suit Stephano that kept her awake, staring into the darkness long after her daughter had fallen back into the innocent sleep of childhood. It was rather, she finally conceded, the probability that he would be gone long before her half-brother returned to see if his orders had been obeyed.

Why should she care if the *gaujo* she'd never laid eyes on until a week ago disappeared from her life? England was full of *gadje*. And most of the ones Nadya had met were more than eager to further their acquaintance with her.

So what could it possibly matter if she never saw this one again? she asked herself with a small shrug of disdain. Feeling that motion, Angeline turned, settling more closely against her. As she returned the little girl's embrace, Nadya reiterated the mantra she'd only tonight found necessary to formulate.

She had everything she needed. A child she loved. Respect in her community. More than enough money to meet her needs and the capacity for earning more.

Everything, she told herself again, she could possibly want.

Even as the thought formed, she knew it for the lie it was. She had the same physical needs of every other woman. And, though the capability to assuage her needs was always at hand, both here in camp and elsewhere, she had so far chosen not to avail herself of those opportunities.

More fool you. If you have an itch for a man, there are far better choices than a gadje *lord.*

That sort of liaison had never meant anything but dishonour and heartbreak for her kind.

She knew that. Had long ago acknowledged it. Yet tonight…

Tonight, when she had leaned down to put the cup to the Englishman's lips, she had instead wanted to fasten her own over them. To taste his kiss. To know, however briefly, what it would feel like to be held in his arms.

And for the first time in her very pragmatic existence, Nadya Argentari couldn't rationalize away the strength of that very emotional response. Or deny its reality.

She was still trying when she fell asleep.

Chapter Four

Rhys opened his eyes to sunlight. The first thing he realized was that it didn't hurt his head. The second was that it allowed him to get a much better look at his surroundings than he had been able to before.

He knew, because the Gypsy girl had told him, that he was in her caravan. Her home on wheels.

This morning, a section of wall in the part where he lay had been propped open to allow both light and fresh air inside. The slightly medicinal scent he'd been aware of last night had been replaced by the crispness of the English countryside in autumn.

He drew a deep, savouring breath of it into his lungs. As he did, he identified other smells, familiar from his campaigning days. Wood smoke. Fresh meat turning on a spit somewhere.

The sounds were the same as well, he realized. A low hum of conversation. The occasional masculine laugh.

A movement at the periphery of his vision caused him to turn his head. The little girl he'd seen yesterday was again standing at his bedside.

This time her lips immediately curved into a smile, which he couldn't have resisted responding to, even if he'd been so inclined. She raised her hand and, holding it directly in front of his face, moved two of her fingers up and down.

Puzzled, he shook his head, attempting to soften the denial with another smile. She repeated the motion, cocking her head to the side when she was through, as if waiting for his response.

Again Rhys shook his head, relieved that the movement, which yesterday would have produced blinding pain, didn't bother him at all this morning. 'I don't understand,' he confessed.

Once more the child made the gesture, clearly frustrated with his lack of understanding.

'I'm sorry, little one…' he began.

Apparently, she'd had enough. She turned, disappearing from his field of vision.

Alone again, Rhys raised his eyes to the opening at the end of the caravan. The beech leaves were molten gold in the morning sun. As they swayed in the wind, they cast dappled patterns of light and shade onto the walls of the caravan, reminding him of the countryside he'd ridden through after he'd left Buxton. And, he realized, that was the last thing he did remember.

I fear you've fallen among the Rom, the woman had told him. But she'd given him no explanation of how that had occurred. Or of how he'd been injured.

No matter how hard he tried, searching his memory for answers, he could remember almost nothing after he left the inn. All he knew was that he'd been thoroughly enjoying his first taste of freedom since he'd returned to England.

It was possible he'd been attacked by robbers. If so, he had no memory of it. Still, being set upon by highwaymen would explain the blow to the head, so that version of events seemed logical. Whether the Gypsies had been his attackers or his rescuers, however—

'Angel said you were awake. How do you feel?'

The woman who'd given him the medicine last night was back. Today the kerchief had been replaced by two gold combs, which glittered among her midnight curls as if bejewelled.

The shawl that had covered her shoulders had also disappeared. The cap-sleeved blouse she wore would offer little protection against the morning's chill, but the white fabric flattered the smooth tan of her shoulders.

Despite its décolleté, something he was suddenly extremely aware of, the garment was no more revealing than the gowns he'd seen at the country party his sister-in-law had dragged him to. Merely the fashion, he told himself. Still, he hadn't reacted to those rounded white shoulders in quite the same way his body was responding to these.

'Angel?' The question was a form of self-defence, since he was certain of the source of her information.

'Her name's Angeline, but…' The woman shrugged, the movement again drawing his eyes to the beginning curve of her breasts, visible above the low neckline.

Rhys raised his eyes, smiling into hers. 'I'm afraid she wasn't very pleased with me.'

'Really? She seemed excited you're awake.'

'She kept doing something with her fingers. I think she expected me to be able to figure out what it was, but…' He shook his head.

'Can you show me?'

Feeling foolish for having brought it up, Rhys repeated the gesture the child had made.

The woman laughed. 'She wanted you to come with

her. And since she is, I'm afraid, too accustomed to having her own way, I'm sure she thought you wouldn't hesitate to oblige.'

'I should have tried. If she'd told me what she wanted.'

'Angel doesn't speak. Nor does she hear what we say.'

'She's deaf,' Rhys spoke the sudden realization aloud, and then wondered at his own stupidity in not understanding the situation sooner. 'Forgive me. You must think me very slow.'

'I think you've had a severe blow to the head. It's to be expected that things seem strange. As all of this certainly must.' One slender hand gestured at their surroundings.

'You said last night I'd "fallen in" with your people. I'm afraid I can't remember how that happened.'

Her eyes widened slightly. 'Nothing?'

'Very little beyond setting out from the inn at Buxton. I assume that was yesterday morning. Unless, that is, I've enjoyed your hospitality longer than I'm aware.' His voice rose questioningly on the last.

'Then…you don't remember Angel at all?'

'She was here once before when I woke up. That must have been…last night?'

'Do you remember being brought here?'

'I thought—' Rhys hesitated, for some reason reluctant to confess that during that journey he had imagined he was back in Spain. 'Perhaps,' he amended. 'Parts of it.'

Even as he said that, it seemed he did remember. They'd put him on a cart of some kind. And the ground they'd pulled the conveyance over had been very uneven.

Rough enough, he thought with an unexpected clarity, that he'd been more than willing to sink back into the unconsciousness their painful ministrations had pulled him from.

'What about my horse?' Another memory that had suddenly risen to the surface of his consciousness.

'A gelded bay with a star on his forehead?'

'That's it. He's my brother's, actually. I should hate to lose him.'

Rhys had had several mounts shot out from under him in Iberia. More than enough to teach him not to become attached to any of them. Still the bay had been responsive, seeming as pleased with the freedom of their journey as Rhys had been.

'One of the men found him this morning. Don't worry. He'll be ready for you when you're well enough to ride.'

'When do you think that will be?' Right now, he couldn't imagine sitting on a horse, but given the crowded conditions of her "home", he also couldn't imagine imposing on her any longer than was absolutely necessary.

'I'm a healer, not a fortune-teller, my lord,' she said with a smile. 'I can send for my grandmother if you'd like to make inquiries about your future.'

'I'm no lord.' Rhys wasn't sure why it was suddenly so important that she understand that.

'All English gentlemen are lords to us.' The smile tugged at the corners of her lips again. 'We discovered long ago that a little flattery goes a long way. Especially when your livelihood depends upon the goodwill of those with whom you conduct business.'

'And what kind of business do you conduct?'

Her chin tilted upward fractionally. 'Assuredly not the kind you're thinking of. As I told you, I have some small skill with herbs and potions. I can set bones and sew flesh so that the limbs involved are still usable. My grandmother can tell you what your future holds, if you're foolish enough to desire that information. As for the others…' She made that expressive movement with her shoulders again. 'We're blacksmiths, tinkers, leather workers, basket weavers, woodworkers. Craftsmen of all kinds. And we buy and sell all manner of things.'

The Rom were known for all those things. And for many others as well. For centuries every type of roguery—from cheating at games of chance to stealing children from their beds—had been laid at their door.

With that thought, the image of the little girl's wide blue eyes surrounded by colourless lashes was in his mind's eye. How did a child like Angeline come to be in a Gypsy camp? Rhys didn't believe for a moment that Angel was her daughter.

That was, however, a subject he couldn't afford to pursue. Not while he was flat on his back and at the mercy of these people. At least one of whom very much wanted him gone.

He wondered what this woman's relationship was with the man who'd ordered her to get him out of camp. Was he the tribal leader? Her father? Husband? Lover?

The last two choices were more distasteful to him than they should be. Despite his attraction to her, the worlds they occupied were separated by an abyss of custom and prejudice. The Gypsy had taken care of him, for which he would always be grateful. As for the other…

The sooner he could leave, the better it would be for all concerned. The woman who had tended to him could once more have her home back. Whoever had demanded she get rid of him would be satisfied. And more important, Rhys would be on his way once more to his godfather's house.

With the memory of his journey's purpose, he realized that unless he sent word to Keddinton that he'd been delayed, his godfather was apt to sound the alarm, which would send Edward rushing into the countryside to find him. It was lucky he hadn't been more exact in his letter about the date of his arrival. Perhaps if he sent Keddinton a message now, he could forestall the humiliation of his family's search.

'Some of you have occasion to travel outside this camp?'

'Of course,' Despite her ready agreement, the woman seemed puzzled by his question.

'I was hoping someone could take a letter to my godfather, Viscount Keddinton. His home is Warrenford Park. Near Wargrave. He's expecting me. If I don't show up there soon, he may institute a hue and cry.'

Although Rhys had attempted to phrase the possible consequence of his non-arrival lightheartedly, the woman's face changed. Only then did he realize that his presence might represent a danger to the Rom. And on reflection, he had no doubt his brother and even Keddinton would assume the worst if he were discovered to be convalescing in a Gypsy encampment.

'Of course,' she said evenly. 'I'll bring you something with which to write your message and see that it's delivered as soon as possible.'

'Thank you. My arrangements were not so exact as to cause immediate concern, but I think it best we forestall any unnecessary worry.'

'Of course,' she said again, but her eyes told him she knew exactly what he was thinking.

He had finally escaped his family's solicitous care of him. Now he must concentrate on regaining his strength in order to escape the possibility of further humiliation. Not all of which, he admitted ruefully, involved his family.

'How is he?' Magda asked.

'Stronger.' Nadya dipped a ladle into the pot of porridge that hung over the fire near her grandmother's caravan. She had already put the writing materials she'd promised the Englishman in the pocket of her apron. 'He doesn't remember what happened with Angel or how he came to be here.'

'He doesn't remember saving her?'

'No. And I'm not sure it's to our advantage to tell him.'

'As it stands now, he believes *he's* beholden to *you*.' Magda had immediately grasped her dilemma. 'If you tell him what he did for your daughter, the shoe is on the other foot.'

'Exactly.'

'And yet you feel like a cheat for not telling him.'

Nadya looked up at the old woman, marvelling again at how easily she was able to read her thoughts. 'He deserves my gratitude, *Mami*. If he hadn't been there…' A tightness in her throat prevented her from finishing the thought.

'It wasn't only that he was there, *chavi*. According to the girl, he put his life at risk to save Angel.'

'I know. And for a child he didn't know. A child who was nothing to him.'

'An English child. One of his own kind,' Magda reminded her. 'If your daughter had looked like you, *chavi*, I wonder if he would have gone into the water to rescue her.'

Nadya couldn't argue with what her grandmother was suggesting. She had lived her entire life with the kind of unthinking prejudice that held her people to be less worthy of every measure of respect accorded to the fairer-skinned population among whom they lived.

'What do you think?' Magda asked.

'About what?' Without meeting her grandmother's eyes, Nadya wiped the rim of the bowl she'd just filled with the edge of her apron.

'Do you think he would have done that for another child? For Tara? Or Racine?'

'How should I know what the *gaujo* would do? All I know is what he did.'

'And that's enough for you?'

'It's enough for today,' Nadya said as she straightened.

'And for tomorrow?'

'Tomorrow he'll be gone, and I won't have to wonder about him ever again.'

The dark, far-seeing eyes of her grandmother held on hers. Then the thin lips, surrounded by their network of fine lines lifted, curving at the corners. 'There are lies more believable than the truth, *chavi*. The one you just told isn't one of them.'

'Your old sayings may work with the *gadje*, *Mami*, who are willing to believe anything you tell them. You've forgotten who you're talking to. Besides, Stephano has decreed I have to get rid of the Englishman before he returns.'

'When have you ever worried about obeying Stephano's orders? Except when they track with your own desires.'

'Then isn't it convenient that in this case they do? Go peddle your fortunes to the villagers. We shall need their shillings come winter.'

'Before it, if we keep feeding strangers.' One dark brow rose in challenge, but the old woman's grin widened.

And when Nadya turned to take the *gaujo's* breakfast to him, she, too, was smiling.

As she rounded the corner of her *vardo*, she discovered the Englishman dressed and sitting on its high seat. Flat on his back, he had sent her normally unflappable senses reeling. Upright, he proved to be even more of a threat to them.

Much the worse for its recent immersion as well as for the now-mended mutilation she'd performed on it, the lawn shirt was stretched across a pair of broad shoulders. She had removed his cravat when she undressed him. He hadn't bothered to replace it today, so that the strong brown column of his neck was visible at the open throat.

'Out for the sun?' She shaded her eyes with her free hand to look up at it.

'I thought it was past time I was up.'

'Then you've discovered the answer to your question.'

'My question?'

'About when you'll be well enough to ride.'

His lips flattened, but he didn't respond to her teasing. She waited a moment, unsure what had just happened, and then held the bowl she carried up to him.

'Do English lords eat porridge?'

'I'm sure they do.' The green eyes again held a trace of amusement.

'Do you?'

'I have been known to partake of porridge. When I was lucky enough to have it at hand.'

'Then…' She lifted the bowl a little higher.

He hesitated a moment before he reached down to take her offering. 'I'll be more than happy to pay you for whatever you've expended on my care. If you'll provide me with—'

She wasn't sure what he saw in her face, but whatever it was stopped him in mid-sentence. 'It's porridge,' she said. 'We've plenty of it. And no matter what you've heard, we aren't accustomed to charging our guests for their food.'

'I'm hardly a guest.'

According to his lights, he was right. He didn't remember what he'd done to earn her gratitude, and she had thus far, for her own selfish reasons, chosen not to tell him. But it was past time for the truth.

'You are my guest. An honoured one. For as long as you wish to stay.'

'That's very kind, but—'

'You saved my daughter's life,' she interrupted. 'At considerable risk to your own.'

'Your daughter? Angel?'

'She'd fallen into a stream, and you rescued her. I'm not sure when or how you struck your head, but it was in the course of that rescue.'

'She told you that? I thought...'

'The girl who was supposed to be watching her witnessed it all. You still don't remember?'

A furrow appeared between his brows as if he were trying to. Finally he shook his head.

'None of it. I remember riding out that morning, revelling in the freedom of being in the saddle, and then...I remember being placed on a cart. At least I think I do. That may have been something else—' Again he hesitated.

'Something else?'

It seemed the Englishman, too, had things he'd chosen not to reveal, but she couldn't imagine what. If he remembered the rescue, then in his situation, it would be to his advantage to lay claim to his heroic actions.

'Another memory, perhaps. I remember thinking at the time that I was being carried from the field. And then...then I thought I must have dreamed it.'

'The field? A battlefield? You were a soldier?'

'Better or worse than being a lord?' The amusement was back.

'From my perspective? I suppose that would depend on whether or not you were a wealthy soldier.'

'Another disappointment, I'm afraid. All the wealthy soldiers *were* lords. It takes a great deal of money to buy a commission these days.' He spooned a bite of the porridge, blowing on it before he put it into his mouth.

'Ah, well,' she comforted as she watched him, 'I suppose you'll just have to share porridge with the rest of us then.'

'And very good porridge it is, too. Thank you.' He lifted

the spoon in a small salute before he used it to secure another bite. 'For this and everything else.'

'I believe the weight of debt is still rather heavily in your favour, my lord. If porridge and a few decoctions can make payments on that balance, perhaps one day it may be paid in full.'

'Consider it paid already. If what you say is true, then I'm glad I was at hand when your Angeline needed a rescuer.' He looked up from the bowl, the green eyes serious now. 'And very glad you were at hand when I needed one.'

'At no risk to myself.'

His gaze left hers to survey the compound. Despite the fact that the normal morning activities were ongoing, more than one pair of eyes had been focused on the two of them.

The Englishman smiled and nodded a greeting to those who seemed interested in their conversation. As he did, most had the grace to turn their attentions back to the daily tasks at hand.

Andrash, who had helped carry the Englishman back to camp, lifted a hand in response. The ex-soldier responded in kind before he looked down at her.

'At no cost to yourself?'

She laughed. 'If you're imagining that my position here is in jeopardy because I choose to take you in, you're mistaken.'

'At least one person objected rather strongly to your kindness. And, although I have no way to verify his claim, he said he had the authority to enforce his displeasure.'

He meant Stephano, Nadya realized. Given their proximity to the caravan when her half-brother had issued his ultimatum, she shouldn't be surprised to find that her patient overheard them.

'Is that why you're up? Because you felt…threatened?'

'I'm up because I felt well enough to try.'

'And well enough to succeed, it seems. Congratulations.'

'You may hold your applause until I can do more than sit in the sun.'

'Granted, your bay will prove more of a challenge.'

'My brother's bay,' he corrected softly.

There was some issue there. A rivalry? Or simple envy of the firstborn's rights under English law?

'Shall I ask Andrash to bring the gelding?' She turned her head, seeking the smith, who had apparently found occupation in another area of the camp while they'd been talking.

'Maybe I'll check on him. Later, I think.' He held the half-empty bowl down to her.

Although she noted the slight tremor in his fingers, she didn't comment on it. 'At your convenience, my lord. I assure you your brother's horse will be here and well tended when you are ready for him.'

'If you insist on a title, then major will do.'

'Aren't majors' commissions purchased?' she teased.

'It happens mine was awarded. My previous ranks were purchased, however. By benefactors,' he added when she cocked her head as if to challenge his denial of wealth. 'My brother and my godfather, actually.'

'That reminds me.' She fished the paper and pencil stub out of her pocket, holding them up to him. As he took them, his fingers brushed hers. 'So, Major…?'

'Morgan. Rhys Morgan.'

'How do you do, Major Morgan.' She lowered her head as she had seen the ladies in the village do.

'Better than yesterday, thank you.'

'And not so well as tomorrow. That I can promise you. Don't be impatient.'

He nodded, his eyes on hers.

After a moment, she deliberately broke the contact between them by looking down at the bowl he'd handed her. 'We can do better than this for dinner.'

He shook his head. 'You'd be surprised how grateful one can be for porridge.'

For some reason she believed him. Of course, as a soldier, he had undoubtedly known deprivation.

Now, however, he was back in England, where his kind wanted for nothing. Except, perhaps, the favours of a well-placed benefactor. Or of a Gypsy girl.

'You didn't tell me your name.'

Surprised, her eyes came up, as she debated whether or not to tell him the truth. And then, deciding that it couldn't possibly matter if he knew, she did. 'My name is Nadya Argentari.'

'Your servant, Miss Argentari.' He repeated her earlier gesture, making rather more of it than she had.

'Somehow I doubt that, my lord.'

'Major,' he corrected again.

'Major Morgan. Now if you'll excuse me, I have other patients who seem to *still* be in need of my skills this morning.'

'But none, I assure you, who will be more grateful for them.'

'No matter your denial, I see that you are indeed a milord.'

'A simple soldier, ma'am, I assure you. And quite willingly at your service.'

He inclined his head slightly. Despite all her strictures to the contrary, Nadya found her senses once more stirred.

Like a schoolgirl taken with the first handsome gentleman she encounters.

Or at least the first she had encountered in a very long

time, Nadya admitted. And, she reiterated, this time strictly to herself, the sooner he is gone, the better it will be for everyone concerned.

Especially for me.

Chapter Five

The following morning Nadya was surprised to discover her half-brother back in camp. As she crossed the centre of the compound, she saw one of the men taking Stephano's black stallion to the horse pens to be cared for. Sadly, the animal appeared to be in need of the attention.

Riding his mount to exhaustion was not something Stephano would normally have done, but the act was typical of his single-mindedness of late. Consumed with events in his past, he was, in her opinion, abdicating his current responsibilities.

Not that he was interested in her opinion.

If only his lack of interest might extend to her activities…

Taking a deep breath, she walked toward her grandmother's caravan. There was no sense in postponing the confrontation she knew would occur. She had deliberately disobeyed Stephano's orders, and he would demand an explanation. And she had none, other than the one he'd already rejected.

As she approached Magda's caravan, eyes on the ground, her half-brother jumped down from it and came toward her. She saw that he had been in camp long enough to change out of his *gadje* attire and back into the traditional garb of their people.

The small gold earring he wore when in camp glinted in the sun. The colourful vest, long-sleeved shirt and loose trousers were exactly the same as those worn by the other men, but Stephano's good looks and air of confidence would make him stand out anywhere.

Even among the English Ton he professed to despise, she thought with a small sense of pride.

Today, nothing about his appearance suggested his mixed heritage. And when he was with the Rom, that was exactly the way Stephano wanted it.

When he reached her, there was no kiss of greeting, as there usually was between them. Apparently her halfbrother had already discovered that the Englishman was still here.

The first words out of his mouth confirmed that impression. 'I told you to get rid of him.'

'And I told you he'll leave as soon as he's well enough.'

'He's well enough now.'

Without slowing, Stephano strode past her and toward her caravan, so that Nadya was forced to run to catch up with him. She grabbed his arm, but he shook her off.

'Listen to me.' This time she used both hands to grasp his wrist, holding tightly enough that he would have had to use force to free himself. She was relieved when he turned toward her instead.

Although his face was closed, Nadya tried once more to argue her case. 'The man saved Angel's life. Surely that means *something* to you, if for no other reason than because it means so much to me.'

The hard black eyes softened almost imperceptibly. If

she had not known him so well, however, she might not have been able to tell her argument had had any impact. The stern lines of Stephano's face hadn't altered.

Which shouldn't be surprising, she conceded, considering he'd had a lifetime of practice in not revealing what he felt.

'Magda says he's well enough to leave,' her brother said.

'The next time you suffer an injury, shall I let Magda decide your treatment?'

His lips tightened, but he didn't dispute her point. She was the *drabarni*. Questions about healing were her domain, not that of their grandmother.

'But he is conscious?' Stephano demanded.

'Yes.'

'So who is he?'

'His name is Rhys Morgan. He's an ex-soldier, recently returned from Spain.' She couldn't see how revealing what his service had cost the Englishman could advance her cause. Stephano had grown so hard that he might instead take those wounds as a sign of weakness.

'And?'

'That's all I know. That and the fact he was travelling to his godfather's house when he rescued Angel.'

As she mentioned Rhys's godfather, she realized that her half-brother would be the ideal person to deliver his message. Not only would he be returning to London shortly, he also knew the ways of the *gadje* and, because of that, would be less likely to raise concerns within Rhys's family.

'He asked me to find someone to deliver a note to him.' She removed the folded paper Rhys had given her from her pocket and held it out to him.

'To his godfather? Did he mention a name?'

'Keddinton, I believe.'

'Keddinton? Are you sure?'

The name had meant nothing to Nadya, but clearly it did to her half-brother. He unfolded the paper to read what Rhys had written, the gesture revealing the silver bracelet her father had made for him.

'Do you know him?'

Stephano laughed. 'I don't travel in the elevated circles Lord Keddinton occupies. Not any more.' The bitterness of the last was apparent.

'Then…?'

'I know *of* him,' he clarified, closing Rhys's note. 'So would you if you weren't so concerned with your "daughter" and your herbs.'

'A concern for which you've had reason to be grateful in the past. And may again.' Stephano suffered debilitating headaches, which with her herbs she had been able to mitigate to some small extent. 'Who is this Keddinton?'

'Someone influential in the capital. More influential than the title he holds would indicate. Your *gaujo* has powerful connections, *jel'enedra*. Which makes me wonder why he's content to recuperate in a cramped *vardo* under the care of a Gypsy healer. I wonder if that could that have anything to do with you, my dear?'

That very English appellation jarred, especially coming so closely on the heels of his usual name for her. Almost from the moment her father had brought Stephano back to them, he had referred to her as *jel'enedra*. His little sister.

'I imagine this is not so different from what he's accustomed to. I told you: he's a soldier.'

'Whose godfather is one of the most powerful men in England.'

'What can that possibly matter to you?' She was beginning to fear that her half-brother was considering how he might benefit from Rhys's connections.

'I'm not sure it does,' Stephano said with a shrug. 'It's simply something I find interesting. And potentially useful.'

'How could that possibly—'

'I said *potentially* useful, *jel'enedra*. Do you think it would come amiss if I inform Lord Keddinton of your kind services to his godson?' He held up the note for emphasis before he pushed it into the pocket of his vest. 'Maybe he'll even see fit to reward you for them.'

'I don't consider caring for the man who saved my daughter's life deserving of a reward.'

'Then it's just as well you're content with your lot. Those who are never use the tools fate hands them to achieve a better one.

'As you have done, I suppose.'

'A lesson I learned early. And too well. But then I had sterner masters than you. You should be grateful for that.'

'You didn't used to be this way, Stephano. Bitter and vindictive.'

'Or perhaps you didn't know me so well as you thought.'

'I know you've changed. Something or someone has changed you.'

Stephano laughed. 'Ask Magda if you want to know why I've changed.'

'*Magda?*'

'Who sees and knows all. Have you ever asked what future she sees for you?'

'You don't believe in her *drabbering*. No more than do I.'

'I believe in destiny. Someone has tampered with mine.'

'Did Magda tell you that?' Nadya's tone was derisive. Leave it to the old woman to try and stir up his ambitions.

'Magda tells me things because I pay attention. Do you?'

'To Magda's prophecies?' Nadya laughed. 'Did you remember to cross her palm with silver, Stephano? Be

warned. If it wasn't enough, she may weave you a bad
fortune. Maybe she'll even put a curse on you.'

'Someone's already done that, my dear. Magda is
simply trying to help me find a way to remove it.'

With that, her half-brother made a sweeping bow, as if
they were in some London ballroom and the cotillion had
just ended. Before Nadya could think of a suitable re-
joinder, he had walked away.

As she watched, he joined a group of men smoking beside
one of the tents. Their heartfelt welcome made her realize
anew how adept Stephano was at playing the chameleon.

*Someone's already done that, my dear. Magda is simply
trying to help me find a way to remove it.*

Clearly Stephano preferred to remain cryptic about his
intentions. Nadya knew the old woman well enough to
know that she would, no doubt, relish the telling of how
the two of them were scheming to get back at the *gadje*
who'd ruined Stephano's life.

Nadya glanced back at her *vardo*. It seemed that her
half-brother might be content to leave Rhys alone until he
had considered every possible way in which he might use
the Englishman and his connections.

That meant that, for now at least, her patient was safe.
And she would have a chance to find out what poison their
grandmother had been feeding Stephano.

'I thought you didn't have any use for the past. That's
what you always tell me. "None of your old stories, *Mami*.
What's done is done."'

Her grandmother wasn't as forthcoming as Nadya had
anticipated. Still, she had years of experience in dealing
with the old woman. Making a mystery of things was part
of Magda's stock in trade.

'People change,' Nadya said. 'Look at Stephano, for example.'

'You think he's changed? Maybe you've simply become more aware of the difficulties your brother faces because of his birth.'

'What difficulties? Stephano does exactly what he wants. He's successful both here and in the *gadje* world. He comes and goes between them as he pleases. If anyone is master of his fate, it's Stephano.'

'And you envy him that.'

Nadya shrugged, but she couldn't deny her grandmother's perception. Nadya knew that she was very lucky not to live under some man's thumb. Neither a husband nor a father.

The influence Stephano exerted as head of their *kumpania* was the closest thing to control she was subject to. Given their blood ties, his rule over her had always been remarkably loose. Now, distracted with whatever was going on in the other world her half-brother inhabited, he had been even less concerned with her affairs.

If it hadn't been for Stephano's increasingly obvious unhappiness, she would have been content to leave matters as they were. But because she loved him, she wanted to know what was driving his self-destructive behaviour.

'Why shouldn't I envy it?'

'Your brother had suffered in ways you can't begin to imagine, *chavi*. As a child, Stephano was assured of everything a man could desire. Money, position, power. With his father's murder, all those promises disappeared. Whatever Stephano has now, he stole from the hands of fate. Nothing was given him.'

The English lord who was Stephano's father had been stabbed by a friend. After his death, his widow's family had quickly seen to it that the half-breed bastard he'd foisted on her was sent away to a foundling home. It didn't bother them in the least that they were throwing a seven-year-old child out of the only home he'd ever known.

'What more can he want than what he has now?'

'Justice,' Magda said simply. 'For his father. And for himself.'

'When has the Rom ever had justice? Especially at the hands of the *gadje*.'

'Ah, but that's the difference between the two of you. You don't expect the world to do right by you, so you'll do right by yourself. Stephano, on the other hand…' Magda's shrug was expressive.

'Stephano expects the *gadje* to treat him fairly? He isn't that naïve.'

'Not expects, *chavi*. *Demands*. There's a difference. Stephano believes justice is his birthright.'

'Stephano is half Rom. That half, if nothing else, precludes justice at the hands of the *gadje*. As for his English half, the courts hanged the man responsible for his father's death. Isn't that justice enough?'

'Your mother didn't think so.'

'Because she was obsessed with the death of her lover.'

'How would you feel if it were *your* father who'd been murdered, *chavi*? Or your lover?'

For an instant, the handsome features of the ex-soldier she'd cared for the past week were in her mind's eye. Nadya banished the memory with the practicality she had learned from both her grandmothers.

'What can Stephano hope to accomplish after all these years? His father's dead. The nobleman who murdered him has been punished by the English courts. Under their laws, Stephano has no claim to his father's title or estate. Instead of encouraging him in this insanity, you should make him realize that what's done can't be undone.'

That was a truth Nadya's mother Jaelle—Magda's beloved daughter—had never accepted. Overcome with grief at her lover's death and obsessed with seeking justice for her lost son, Jaelle had eventually hanged herself.

In doing so, she had left Nadya motherless and her Romany husband heartbroken. Thom Argentari had never recovered from the loss of his wife or from the sense of betrayal her suicide had engendered. Nadya would always believe that had played a role is his own too-early death.

Left in the care of her beloved grandmothers, Nadya had thrived, despite her grief. Perhaps if Stephano had been returned to the Rom after his father's death, he might not have been scarred to the extent Magda suggested he had been. As for what he was doing now…

'I don't understand why Stephano would choose their world over ours,' Nadya said. 'Here he's loved and re-spected. There…' She shook her head. 'Whatever success he has will never be enough. The fact that he can never be all those things his father promised eats at his soul. If you encourage him in that, Magda, you'll destroy him.'

'It's his destiny, *chavi*, and he must follow it. Just as you must follow yours.'

'I don't want your fortune-telling, thank you. I have quite enough trouble living in the present.'

'You don't reject what your Argentari grandmother taught you.'

'She taught me to save lives, to heal and to mend. You wanted to teach me how to cheat and deceive those who are gullible enough to believe that someone can see their future by looking into their palms.'

'Then you are no different than your brother, *chavi*. You, too, reject your heritage.'

'You think that's my heritage? No wonder the *gadje* believe we're all thieves and liars.'

'Does he think that? Your *gaujo*?'

'He isn't *my gaujo*. And I don't know what he thinks.'

'Stephano wants him gone.'

'So he said. And he will be. As soon as he's well enough.'

'And that day can't come soon enough for you, I suppose.'

Her grandmother's lined face was devoid of expression, but Nadya wasn't fooled. 'What does that mean?'

'It's too late to reject what I offer. I've already seen your palm, *chavi*. I saw it the day you were born. Neither it— nor your future—hold any secrets for me.'

Nadya laughed. 'Whatever you're expecting from it, *Mami*, I hope you aren't disappointed.'

'I won't be, *chavi*. I can promise you that, if nothing else.'

Although Stephano had been in camp less than a day, when Nadya returned from taking the evening meal to her patient, her brother was saddling his stallion. Nadya stopped to run her hand down the horse's silken nose, smiling when the animal pushed against her chest in response.

'Off so soon?' she asked as she watched Stephano's hands smooth the blanket he'd thrown over his mount's back.

His Romany clothing had again been packed away in the trunk he kept in Magda's caravan. Her half-brother looked every inch the English gentleman once more.

'Don't pretend you aren't delighted to be rid of me.'

'Why should I be?' Nadya asked. 'Your place is here, among people who love you. I know that, even if you seem to have forgotten it.'

Stephano turned, looking directly at her for the first time. 'I haven't forgotten.'

'Then why go? They turned their backs on you, Stephano. All of them. No one here has ever done that.'

'Unfinished business.' His attention was deliberately refocused on the task at hand.

'And you think you can finish it? Your father's dead. You can't bring him back to life. Or force his family to accept you.'

He laughed at her suggestion. 'Is that what you think I want? Acceptance? From them? I'm not that big a fool.'

'Then what do you want? Revenge? Against whom? Your father's murderer was hanged. By the Crown. What possible—'

'Those who helped to bring about his death don't deserve to prosper.'

Nadya shook her head. 'You're going to right the world, to set it spinning anew on its axis so that only the righteous prosper? And you think *me* naïve.'

'I think you know nothing about what I'm doing.'

'I know it takes you away from your people. And that this quest has cost you—both physically and emotionally. It may even be the cause of your headaches.'

'If your drugs come with the price of meddling in my affairs, I'm afraid I shall have to do without them.'

'Other than Magda, I'm the only family you have left. Perhaps that means nothing to you, but it means a great deal to me.'

'Then wish me well in my undertaking.'

'I would, if I thought this…whatever it is…would make you well.'

For a moment, he seemed to consider the beech trees, golden in the evening sunlight. When he looked down at her again, his face was more relaxed than she'd seen it in months.

'If it doesn't, *jel'enedra*,' he said softly, 'then nothing will.'

Nadya tried to analyze the emotion she heard in his voice. Regret? Or was it despair?

'What you're doing is dangerous,' she warned.

The line of his lips, once so mobile and quick to smile, ticked upward slightly at the corners. 'Not to me. Or rather,' he conceded, 'not only to me.'

'But since you are the only brother I have, lost to me once and then returned, I don't want to have you lost again.'

'Then be at peace, little one. Magda assures me this is the only way I shall ever resolve the things that trouble me.'

'And you believe her?' Nadya mocked.

'You doubt her gifts because your father's family devalued them.'

'I doubt her "gifts," as you call them, because I've seen too many fortune-tellers through the years. I'm not a woman of the *gadje*, willing to be taken in by promises of a meeting with a handsome stranger or of finding untold wealth waiting around the next bend.'

'Nor am I. Have a little faith, I beg of you.'

'In you? All you wish. In Magda's fortunes? I'm not that gullible.'

'And in Jaelle's curse against those who brought about my father's death?' Stephano asked quietly.

'Our mother gave you to another woman to rear as her son. And when she couldn't cope with her grief over your father's death, she killed herself rather than making a life with me and my father. Do I believe in her curses? I believe that with her death she cursed us both, Stephano. She cursed us not to think love can be true or faithful. She cursed us to value death over life. Jaelle's legacy isn't one I would be proud to claim. Nor should you.'

'You blame her for making the choice she did. I blame those who drove her to that choice.'

'But it *was* a choice. My father was a good man. One who loved her. He would have done anything in his power to make her happy.'

'The only person who could have done that had already been murdered. Those responsible for his death have much to answer for.'

'And you're going to see to it that they do.' Nadya's voice was flat, past anger and argument.

'If I can.'

'No matter what it costs you.'

'They have already cost me everything I ever valued.'

Despite her determination not to let him see how much those words hurt, Nadya's eyes stung with tears. 'So revenge is all you have left.'

'It's enough.'

'It's never enough. Even our mother knew that, at least at the last.'

Stephano's face tightened. 'It has to be enough, *jel'enedra*. It's all I have.'

He put his foot into the stirrup and vaulted into the saddle. Then he dug his heels into the eager stallion's side, urging him through the woods toward the road that would lead him to London and back to that other world he inhabited.

The child whose rescue Rhys had no memory of came to visit him every day. At first he'd been uncertain about trying to communicate with her, but he'd soon discovered that, in spite of her disability, she was as bright and as eager to learn as his brother's children had been at her age.

More importantly, from his standpoint at least, she seemed to accept his presence in the Romany encampment without any trace of reservation. Although Nadya's visits had become less frequent since he'd begun to regain his strength, Angel's had increased. Hugging her rag doll tightly, with fascinated eyes she had followed his careful progress up and down the narrow central aisle of the caravan. On the afternoons when the weather allowed it, she joined him on the high seat of her mother's *vardo*, content to play with her baby while he watched the busy camp.

He had even learned some of the finger signs the little girl used in place of words. Those had served as an introduction to other members of the tribe, each of whom took time to greet Angel—and frequently her new companion as well—as they passed the caravan.

Sometimes Rhys imagined that he could see the same question in their eyes that had occurred to him. Was Angel drawn to him, a stranger, because they shared a nationality? Nadya had offered no explanation of the child's origins, and although she referred to Angel as her daughter, during the conversation Rhys had overheard, the man Nadya argued with had disputed that title.

What was clear was that the little girl was both well cared for and dearly loved, not only by her mother, but by the other Rom as well. He told himself that how she had come to be here was none of his concern, but despite his gratitude to Nadya, those niggling questions remained in the back of his mind.

Small fingers tugged at his sleeve, bringing his eyes up from his whittling. It was an art he'd picked up from the batman who'd served him in Portugal. He would never be as skilful as Williams, but he had found that he enjoyed bringing the objects he saw in the wood to life.

The cat he was working on had been so clearly visible in the piece of deadfall he'd noticed that he had borrowed one of Nadya's knives from inside the wagon and begun to free it. Angel had watched his every stroke. Now, under the insistent command of her fingers, he stopped his carving to hold the animal up in the sunlight.

Exactly as it had the first time he spoke to her, her mouth formed a perfect circle of delight as she identified the creature he'd created. She touched the wood, whose stripes Rhys had incorporated into his mock feline and then pointed toward one of the bender tents scattered around the central clearing. Eyes wide, she turned back to him, her tongue bathing her hand in perfect imitation of a cat.

When he nodded agreement, laughing at her cleverness, she smiled in response. Deciding he couldn't improve on his work enough to make her waiting for it worthwhile, he held the carving out to her. Her smile changed into a look of such amazement and joy that he wondered how many presents she'd been given in her brief life.

Not enough, he decided, watching her careful fingers examine each detail of her new toy. When she finished, she drew the cat to her chest, holding it in exactly the same position as she so often did her beloved doll.

Then, unexpectedly, she leaned forward to put her lips against his cheek. She made some sign he didn't recognize, but took to be an expression of her thanks before she nimbly climbed down the steps of the wagon and ran toward the opposite side of the encampment, where the only other caravan stood.

'She likes it. And you.'

The comment drew Rhys's eyes to the man who'd uttered it. He was the Rom who'd raised his hand in greeting the first day Rhys had ventured out onto the wagon's high seat.

'I doubt it will take the place of her doll, but she deserves more than one toy, I think.' Rhys smiled, lest the man take his words as criticism of the little girl's circumstances.

'Many more,' the man agreed.

'And a small repayment for her mother's kindness to me.'

'Which was given without any expectation of return. Perhaps that isn't the custom among your people.'

'I'm not sure it is,' Rhys agreed, as he raised his eyes to follow Angel's ascent of the steps of the other wagon.

The old woman who opened its curtained entrance for her bent to admire the carving. Her eyes then followed Angel's finger as it pointed him out. The grey head bowed in Rhys's direction before, with a hand on the little girl's back, the woman directed her inside.

'You've made a friend,' the man who'd spoken to him said. 'A valuable acquisition, too.'

'Angel? For some reason liked me even before the cat.'

'I didn't mean the child. I meant the other. That's Magda Beshaley, our *phuri dai*. Our wise woman, as you would say. Your kindness to her great-granddaughter may reap more rewards than you can know, my friend. Enjoy the sun.' The Rom touched his hand briefly to his forehead before he continued on his way.

The gesture's origin probably lay in the traditional tug of the forelock, although nothing about it had hinted at servitude or humility. It seemed more like the casual salute one officer might make to another of equal rank. Whatever the English might think about the Gypsies living among them, apparently the Rom did not consider themselves to be a lesser people.

Rhys's gaze focused again on the caravan into which Angel had disappeared. The tone of the Rom's voice when he spoke of Nadya's grandmother expressed a deep respect.

Your kindness may reap more rewards than you can know.

The child's pleasure had been reward enough. Despite Nadya's denial of the indebtedness he felt, Angel's reception of his gift had been more gratifying than he could have imagined.

And whatever question he might have about how the child came to be here would have to remain unanswered. He owed her mother too much to think of causing her trouble.

Or her people, he thought, his eyes again considering the bustling encampment. The old wives' tales about the Rom were one-by-one being proven false.

Except, he admitted with a reluctant self-knowledge, the ones having to do with the charms of their women. Those he had found to be not the least exaggerated.

Chapter Six

Two days after Stephano's departure, Nadya's guest professed himself well enough to ride—a proclamation she was on some level relieved to hear, despite her qualms about its accuracy. Although her half-brother had promised to deliver Rhys's note to his godfather, she knew Rhys was concerned that his continued absence might trouble his family.

A feeling she could sympathize with, Nadya acknowledged as she walked across the clearing. Every time her half-brother departed, a knot of anxiety formed in her chest that didn't dissolve until his return.

When she reached the steps leading up to her caravan, she hesitated, trying to put those thoughts out of her head. She had never been able to sympathize with the loss Stephano felt when his English family had rejected him. But now, she, too, had felt the lure of the *gadje* world. All of it embodied in the smiling green eyes of a man who was as much out of her reach as the home Stephano remembered with such fondness was out of his.

Drawing a steadying breath, she climbed the steps, pausing at the top to call, 'Major Morgan?'

After a moment, the curtain that barred the entrance to the caravan was pushed aside. Rhys had been shaving, the task only half completed.

She tried unsuccessfully to stifle her smile at the effect of his partially lathered face. 'I can come back,' she offered. 'Or I could finish that for you.'

The words were out of her mouth before she had fully realized their implications. Shaving Rhys while he was unconscious was one thing. The physical proximity such a service would demand now was quite another.

'You shaved me before.' It was not a question.

'Once. You'd been clean-shaven when you arrived. I hated for you to find yourself less than properly groomed when you woke up.'

'That's why I didn't realize at first how long I'd been unconscious.'

'Your fever was high enough that you were bound to lose track of the days.'

'And during all that time you took care of me?'

'Not alone.' In truth, she had sent for the men to finish undressing him and to help with some of the other tasks his illness had entailed.

Besides, there was no need for him to know the level of intimacy her care of him involved. As a healer, she had long ago lost any sense of embarrassment about the human body, but she was certain that would not be the case for Rhys.

He moved aside, holding the curtain back for her to enter. She laid down his coat, which she and Magda had painstakingly repaired, and turned to find him watching her.

She held out her hand, palm up, for the razor he'd been using. As soon as he gave it to her, she indicated that he should sit down on the edge of the bed.

Working without a mirror—and there was none in this

part of the caravan—it was surprising he'd done as well as he had. Refusing to meet his eyes, she dipped the blade into the basin of tepid water he had placed on the nearby shelf.

When she'd removed most of the soap from the blade, she took his chin in her left hand, lifting his head and turning the unshaven side of his face toward the light. His skin was warm against her fingers. She bent toward him, willing the hand that held the razor not to tremble.

'You're very trusting,' she said as she made the first stroke.

'I have no reason not to be. If you meant me harm, there were ample opportunities for it when I was more vulnerable.'

Despite how sick he'd been, he didn't seem the least bit vulnerable to her now. She was aware once more of his size. Of the breadth of his shoulders. Of the determined strength of the jaw she drew the blade along.

She increased the upward angle of his chin, taking off the whiskers beneath it with three careful strokes. Then she turned his head to the right, trying to make sure that area was totally smooth.

Satisfied, she lifted her eyes in preparation for finishing the job and found herself staring into his. She had never realized there were flecks of gold in their clear green depths.

Of course, for most of the time she'd known him, his eyes had been closed. It was no wonder that, surrounded as they were by those long, thick lashes, they were having such an effect on her now.

'Almost done.' Deliberately she pulled her gaze from his, concentrating on the narrow space between his nose and top lip.

If anything, that area was even more distracting than the line of his jaw or his eyes. Magda would have told her the fullness of his bottom lip signified a passionate nature.

Despite her disdain for the old woman's mumbo-jumbo, Nadya would have wagered that in this instance her grandmother would be correct.

Hurrying now, Nadya rinsed the razor again, refusing this time to meet Rhys's eyes. She was only adding fuel to a fire that should never have been allowed to spark.

Three more strokes, decisively made, and she had succeeded in removing all the lather from his cheek. She stepped back to survey her handiwork, grateful to be able to put even that small space between them.

'That should do, I think. There's a mirror behind the partition.' She handed him the cloth she'd been using to wipe soap from the blade.

'Thank you.' Rhys was forced to duck his head as he entered the sleeping alcove.

Although her father had been considered a tall man by the standards of their people, she couldn't remember that he'd ever had to do that. Nor did Stephano.

After a moment, Rhys emerged from the back. 'Much better than I should have done.'

'But not, I'm sure, so good as your valet would have managed,' she suggested with a smile.

'I told you. I have no valet. I'm a soldier.'

'A soldier who doesn't know hot water can be obtained from a campfire?' she teased.

'I wasn't sure that was allowed.'

'Why wouldn't it be?'

He shrugged. 'It was my understanding that not everyone approves of what you're doing.'

'Has someone…said something?' She wondered if Magda had told him that Stephano wanted him gone. She didn't believe any of the others would take it upon themselves to turn out someone she was treating.

'I overheard a conversation to that effect, if you remember. Your father? Or…husband, perhaps?'

Although the last had been casually added, there was a decided undercurrent to the word. As if she were that silly schoolgirl she'd mockingly compared herself to, Nadya's heart rate increased with the realization Rhys was looking for that information.

'My brother. Half-brother, actually. And head of our *kumpania*. He's undertaken to deliver your note, by the way.'

'Thank you for seeing to that. Considering how adamantly he wanted me gone, I'm surprised he was willing to do it. Perhaps he felt questions about my whereabouts might have had unpleasant repercussions for your people.'

'Perhaps. Or he might simply have been feeling more dictatorial than usual the day you overheard him. If you don't yet feel well enough to ride, you're more than welcome to stay.'

Stephano had become slightly less adamant about Rhys leaving immediately. Especially since he'd discovered how influential his connections were, she acknowledged cynically.

'I've managed to stay in the saddle in worse straits than I'm in today. I owe you for that.'

'A conversation we've had already, I think. If there is indebtedness, the balance is on my side.'

'Then consider it paid. And with my most sincere thanks. Do you suppose the morning would be soon enough to suit your brother?'

'I'm sure it will be.' With Stephano safely away in London, he would never know when the Englishman departed.

'If you'll arrange for whoever has the bay to bring him around then…' he hesitated. 'Or tell me where to find him.'

'I'll have them bring him. And my grandmother and I

repaired your coat.' She stepped across to the foot of the bed where she'd laid the garment. Holding it up for his inspection, she added, 'Although not perfect, I think it will pass a cursory examination.'

He walked down the narrow aisle to examine their handiwork. When he had, he smiled at her. 'On a less-than-cursory examination it passes muster. Thank you. And please convey my thanks to your grandmother as well. Did she teach you to sew?'

'Among other things.' That was true enough. Like her father's mother, Magda had shared much of her store of knowledge. Some of which the Englishman would find exceedingly strange.

Of course, he might have found everything associated with the Rom exceedingly strange. Never having lived among the English, Nadya had no way to compare his day-to-day life to this.

'Did she teach you all this?' Rhys indicated the shelves piled with the plants, roots and herbs she used in her craft.

'That was my other grandmother. My father's mother. She was our healer before me. She's the one who taught me about the bark I used to break your fever.'

'Bark?'

'Peruvian bark. It's been used for years as a remedy for recurring fever. I wonder that your physicians didn't dose you with it.'

'I'm not sure they're so well versed in the healing properties of bark.'

'Peruvian bark.' If he had known her better, he might have realized the softness of her voice indicated anger. 'If not, then they're as ignorant as their patients about pharmacology. Unforgivable in men who profess to be healers.'

'Forgive me. I wasn't mocking you. My doctors did

little to treat fever beyond bleeding the sufferer. Or applying plasters. They seemed to feel that one either survived or succumbed, and it wasn't up to them to influence the outcome.'

'As I said.' His humility had mitigated her anger with him, but not his surgeons. 'Unforgivable.'

'Perhaps they weren't as knowledgeable as they should have been in…pharmacology, was it? But I have other reasons to be grateful for their skills.'

He was referring to his shoulder. Even if she found fault with them for their ignorance about the proper treatment of recurring fever, she had to give the surgeon credit for keeping him alive despite the terrible damage that had been inflicted on his body.

'Grapeshot,' she guessed.

She'd had no experience treating that, of course, but her grandmother had described the grievous injuries it typically caused. Rhys's wounds seemed severe enough to meet the criteria the old woman had set out.

'If I'd been standing a few yards closer to where it struck…' He let the sentence trail, shrugging fatalistically.

'You would have been killed.'

'So they tell me.'

'Even so, you're very lucky to have the use of your arm.'

He raised his left hand, opening and then closing his fingers into a fist. 'So they tell me,' he said again, smiling at her.

Despite the seriousness of the subject, she couldn't prevent her answering smile. Then, even as she watched, his slowly faded.

His eyes held hers. And what she saw within them made it impossible to breathe.

She was no green girl in the throes of her first infatuation. Nor was she easily beguiled by a charming answer or some other evidence of good breeding and culture. Yet from the moment she'd looked down on his face in the wavering torchlight, she'd fallen under the spell of this *gaujo*, almost as if she'd drunk one of the love potions Magda peddled.

Rhys's lips parted, causing her pulse to race. She waited, anticipating, for him to cover her mouth with his own.

Instead he straightened, swallowing against an emotion he chose not to confess. 'I'll be ready to leave in the morning.'

That, then, was the reality. He would be gone tomorrow. Back to his world, whose pull she had reason to know was incredibly powerful. Even for someone like Stephano, whose blood was half Romany.

The choice of how she should deal with what she felt was hers. She could continue the politely distant relationship they'd shared up to now. Or she could offer herself to him with no expectation of anything beyond a few short hours of pleasure. From what she had just seen in his eyes, she believed he would not refuse.

And yet, still he would leave. If not tomorrow, then when he'd had his fill of what she offered.

The *gadje* did not make Romany women their wives. At least those in the highest circles of English society didn't. And surely she had learned from her mother the cost of settling for anything less than marriage.

No matter how much she wanted to.

'I'll have them bring the bay to you then. Sleep well,' she said.

'Will I see you before I leave?'

'I'm sure Angel will want to say goodbye.' She had no doubt about that. Her daughter, it seemed, was as enamoured of the Englishman as she.

Rhys didn't respond, and after a moment she realized that whatever they felt for one another had come to this. A small, awkward silence between two strangers.

'Then…good night.' All she wanted was to be gone. Away from a temptation stronger than any she'd ever known.

'Good night,' he echoed. 'Thank you again for everything.'

She shook her head as she turned away, unwilling to repeat the arguments she'd made before. Besides, if there was anything she wanted from this man right now less than his gratitude, she couldn't begin to think what it might be.

Rhys lay on his back, eyes wide open, staring up into the darkness. This was the last night he would spend in Nadya's caravan. Tomorrow he would continue his interrupted journey to Keddinton's country estate. A journey he had, not long ago, been elated to begin.

This interlude in the Gypsy camp seemed almost like a dream. Part of that, he knew, was the result of his fever. And the rest…

He couldn't explain the rest. Or rather, he refused to.

He had closed his mind to the strength of his attraction to the Gypsy healer. He had refused to think about it since he'd been capable of making that decision. In the morning he would leave, never to see her or her child again.

Which was for the best, he told himself for the hundredth time. No matter the physical attraction he felt for Nadya Argentari, he could not act on it. He owed her more than that kind of disrespect.

He closed his eyes, willing himself to think of something else. Anything else.

He concentrated on the subtle sounds that had become part of the fabric of the time he'd spent here. The hiss and crackle of the fires that were kept burning all night. The brush of wind through the leaves overhead. The distant movements of the penned horses.

Tonight the familiar night-time stillness seemed deeper somehow. As if every soul in the encampment were asleep except for him.

Then, flickering on the edges of his consciousness, like a melody once heard and never forgotten, came a sound he couldn't quite identify, yet knew he should. Breathing suspended, he listened for the noise he'd heard only seconds before.

It had been alien somehow. Out of place in the peace-fulness of the sleeping camp.

When it drifted again through the stillness, he threw the covers off and bent to pull on the boots Nadya had so care-fully polished this afternoon. As he hurried to the front of the caravan, the sound grew louder, whispering through the trees like the wind that presages a storm.

Even before he'd reached the caravan's entrance, he could see a faint glow among the trees. As he pushed aside the curtain, he smelled the burning pitch of the torches the men carried and heard the murmur of angry voices, which grew louder and louder as the mob poured through the forest toward the encampment.

His gaze flew to the caravan on the far side of the clearing. Illuminated by the campfires between, dark figures moved silently from tent to tent.

For an instant, he thought the invaders had breeched the camp's defences. Then he realized the Rom were prepar-ing to defend themselves.

As Rhys descended the steps of the *vardo*, he became aware of the controlled chaos that surrounded him. Men pushed their wives and sleep-befuddled children toward the safety of the dark forest.

He ran toward the old woman's caravan, hoping its occupants were among the silent wraiths already disappearing into the trees. He hurried up its steps, pushing aside the concealing curtain without knocking.

Despite the lack of light, he could tell that the interior of this wagon followed the same basic design as the one he'd recuperated in. He rushed down the narrow central corridor toward the sleeping compartment in the rear, his heart dropping into his stomach when he found it still occupied. Nadya and her daughter were sleeping soundly despite what was happening outside.

'Get up.'

'What is it?' Like a soldier, Nadya had come awake instantly, every sense alert.

'There's a mob coming through the woods.'

She slipped out of bed and then scooped up her daughter. She didn't protest when Rhys took the still-groggy child from her arms.

'Get your shoes,' he ordered over his shoulder as he carried the little girl toward the entrance.

'Oh, my God.' Nadya's soft exclamation told him she was close enough to see the torches, which were now much nearer the clearing than when he'd first seen them.

'Who's out there?' Rhys dragged one of the blankets off the shelf beside the door and wrapped it around the child.

'Someone missing a cow,' Nadya said bitterly. 'Someone whose child's fallen ill. Or whose crops failed.'

As Rhys listened to the litany of things traditionally blamed on the Rom, he tried to decide if defending the wagon would be safer than taking the two of them into the forest. The sound of one of the light wheeled carts the band used for transport being overturned decided him.

As he carried Angel down the steps, Rhys realized that the Romany men were mounting a counterattack. Despite their efforts, one of the bender tents had been put to the torch. The speed with which the fire caught and the eerie glow it cast on the faces of the invaders created an additional sense of urgency.

'Come on.' Rhys put his hand against Nadya's back, pushing her toward the trees.

'That leads to the river.' Taking his hand, Nadya began to draw him in the opposite direction. The same one from which the mob had approached.

In order to do what she was suggesting, Rhys realized, they would have to skirt the clearing and then enter the woods on its far side. Given the ongoing pandemonium, that longer journey might ultimately be less hazardous than becoming trapped between the enemy and the river.

As he trailed Nadya, who kept to the shadows beneath the overarching beech trees, his eyes surveyed the madness around them. She and the little girl whose arms were wrapped tightly around his neck were his primary concerns, but seeing the destruction of the Rom encampment, he vowed that if he could find refuge for them, he would come back and join the fight.

They skirted another overturned cart, its load spilled out onto the close-packed earth. Ahead, a small group of the invaders had surrounded one of the men of the tribe.

Two were holding the Gypsy upright, his arms behind his back, while a third shouted questions at him. Those were periodically punctuated by the sound of the questioner's fists striking the helpless Rom.

Nadya stopped so suddenly Rhys ran into her. She turned, her eyes pleading with him to do something.

Rhys's background and training made it impossible to refuse. He shoved the little girl into her mother's arms and ran to where the one-sided attack was taking place.

As he passed the nearest of the campfires, he bent and unhooked the iron kettle that hung from its tripod. He swung his makeshift weapon at the unprotected head of the first Englishman he encountered, dropping him unceremoniously.

The rest turned, their eyes widening in shock at the interruption of their entertainment. One of them shouted, 'Watch out, Oliver.'

Rhys swung the kettle again, this time at the nearer of the two holding the Rom. His intended target, warned of his intent, raised his arm to ward off the blow.

The metal pot resounded hollowly as it struck. Still hot from the fire, its heat rather than the force of the blow dispatched Rhys's second victim, who leaped away, cursing.

Rhys turned then to the man who'd been systematically pummelling the Gypsy. In the light of the burning tents, Rhys recognized the battered face as belonging to the Rom who'd talked to him the afternoon he'd carved the cat for Angel.

The recognition caused a split-second's hesitation in his forward progress, one the man beating the Rom used to his advantage. He charged, ham-sized fists lifted like a prizefighter. Rhys managed to duck the first, but the second— a hard right aimed at his ribs—landed a glancing blow to his damaged shoulder instead.

The resulting agony robbed him not only of breath, but of the ability to think. He sank to his knees under its force.

Instinct alone made him struggle to his feet as the man came at him again. Bent over from the pain, Rhys still managed to drive his head into his attacker's solar plexus, forcing him backward and into the bottom of an overturned cart.

The man recovered more quickly than Rhys, launching himself once more into the fray. As Rhys staggered forward, he again ran into the man's punishing fists. The left struck his jaw, rocking his head back. The right, as if in payment for his previous momentary success, came up under his ribcage.

Deprived again of the ability to breathe, this time for a very different reason, all Rhys could do was cling to the man's thickset shoulders with both hands. From his limited experience with the kind of bare-knuckle brawler he now knew he faced, he understood that once he went down, the man's boots would replace his fists.

Rhys braced for the next blow, knowing that whatever happened, he had to hang onto consciousness so he could get Nadya and Angel away. Motivated by fear, not for his own life, but for theirs, Rhys gathered waning reserves.

He sagged against his opponent, feigning a greater weakness than he felt. At the same time he brought his knee up and, with every ounce of strength in his lower body, drove it into the vulnerable area between the man's thighs. His adversary crumbled, slipping from Rhys's grasp with a drawn-out scream.

Knowing that one posed no further threat, Rhys turned, looking for the rest of the men who'd surrounded the Gypsy. He realized with a jolt of terror that he and the bare-knuckled bruiser he'd fought, now writhing on the ground, were alone.

Everyone else, including Nadya and her daughter, had disappeared.

Chapter Seven

Nadya had watched Rhys fight with her heart in her throat. She now realized that with her request she'd put the ex-soldier into an impossible situation. It was unlikely that, recently recovered from a debilitating fever, he could hold his own against such a physically imposing opponent.

When he fell to his knees, head hanging in exhaustion, she'd set Angel down on the ground, quickly making the sign for 'stay.' Then she'd begun to search frantically among Andrash's scattered belongings for a weapon—any weapon—to use against Rhys's foe.

Before she could discover one, she'd watched unbelievingly as Rhys seemed to explode upward, driving the bull-necked man into the blacksmith's overturned cart. At that point, she had taken her eyes off the fight to check on her daughter, only to find Angel was no longer where she'd put her.

Nadya turned in a tight circle, desperately searching for a glimpse of her child. First in her immediate vicinity. And then among the shadowed figures rushing through the smoke-filled clearing.

The encampment was like a scene from a nightmare. And no matter how hard she strained to see through the haze, she could find no trace of her daughter.

She glanced back at Rhys, who was braced for his opponent's next assault. Without a weapon, she could be of little help.

Besides, her greater responsibility was to her daughter. She had to find Angel and get her away from the dangers around them. Dangers that increased by the second.

The two places the child might consider to be safe havens were Nadya's caravan and that of her grandmother. The little girl had spent time in both and each was associated in her mind with people who loved her.

Her own *vardo* was closer now than Magda's. With that alone as the deciding factor, Nadya began to run toward it.

Panicked at the thought of her daughter's danger, she never considered her own. When they'd set out, she had instinctively led Rhys through the shadows cast by the trees. Now she flew through the centre of the camp, skirting the knots of men engaged in hand-to-hand combat.

When she reached her wagon, she gathered the skirt of her nightgown in one hand to scramble up its steps. There were half a dozen places inside that might offer concealment. Since Angel was unable to hear or respond to her voice, Nadya would have to search them all. And without light, she decided, which might bring unwanted attention.

Frantically she ran her hands along shelves, into cupboards and under the narrow beds. As she searched, the cacophony of sounds from outside seemed to grow in volume and hysteria.

It was somehow more frightening not to be able to see the darting figures, but only to hear the hate-filled shouts and the occasional scream. And even more terrifying to think Angel might be somewhere in the midst of that insanity.

Satisfied at last that her *vardo* was empty, Nadya descended its high steps, only to realize that someone was running toward the caravan. She had a fraction of a second to decide whether to try to hide or to fight her way past the approaching man.

'*Drabarni?*'

Nicolaus, she realized in relief. 'Have you seen Angel?'

'No, *drabarni*. Have they taken her?'

The concern in his voice was almost her undoing. Up until now Nadya hadn't even thought of that possibility.

Now she knew she must. An English child in the middle of a Romany camp might well be considered someone in need of rescue. Someone to be taken back to 'civilization.' Someone who would eventually, perhaps, be returned to that awful existence from which Nadya had wrenched her away.

'I don't know. Please help me find her, Nicolaus. Will you go into the forest and see if she's there?'

'Of course, *drabarni*. What will you do?'

'Make sure she didn't go to Magda's caravan. If you see her—' She hesitated, unsure what to tell him. 'If you see her, take her with you. Keep her safe, Nicolaus.'

Nadya was off before he had a chance to reply. She headed back in the direction from which she'd come, again cutting straight across the disordered compound.

A dozen of the tents had been set afire. Here and there were upended carts, some of those ablaze as well. A few fights still raged, but it quickly became apparent that more and more of the Rom had slipped away, recognizing that they couldn't defend the camp against the larger force.

Theirs was a strategy perfected through the centuries. They would melt into the forest, carrying their most valuable possessions, mostly gold and gems, which were always kept hidden where they could be snatched up with a few seconds' warning.

The rest—the pots and pans, clothing and bedding, even the implements of their trades—could all be replaced. Their lives could not.

Their lives.

Someone in the *kumpania* would surely have scooped up a wandering child and carried her with them, Nadya told herself. If Angel wasn't in Magda's caravan, then she'd been taken to the woods. The Rom, any one of them, would keep her safe.

Please, dear God, let her be safe.

By some miracle she managed to reach the other side of the clearing without incident. Her grandmother's *vardo*, too heavy for the marauders to tip over, appeared unmolested.

She hurried up its steps, flinging aside the curtain at the top. The fires outside were bright enough to illuminate the front. After a cursory search of that, Nadya ran toward the sleeping partition at the rear. Angel sat upright in the middle of the bed they'd shared since Rhys had regained consciousness. Her rag doll and the cat Rhys had carved for her—forgotten in the initial terror—were clasped to her chest.

In the dimness, the child's eyes were wide and dark with fear. As Nadya bent toward her, the little girl's trembling thumb made a familiar stroke down her cheek—the sign Nadya used for reassurance. Quickly echoing that gesture, Nadya picked up her daughter, hugging her close.

Tears of joy sprang to her eyes at the feel of the small solid body against hers, but despite the overwhelming flood of relief she felt, there was no time for emotion. They were back where they'd started, and the journey they must undertake to safety seemed even more fraught with peril than before.

Nadya wrapped her own shawl around the child, who shook with cold or fear, and carried her toward the front of the wagon. Shifting Angel into a more upright position, she managed to negotiate the steps. Once on the ground, she took a moment to assess the situation.

The myriad fires had made the clearing as bright as day. Only a few of the Rom still resisted, a rear-guard action intended to give the women and children as much time as possible to get away. As she hesitated, her eyes searching for the best path into the forest, one of the remaining men called to her.

'You found the girl, *drabarni*?'

Panuel. She nodded to him, her arms automatically tightening around her daughter. 'I have her. She's safe.'

'I'll tell the others. Nicolaus told us to look for her.' He glanced over his shoulder at the smoke-shrouded centre of what had been their encampment before he turned back to her, his eyes troubled. 'You should go now, *drabarni*. There are too few of us left to hold them off for long.'

Nodding her thanks, Nadya turned to run in the direction she'd decided was her best chance of escape. Before she had taken more than a dozen steps, a dark shape loomed out of the smoke in front of her.

'Here she is! I found her!' the man shouted.

Nadya sidestepped as he lunged at her, evading his hand. He came at her again, eyes shining in the light reflected from the torches that were approaching in response to his call.

This time the man's fingers closed over her shoulder, locking on it painfully. Knowing she would soon be outnumbered, Nadya reacted with desperation.

She turned her head and sank her teeth into the fingers that held her, biting down to the bone. The man released her with a strangled cry, shaking his hand as he danced away.

As soon as his grip had relaxed, Nadya jerked free. She sprinted toward the woods, uncaring, now that she had Angel, about anything other than losing her pursuers in the welcoming darkness of the forest.

Despite telling himself over and over that Nadya had taken her daughter and fled into the nearby woods, Rhys knew something was wrong. She had asked him to intervene on the Rom's behalf. Would she have deserted him in the middle of that intervention?

A few of the English were still applying their torches to anything that hadn't yet been burned. The Rom, who had fought so valiantly at the beginning of the attack, seemed to have disappeared.

A strategic retreat, based on the disparity in numbers? Or cowardice on a scale he hadn't seen in all his years of combat?

Whatever the case, Rhys knew his efforts alone couldn't turn the tide of this battle. And if Nadya and her daughter were safe...

If.

Maybe she'd gone to check on her grandmother. Or maybe she had remembered something of value she'd left in her own caravan.

After an unconscious assessment of which would be more likely for Nadya to do, he found himself running toward the wagon where Angel had taken the wooden cat that afternoon. As he ran, he realized that despite the fight, his body was still able to function with relative effectiveness.

The effects of the fever seemed to have passed. As long as he didn't receive another blow to his damaged shoulder—

A cart was overturned almost in front of him. It hit the ground with a clatter of pots and pans, the force of its fall causing the shroud of smoke that choked the camp to waft aside momentarily. In that brief window of visibility, Rhys saw the old woman's *vardo*.

That it was still standing elated him after the destruction around him. That emotion that was quickly replaced by another.

One of the attackers, easily identifiable as English by his clothing, stood near the bottom of its steps. He pointed toward the edge of the clearing, shouting something unintelligible.

Rhys's gaze automatically tracked in the direction of the Englishman's outstretched arm. A woman ran toward the woods. A woman who carried what appeared to be a child wrapped in a shawl. A woman in a long, white gown.

Rhys's heart had begun to pound before the smoke once more obscured the scene. He broke through it, running as if his life depended on it.

Because he had seen what the woman could not.

Under the direction of the man at Magda's caravan, two others rushed toward her, approaching at an angle. Their paths would intersect before she could reach the safety of the trees.

It wasn't Nadya. She'd had more than enough time to reach the woods since she'd disappeared. She wouldn't still be in camp.

Even as his brain supplied those assurances, Rhys ran. His breath sawed in and out of lungs that burned with exertion. The ache in his shoulder, which seconds before had seemed a mere inconvenience, was once more nearly paralyzing in its intensity.

At last he broke through the pall of smoke that hovered over the encampment. The woman he followed had reached the shadows under the trees. And the men he'd seen before—

As he watched, one of them reached out to catch her arm

and drag her away from the relative safety of the woods. She fought back, striking at her attacker with her free hand.

As she struggled, the shawl fell away from the head of the child she carried. Firelight danced over long, fair hair, leaving no doubt in Rhys's mind about her identity.

Calling on reserves he couldn't believe he possessed, he increased his speed. The heavyset man who'd been shouting directions to the others was almost to them as well.

Operating under the military principle that one should take out the leader first, Rhys threw himself at the person he perceived to be in charge. The shouting man went down, the air forced out of his lungs in a great whoosh as Rhys landed on top of him.

Knowing that Englishman would be out of action for at least a couple of minutes, Rhys clambered up and headed for the one still struggling to control Nadya. The invader's eyes widened as he realized he was about to come under attack. That realization didn't happen in time to allow him to evade the blow Rhys aimed at his chin.

He went down as if poleaxed. Without breaking stride, Rhys gripped Nadya's elbow, pulling her with him into the shelter of the beeches. After progressing only a few feet, he recognized that, burdened as she was, they would never be able to outrun their pursuers.

'Give her to me.' Breathless and exhausted, he could barely get the words out.

'I can carry her,' Nadya protested.

'Not fast enough to keep her safe.'

She hesitated only a heartbeat before she handed the little girl to him.

'Now run,' he ordered. 'I'll be right behind you.'

Her eyes expressed doubt, but despite it, she nodded. She knew these environs far better than he did. And hopefully better than the invaders as well. That might be the sole advantage they had.

As Rhys wrapped his good arm around Angel and prepared to follow the blur of white that was Nadya's gown, he could only pray it would be enough.

Nadya leaned against the trunk of one of the trees and listened. The only sound was their laboured breathing.

Somehow they had managed to elude the men who'd pursued them. Through luck or justice or divine intervention, nothing else was moving in the darkness at the heart of the forest.

As she waited, straining to hear footfalls among the fallen leaves, her pulse began to slow, the terror that had fuelled her run draining from her body. She turned, looking at the man who had, as he'd promised, carried her daughter to safety.

His profile was limned by the distant light of the fires they'd left behind. Still intent on the possibility of pursuit, Rhys seemed unaware of her scrutiny.

Her eyes fell to the child he held. The doll Magda had made her was clutched to her chest. Her other hand, its fingers holding the wooden cat, was around Rhys's neck.

Angel's gaze, however, was focused on her mother. Nadya smiled at her, reaching out to run her thumb down the child's cheek. There was no response. The blue eyes appeared to rest on her face, but they were unseeing.

They'd come so far, Nadya thought in despair. Too far to allow the little girl to sink back into that state of apathy in which she'd found her.

Reaching out, she pulled her daughter from Rhys's arms. He seemed surprised, but released the child as soon as he understood what she wanted.

'Is she all right?' he whispered.

Wordlessly, Nadya nodded. She tucked Angel's head into the crook of her neck, laying her cheek against the child's. With her right hand, she stroked her hair comfortingly.

There was no response. The child's body was cold. Almost rigid. Just as it had been so long ago.

Had this night of terror destroyed the sense of security she and Magda had worked so hard to instil? Had all their efforts been for naught?

She denied the possibility, because she couldn't bear to believe it. As soon as they were somewhere warm and quiet, Angel would recover. All they needed was a place where fires didn't light the sky and screams didn't echo through a terrifying darkness.

'Do you know where we are?' Rhys whispered.

'Of course.'

She wasn't as confident as she sounded. But just as there was no reason to tell him about her concerns over Angel, there was no need to let him know that as they'd fled, she had obeyed his instructions. She'd run with one goal in mind. To outpace the men who followed and lose them in the vast forest.

Apparently, she'd succeeded. Eventually, she would be able to lead them to the place where the tribe would reassemble.

And when she had, she would once more begin the slow, painstaking process of recreating that blessed sense of safety for her daughter.

Rhys had been relieved when Nadya made the very sensible suggestion that they should devote the remaining hours of darkness to rest. Despite her confidence, he'd grown increasingly concerned that they might be travelling in circles. Or even worse, that the path they were on might take them into contact with the men who'd pursued them. Besides, it was evident they'd both reached the limits of their endurance.

Nadya had insisted on carrying her daughter, refusing all offers of help. And although yesterday he'd thought himself well enough to travel, he had discovered tonight that his recovery had not progressed so far as to prepare him for fisticuffs as well as a run for his life.

The thick trunk of the tree they'd taken refuge under provided what had seemed an adequate backrest. Rhys's intent had been to sit upright and vigilant. With the ache in his shoulder, he'd had no doubt he would be able to stay awake.

He hadn't. Despite the pain, despite the discomfort of the cold, hard ground and the even harder wood against his spine, exhaustion had won out.

He awoke with a start, uncertain for a moment where he was. When he remembered, he turned his head to be sure the woman over whom he'd planned to stand guard was still safe.

His chin brushed her hair. That was because, he discovered, her head now lay against his shoulder, the dozing child cradled in her arms.

He drew a deep, unsteady breath at Nadya's closeness. Despite the days during which she had cared for him, this was a vastly different kind of intimacy.

Because *he* was different. No longer her patient. No longer an invalid.

He had acknowledged from the beginning that she was a desirable woman. And while society might wink at a sexual liaison with someone like Nadya, as it accepted the reality of soldiers who satisfied their needs with camp followers, it would brook no other association between them.

Besides, Nadya was someone to whom he owed his life. To him, that meant any carnal relationship between them was quite beyond the pale.

The feel of her body against his now evoked none of that moral high ground. He wanted her. He wanted to tilt her face up to his. To press his mouth against hers until her lips opened, welcoming his tongue.

He eased another breath, trying to ignore the growing clamour of his senses. As he did, he became aware of the lingering smell of smoke in her hair. And underlying it, the sweetly subtle, now-familiar scent that was uniquely hers.

Like everything about her, that, too was slightly alien. Not the flower-based perfumes favoured by the women of the Ton. Nor the sensuous musk preferred by the high-born Spanish ladies he'd encountered. Nadya's scent was elemental. The way air smelled after a rain. Clean and fresh and lovely.

As she was.

A loveliness that he admitted was vastly different from the image that word had once evoked of blue-eyed blondes, their pale arms and rounded bosoms encased in delicate pastels, a scrap of lace at their throats.

Now it suggested dusky arms, shapely from hard work. Hands that healed. Dark eyes that flashed as often with amusement as temper. Hair that smelled of sunlight.

So close now that he could touch it with his lips.

He must have moved. Drawn another breath. Something. Nadya stirred, turning her face into his shirt. Through its thin fabric, he felt the warmth of her breath on his skin.

She was cold. Or that's what he told himself. He eased his arm behind her back, settling her more closely against his side. The movement changed the angle of her head, so that her face was now raised to his, her lips parted, exactly as he'd envisioned them awaiting his kiss.

Tempted beyond rational thought by their unintended invitation, he lowered his head to press his own against them and realized that he would wake her if he did. He brushed her forehead with his mouth instead, the motion as light as the breath that fluttered over his chin.

When he lifted his head, he hoped her eyes would open in response. Both she and the child slept on, however, unaware of what had just occurred.

Unaware that whatever their relationship had been before—whatever noble nonsense he had told himself in a fruitless attempt to place this woman off limits—it had all changed. Erased by the feel of her body against his. An experience that, like all the others from the days he'd spent in the Gypsy encampment, he would never be able to put out of his mind.

Nadya Argentari was not of his world. Nor he of hers. Together, they would be welcome in neither.

Despite what he felt, it would be better, safer, easier for them both if he did exactly what he had intended. He would leave in the morning. Once away...

Although he knew them for a lie, he repeated the words, trying to instil the concept more firmly into his rejecting brain. Once away, what he felt for her would fade. He would again find attractive the women who inhabited his world. Those inane simpering blondes, with their pale skin and soft useless hands.

Someday...

Chapter Eight

'Here.'

Nadya had bent to examine what appeared to be a broken twig. On closer examination, Rhys could see a bit of thread had been wound around its stem, pulling it down at an angle.

She'd been searching since sunrise for *patrin*, the signs the Rom always left to mark their trail. Despite the bedlam of last night, Nadya had had no doubt she would find them.

'What does that tell you?'

She glanced up, as if surprised by the question. Her eyes were still reddened from the smoke, the circles under them like old bruises. The dawn chill brushed colour along her cheekbones, emphasizing the slight hollows that seemed to have formed beneath them overnight.

'That they went in this direction.' She pointed toward the sun, its first rays turning the leaves of the beech trees gold.

Rhys shook his head, unable to see how the twisted thread could possibly provide that information. Still, they were her people. She had told him they would mark the trail they'd taken, and evidence that they had was before his eyes.

'We'll make better time if you let me carry Angel a while.' Rhys anticipated that Nadya would again refuse, as she had since she'd taken the child from his arms last night. In truth, he was paying a price this morning for his attempted heroics. He had slipped his left hand into the waist of his trousers in an attempt to relieve the steady ache of his shoulder.

'I don't want to wake her.' Without another word, Nadya set off again.

Seemingly indefatigable, despite her burden, she walked steadily for the next two hours, stopping only to examine the signs that appeared with regularity. After she'd examined the last she'd found, she turned to him.

'There's a stream just beyond that rise.'

Rhys had been wondering how much longer he could stay on his feet. Until she'd mentioned water, however, he hadn't been aware of his thirst.

'Did they tell you that?' He lifted his chin to indicate the bit of thread.

She shook her head. 'We camped here occasionally when I was a child. *Because* of the water.'

'But you don't now?'

She shrugged. 'It's too close to the village.'

The one from which last night's marauders had come? Rhys wondered before he realized it didn't matter. Ever the outcasts of society, the first to be suspected when things went wrong, the Rom might well have been attacked by the inhabitants of any of the small hamlets scattered around the vast forest.

'I'm sorry about what happened.'

She looked surprised. 'Why? It wasn't your fault.'

'Because it shouldn't happen. Not here. Not now.'

She laughed at his naivety. 'It's *always* happened. Here. Everywhere. People fear what they don't understand.'

'You're more accepting than I could ever be.'

'Because you've never *had* to accept it. We always have.'

'What about your caravan? And your horses?'

'The horses would have been taken into the woods last night as people fled. As for the rest, someone will return to the encampment to recover whatever's left. Everyone knows what's expected of them in this situation.'

'What's expected of you?'

'First, escape. Afterward to care for those who were injured. And the quicker we catch up to the rest, the quicker I'll be able to do that.'

'Do you ever offer your services to the villagers?'

That would seem a dangerous practice, given what she'd said last night about the possible motives for the attack. What if someone she had treated died? Or if the illness worsened or spread?

'I have, but…' She shrugged. 'There are risks involved. Not unlike those in any of our dealings with the *gadje*. But if I feel I can help someone, it's difficult to refuse.'

'Have you helped—or refused your help—lately?'

She shook her head, her laugh rueful. 'Mostly they come for charms or potions or to have their fortunes told. None of those are my domain. And Magda is very skilful in handling those dissatisfied with the services she provides. After all these years, she should be.'

There were probably no answers for the questions last night's raid had created in his mind. Unless…

He hesitated because he knew how Nadya would respond. Still, this was something that had troubled him from the beginning of their acquaintance. Might it not also trouble the villagers?

'What about Angel?'

'Angel? I don't understand.' Despite her disclaimer, her tone was defensive.

'I thought someone might have questioned how she came to be with you.'

'Why would they? Angeline is my daughter.'

Rhys allowed his gaze to fall to the face of the sleeping child. The fair hair and pale skin contrasted with the rich colours of the shawl that covered her.

Still, it didn't take a great deal of perception to know he was treading in sensitive territory. 'I don't mean to pry—'

'Then don't. Angel isn't your concern. None of this is. Someone will have brought your bay out of camp. As soon as we find the rest, you can be on your way. Just as you'd planned. I'm sure your family is becoming anxious.'

That door had been firmly shut. And actually, Nadya was right. Unless he seriously believed she had stolen the child, who was obviously happy and well cared for, the fact that Angel was with the Rom was none of his affair.

'I think we have time to find the water you spoke of before they send out a search party.' He smiled at her, trying to soften the taut lines of her face.

She didn't return his smile, but Nadya, too, seemed more than ready to end any discussion of Angel's origins. 'It isn't far. Are you close to your godfather?' she asked as she turned to lead the way.

Rhys accepted the change of subject, thinking about his relationship to Keddinton. 'He was a boyhood friend of my father's. I'm not sure anyone, including my father, believed he would climb to the heights he's achieved.'

'Friends in high places. If only we had those…' She let the sentence trail as she began the climb up the rise.

As Rhys followed, he was forced to acknowledge the accuracy of her last statement. In a country dominated by

men of means and position—men like Lord Keddinton—
Nadya and her people would always be on the outside
looking in. Outsiders even among those on the fringes of
society. Like their attackers last night.

And despite his gratitude to the woman who had saved
his life, there was nothing he could do to change that.

Although she hadn't confided as much to Rhys, Nadya
had had a very good idea where the *kumpania* would
gather. Their nomadic existence was far more ordered than
the *gadje* were aware, since they had visited and revisited
the same areas for the last two hundred years.

People became accustomed to finding them in the same
spots at certain times of the year. Establishing that routine
was good for the tradesmen within their group, who
enjoyed the patronage of many repeat customers.

And in spite of the bitterness of her tirade when she'd
seen the torches winding their way through the woods last
night, most of the time their relations with the people
among whom they lived were, of a necessity, both cordial
and productive. That wasn't to say events like the raid were
unknown. Only that they had become increasingly rare.

She hadn't shared any of that with Rhys, who seemed determined to believe the cause of the attack had something to
do with her. And in the back of her own mind were the words
of the man who'd accosted her: *Here she is! I found her!*

Perhaps some of the others had gleaned some information about what precipitated the raid. After Rhys left, she
would ask around to see what the consensus was.

As they entered the new encampment, everyone was
already hard at work. Whatever could be salvaged from the
destruction would be repaired and again put to use. What
had to be replaced would quickly be made, or purchased,

either in one of the nearby villages or from one of the itin-
erant tradesman.

As for the human toll, that was her job. She hoped no
one had been seriously injured, of course, but she knew she
would welcome the demands on her intellect that using her
skills would make. She needed something to think about
besides the troubling thoughts that had occupied her
emotions the last few days.

'*Drabarni.*' A man repairing a broken axel straightened
to speak to her, his eyes examining the Englishman beside
her suspiciously. 'Welcome back.'

'Thank you, Paul.'

'You found your baby, I see. We all looked for her after
Nicolaus told us she was missing.'

'She'd gone back to the *vardo* to get her doll. I should
have known that's where she'd be.'

The Rom laughed, his ready good humour restored,
despite the job that lay ahead. But then, as she had told Rhys,
they were accustomed to bearing the brunt of others' anger.

'Do you know where my grandmother is?'

'Seeing to Andrash.' He pointed across the clearing,
which under the experienced hands of the *kumpania*, was
rapidly filling with tents and stacks of firewood and the
smell of cooking. 'That one will welcome your return, I
think.' Then, nodding politely to them both, he bent again
to his work.

Nadya turned to Rhys, once more aware of the gulf that
separated her world from his. While she'd talked to Paul,
his eyes had been surveying the emerging camp. She
couldn't help but wonder what he thought about it all.

'After I see what is wrong with Andrash, I'll send
someone to find your horse.'

'You have enough to do. I can scout around for him.'

She wasn't sure how to explain to him her concerns with that plan. 'It might go better if you let me make inquiries.'

A raised brow expressed his puzzlement.

'In situations as chaotic as last night, questions of ownership arise.'

'Are you suggesting someone may lay claim to him?'

'If they feel they rescued him when you didn't.'

'An interesting view of property rights.'

'Learned from the *gadje*, I believe.' Unkind, perhaps. And almost certainly untrue. In light of the viciousness of the attack that had been launched against her people last night, she didn't particularly care.

'If that's the case, I should probably present my claim as soon as possible. If you'll excuse me.' Rhys bowed slightly before he turned and walked away.

Nadya fought the urge to apologize for her rudeness, but there was nothing to be gained by prolonging his stay. Rhys needed to return to his world. To get on with whatever he'd been doing before he'd encountered her daughter.

And saved her life. Despite the gulf she'd just acknowledged, Nadya would always be joined to this particular *gaujo* by that debt.

The problem was that gratitude was no longer the primary emotion she felt when she thought about him, and yet it was, no doubt, the only one he'd be willing to accept from the likes of her.

Surprisingly, Rhys seemed in no hurry to leave the encampment. Although she didn't have an opportunity to talk with him again, Nadya spotted him several times during the course of the day working with one or another of the people trying to put their lives back together. Paradoxically, in spite of the fact that he was a member of the race who'd caused the destruction, they all seemed to welcome his help.

Magda had offered to watch over Angel while Nadya tended the wounded, but she had chosen instead to keep the child with her as she worked. Normally too active for that, today Angel seemed content to watch as her mother applied salves to burns and bound cuts.

As Nadya had suspected they might be, Andrash's injuries were among the most severe. Like most of those she'd tended during the long day, he, too, seemed in re-markably good spirits.

Only much later, her concentration was broken by a commotion at the centre of the camp, did she realize it was almost sundown. She glanced up from yet another patient to see Stephano's stallion protesting the attempt the men were making to unsaddle him.

The black's owner strode across the clearing to the table where she worked. Her half-brother hadn't yet changed into his Romany clothes. The tailoring of the dark blue jacket he wore above tight-fitting pantaloons and gleaming Hessians was far more stylish than the jacket she'd cut off Rhys.

Obviously someone had sent word to Stephano about last night's troubles. Judging by lathered flanks of his mount, he'd come as soon as he'd heard.

Nadya lifted her hand to push a strand of hair out of her eyes. Physically and emotionally drained, she didn't relish having to deal with her hot-tempered half-brother.

'What happened?' Stephano demanded.

'We were attacked.' As she answered, she turned her attention back to the splinter she'd been trying to remove from the hand of Anna's grandson. The waning light would make the job more difficult.

'By whom?'

'By someone who didn't like something we'd done. Perhaps our breathing offended them.' She didn't lift her eyes from what she was doing.

'You'd had no trouble before?'

'None I'm aware of,' she said truthfully.

She had at last managed to grasp the sliver of wood imbedded in the child's palm. Her half-brother had the courtesy to hold his questions until she'd successfully manoeuvered it out and sent the boy away with a smile in lieu of the sweet she would normally have offered for his braveness.

With his next inquiry, Stephano discredited the consideration she'd just ascribed to him. 'But then you have been occupied with other, more pressing matters, haven't you?'

Exhaustion and despair at once more seeing her people under attack suddenly boiled over in an unexpected—and for her, uncharacteristic—fury. 'No busier than you, Stephano. At least I was here.'

Her half-brother's lips flattened, but he didn't deny the unspoken accusation. His eyes fell instead to Angel, who'd finally fallen asleep on the nest of blankets Nadya had spread for her. 'Was she hurt?'

At the concern in his voice, Nadya's anger dissolved, leaving nothing behind but the despair she'd fought all day. 'She was terrified. For all I know, she still is. She's shut out everything—and everyone—again.'

'Bastards.' Before the sibilance of Stephano's expletive had faded, he stooped, balancing on the balls of his feet in front of the little girl's pallet. With his thumb, he traced along the upturned nose and then down to the Cupid's bow mouth.

Angel's lids fluttered open. The blankness that had been in her eyes since last night vanished in an instant. A flash of joy replaced it, as she launched herself into Stephano's arms.

They closed around her as he straightened, lifting her high into the air. Laughing, he swung her around and around. As he did, the little girl raised her face to the sky, closing her eyes in ecstasy.

Tears stung Nadya's eyes, but she denied them. She revelled, instead, as her daughter seemed to, in her half-brother's laughter. For Angel, apparently all was right in any world her beloved uncle occupied.

'I believe she's glad to see me.' Stephano smiled at Nadya.

'We're all glad to see you.' Although her words had been softly spoken, she knew he'd heard them by the upward tick of his lips. 'Your place is here.'

'When it's done, *jel'enedra*. When it's all done, I promise you.'

'And what if the pull their world exerts is still stronger than your love of this?' With her hand, she gestured toward the camp that had literally sprung up around her as she'd worked.

'It isn't. It could never be.'

She wished she could believe him. Not only for the sake of his people, but also for the sake of her child, who so clearly adored him.

Whatever enticement she might have come up with to keep him here was interrupted by another commotion. Her hand shading her eyes against the glare of the sinking sun, Nadya watched as Rhys drove her *vardo* along the cart path that led from the main road. His brother's bay and a piebald mare, which she recognized as belonging to Andrash, had been fastened between its traces.

At first glance, the caravan seemed undamaged. She could only hope its contents had fared so well.

Even if they hadn't, she knew she was lucky to recover anything at all. Far luckier than so many of the others.

Andrash was seated on the high seat beside the Englishman, who now directed his team toward the place where she and Stephano stood. And with that realization, Nadya knew the confrontation she'd hoped to avoid for so long was finally at hand.

Chapter Nine

Nadya glanced at her half-brother. Stephano's eyes were narrowed as they followed the approach of her *vardo*.

'If you desire so ardently to have me stay, *jel'enedra*, why do you continue to defy me?'

'If it hadn't been for the raid—'

'Your *gaujo* would be gone?' Stephano mocked.

'You should be grateful he was there last night. He's the one who awakened us.' Her eyes touched on the child Stephano held. 'He rescued Andrash from the *gadje* who were beating him. He fought off the men—' She hesitated, trying to decide if she wanted Stephano to have that information.

'What men?' Her half-brother's gaze left the approaching caravan to search her face.

If she told him that some of the attackers had apparently been looking for her, it might tip the scales in Rhys's favour. She wasn't sure why she felt it was so important to have Stephano approve of the ex-soldier. After all, Rhys would be gone soon enough. If it would make the next few minutes any easier, however…

'Some of them seemed to be looking for me.'

'Some of the English?' It was strange to hear the word on Stephano's tongue, since he had for so long been one of them.

She nodded, refusing to meet his eyes, keeping hers focused on the approaching caravan instead.

Andrash had leaned over to whisper something to Rhys. Warning him about what he should expect from Stephano? If so, that was not without justification.

'Why would the *gadje* be looking for you?' her half-brother prodded.

She shook her head. 'I don't know. All I know is if Rhys hadn't been there, neither Angel nor I would have escaped.'

'Then it seems we owe him another debt of gratitude. Unless, of course, those were his people who came last night.'

'Why would you possibly think—'

'As good as when you left it, *drabarni*.' Andrash interrupted her question. Despite the bruises and abrasions that marred his face, the blacksmith was smiling broadly.

Nadya forced an answering smile. 'Thank you for bringing it to me, Andrash. I didn't expect to have it back so soon.'

'Everything inside seems undamaged as well,' Rhys added, his eyes considering the man at her side. 'Of course, no one but you can be certain of that.'

'Whatever's left, I'm grateful for it. Thank you both.'

What they had done did involve some degree of danger. It was always possible the attackers might be lying in wait for anyone foolish enough to come back for possessions.

Rhys pulled his team up so expertly that the high seat of the caravan was now directly in front of them. To occupy her suddenly trembling hands, Nadya adjusted her shawl, which had slipped to her elbows as she'd worked.

'Won't you introduce us, Andrash?' Stephano said smoothly.

The blacksmith didn't have as much experience as Nadya in reading her half-brother's tone. Still smiling, Andrash turned, putting his hand on the Englishman's shoulder.

'This is my friend Rhys Morgan, *Rom Baro*. He saved me from a beating last night.'

'And today he is as close to you as any brother. Despite the fact it was his kind who beat you,' Stephano added maliciously. 'How easily duped you are, Andrash.'

The smile faded from the smith's abused face, replaced by a look of bewilderment. 'You don't understand, *Rom Baro*. He fought on our side last night.'

'The better to ingratiate himself into your good graces, no doubt. And those of my sister as well.'

'Rhys has no need to ingratiate himself with me,' Nadya said evenly. 'Although I am now doubly grateful to him for again safeguarding my daughter's life.'

Stephano ignored her, speaking directly to the Englishman. 'Were they friends of yours last night? Or did your enemies follow you to our camp?'

'No acquaintances of mine, I assure you. And if I have enemies, I'm unaware of them.'

Rhys's tone and demeanour suddenly reminded Nadya of the title she'd given him in the beginning. *My lord*. Despite his claim to be nothing more than a simple soldier, right now he seemed every inch the English aristocrat.

'How could they have been either,' she challenged her brother, 'when no one knew Rhys was with us?'

Stephano was quiet long enough she wondered what she'd said that had given him pause. She certainly didn't believe that convincing him Rhys wasn't a threat would be this easy.

'It seems, then, we are all indebted to you for your heroic actions last night,' Stephano said finally.

'There could hardly be indebtedness, considering the circumstances of my being there. As for heroics, I've seen too much of the real kind to classify any action of mine that way.'

'Nicely played.' Stephano's tone was openly sardonic.

'The simple truth,' Rhys said quietly.

'Truth is seldom simple, my friend. A lesson my people learned long ago.'

'It's simple to soldiers. You fight for king and for country. And to protect those…deserving of your protection.' The hesitation, although slight, was unmistakable.

'Then I thank you for fighting to protect my people. Now that I'm back, I hope you'll no longer feel an obligation to delay your journey. Nadya tells me we've kept you from an important appointment.'

Rhys's eyes briefly considered her face. She refused to allow anything of what she was feeling to be expressed there.

'A meeting with my godfather,' Rhys agreed. 'But its importance is merely personal.'

'Then Godspeed,' Stephano said pleasantly. 'Andrash, would you see to the gentleman's horse.'

'Of course, *Rom Baro*.'

The smith hopped down from the seat of the caravan and began to remove the bay from the traces. He still seemed troubled by what Stephano had suggested about the Englishman, his eyes darting uneasily between his leader and his saviour.

'Now if you'll be so kind as to excuse my sister…' Stephano once more addressed Rhys. 'Her patients take priority over everything else. As you have reason to know, I believe.'

It appeared that Stephano was determined to get Rhys away as soon as possible. Nadya knew that any objection on her part, no matter how reasoned, would only strengthen his resolve. That didn't prevent her from making one.

'If Rhys leaves now, he won't be able to reach an inn before nightfall.'

'What a shame he didn't think of that sooner.' Her half-brother's tone was perfectly amiable. 'No matter. Our stalwart hero was a soldier, Nadya. I'm sure he's undertaken more dangerous enterprises than a solitary ride in the moonlight.'

It wasn't simply that Stephano wanted Rhys gone, she realized. He wanted that to happen without their having an opportunity to say goodbye.

'It's all right,' Rhys assured her as he climbed down from the caravan. He seemed almost amused by her half-brother's machinations.

Of course, he hadn't been subjected to them for as many years as she. 'No, it isn't.' And then to her brother, 'This is against every tenet of hospitality. Even Andrash is troubled by what you're doing.'

'If he is, he knows better than to say so. As should you.'

It was a battle of wills she would lose. If she continued to protest, Stephano was perfectly capable of ordering the men to throw Rhys out of camp—possibly without the gelding. And in spite of the Englishman's hard work among them today, she had no doubt they would obey.

In order to prevent such petty vindictiveness, Nadya held out her hand to him. 'Thank you again for all you've done for us. I apologize for my brother's behaviour. The only excuse for his lack of hospitality is that he was raised by the English.'

Rhys's eyes considered the well-dressed man at her side before they came back to smile down into hers. 'I've found no lack of that among your people. Or from you. I owe you more for that kindness than I can ever express.' Then, in spite of Stephano's watchful gaze, he took her hand, carrying it to his lips. 'Thank you for my life, *drabarni.*'

Her throat thick with all the things she could not say to him, even if her half-brother had not been listening, Nadya nodded.

Rhys held her fingers a heartbeat longer than politeness decreed before he smiled at her again and released them. As he began to turn away, Angel leaned forward in her uncle's arms, clearly reaching for him.

'May I?' Rhys said to Stephano.

'You believe your blood calls to hers?'

'I *believe* we've become friends.'

'Angel has all the friends she needs among the *kumpania*. And none of them will disappear from her life forever.'

The child continued to try and touch him, but short of attempting to wrest the little girl from Stephano's arms, there was little Rhys could do. He took her outstretched hand and, exactly as he had done with Nadya's, brought it to his lips.

When he released her, Angel ran her thumb down his cheek, Nadya's sign for reassurance. Sensing tension among the adults, the little girl offered him comfort.

'Goodbye, little one,' Rhys said softly. 'Take good care of your mother.'

In response, Angel put her hands beside her ears, fingers pointing upward. Confused by the gesture, Rhys shook his head.

Angel's brow furrowed and then cleared. She brought one of her hands down, licking it delicately before she rubbed it against the side of her face.

'Cat?' Rhys guessed. 'Did you lose your cat?'

'It's here,' Nadya told him. 'She's held it all day. I think she may be thanking you for making it for her.'

Smiling, Rhys again touched the tiny hand, still slightly damp from Angel's demonstration. Only as he turned to mount the bay Andrash had quickly saddled, did Nadya realize this might be the last time she'd ever see him.

The horse danced a little under his weight, but Rhys easily controlled him. He nodded to Stephano before his eyes found her face. They held on it a long moment before he touched his heels to the gelding, sending him down the same trail along which he had so expertly driven her caravan.

The three of them watched until even the dust from his passage had faded into the twilight gloom. Nadya turned, holding out her arms for her daughter.

As Stephano gave Angel into them, he said, 'I think I may have returned just in time.'

'Don't make assumptions about things you can't possibly understand,' Nadya warned.

'What can't I understand?'

'Friendship. Respect. Honour.'

'Honour? From a *gaujo*?' he mocked.

'A *gaujo* like your father.'

'You think that one honours you, *jel'enedra*? Whatever he feels for you, believe me, has nothing to do with honour. You are no more to him than a serving wench at the next tavern he comes to. He may enjoy her tonight because of a lust you engendered, but that's all he'll ever feel for you. An itch he's far too fastidious to act upon.'

She had raised her hand to strike him, but Stephano caught her wrist with fingers that enclosed it like a vice.

'Another of his simple truths. In his eyes you are nothing more than trash blown about by the wind. Remember what I have told you, *jel'enedra*, but forget him.'

He held her until the fury in her eyes had been replaced by a sheen of moisture. Then, with the thumb of the hand that had bruised her arm, he wiped away the single escaping tear, bringing it to his lips, which slowly curved into a smile.

'His kind aren't for us. And we aren't for them. Our mother should have taught you that.'

'At least she didn't teach me to hate.'

'Hate is a shield to stop you from being hurt.'

'Or being loved.'

'There are worse things.'

Nadya glanced down at the child she held before she shook her head. 'No. No, there aren't. Maybe one day you'll understand.'

Stephano laughed. 'Don't try to reform me, *chavi*. You'll only break your heart.'

That it was already broken was something she would never confess. Not to him. Because, whether protective or simply vindictive, Stephano would use any excuse she gave him to take revenge on another member of the class he blamed for ruining his life.

Chapter Ten

'Believe me, Rhys, I should like to help you,' Robert Veryan, Lord Keddinton said, 'if for no other reason than the normal expectations of our relationship and my friendship with your father. Your commendations and service record, however, take precedence even over those.'

The ladies had finally departed, leaving the two of them alone in the vast dining room of Warrenford Park, the viscount's country estate. Keddinton's daughters, who had flirted with Rhys quite openly, had resisted all their mother's efforts to shepherd them away.

Although he had been waiting for this meeting with his godfather through the long months of his convalescence, Rhys had concealed his impatience and answered their endless questions about his adventures in Iberia. In the course of that conversation, the girls had let slip something Rhys had not been aware of. Apparently the crown, grateful for Keddinton's valuable, if clandestine, activities during the war, intended to reward him shortly with an earldom. Which should, he thought, bode well for the success of his mission.

'Thank you, sir. For considering both.'

'You must understand, however,' Keddinton went on, swirling the dregs of his brandy, 'that the capital is flooded with ex-soldiers, all of whom believe they have the same expertise to offer. And many of them have connections that, quite frankly, trump any you might claim.'

Since Keddinton was Rhys's only connection to any seat of power, he realized he'd been counting too heavily on his godfather's help. It wasn't that he believed Keddinton lacked the influence to secure him a position. It seemed that, for whatever reason, he wasn't inclined to do so.

'I quite understand,' Rhys said, attempting to mitigate the embarrassment of having asked for a favour that the man had no desire to grant. 'I appreciate your time in hearing me out.'

'Go home, my boy. Help Edward with the responsibilities of running the estate. You've sacrificed more than enough in the service of your country.'

'I've never considered my service to be a sacrifice. It's all I've ever wanted to do.'

'England's been at war for almost a dozen years. You've known nothing else your adult life. It's time to enjoy the fruits of your labour, Rhys. Particularly the blessed fruits of peace, which has accrued to all of us because of the sacrifices made by you and others of your generation. Now it's up to my generation to secure a lasting peace in Vienna, so that your children and grandchildren won't be called upon to put down another tyrant.'

'And that's exactly the task I should like to help with. Believe me, sir, I would consider no post beneath me.'

'Don't undervalue your gifts, Rhys. I can't see you as someone's undersecretary or clerk. You're too fine a man for that. And too valuable to your family. Go home. Enjoy what you've helped to secure. Your father would have wished that for you, I'm sure.'

'Thank you, sir.' Rhys lowered his eyes, afraid his host would read the bitter disappointment in them.

He was vain enough to wonder, at least briefly, if Edward, acting behind his back, had urged Keddinton to take this tack.

And why should he have done that? Edward doesn't need my help anymore than England apparently does.

'I know you're disappointed,' Keddinton said kindly, 'but believe me, this is for the best.'

'I'm sure you're right,' Rhys agreed, lifting his own glass to drain it.

'Now tell me more about the accident you suffered on your journey here,' Keddinton urged. A change of subject they probably both welcomed.

'A minor mishap,' Rhys said. 'Unfortunately, it coincided with a recurrence of the relapsing fever I contracted on the Continent, delaying my arrival. I apologize for the inconvenience that may have caused you.'

'No inconvenience at all. I only wish your note had provided more information about your location. Our local man is quite renowned for his skills. As a matter of fact, you should let him take a look at that shoulder while you're here.'

'It's much improved, thank you.'

If there was anything Rhys desired less now than having another sawbones prodding about among his wounds, he couldn't think what it might be. He knew he would judge any other 'healer' by a standard that had been set impossibly high.

'And the fever?'

'Successfully treated with bark from a tree in Peru.'

'Indeed. I shall ask Dr Jennings if he's familiar with the remedy the next time I see him. Who did you say dosed you?'

Rhys hadn't said, but with the heady effects of the

brandy he'd just downed, he could see no reason not to. 'A Gypsy healer.'

'How did you come to be involved with the Rom?'

'It's a long story.'

His godfather had already informed Rhys upon his arrival that he was off to London on the morrow. Although the conference in Vienna had cut into the normal autumn activities in town, his daughters had begged to be taken to the capital, and their indulgent father had agreed.

Despite his impending journey, Keddinton signalled the hovering butler to pour out another measure for each of them. After the servant replaced the bottle on the sideboard, the viscount said, 'That will be all, Simmons. I shall call you if we need anything more.'

As soon as the door closed behind him, Keddinton smiled at Rhys. 'Believe it or not, I knew a Gypsy girl once. More given to curses than healing, I'm afraid. I should be very interested to hear your story. And if it takes a while, we can always call Simmons back for another round.'

It seemed the brandy had mellowed his godfather's mood. Although Rhys refused to allow himself to hope, he raised his glass in a small salute to the older man's request.

'No curses involved in this. Actually, it all started with the most bucolic of scenes—a small fair-haired child running across a country meadow.'

After Rhys finished his tale, their talk had ranged on for another hour or so, touching on a variety of topics. Keddinton attempted to catch him up on the current affairs of his father's boyhood friends, most of whom represented to Rhys nothing more than a vaguely remembered name.

Despite their advantages of birth and wealth, few of them, it seemed, had reached the heights to which the viscount himself had climbed. Despite having refused Rhys's request, Keddinton didn't hesitate to refer to those in power with whom he enjoyed a deep and abiding friendship.

'Come up to town with me tomorrow, and I'll introduce you to him,' he said of one such acquaintance. 'Actually, I've been invited to a soirée at Fairmont's townhouse on Friday night. I'm sure you'd be welcome.'

'I thank you, sir, but perhaps you're right. I should go home and offer Edward my services—belated though that offer might be.'

'I'm certain your brother wouldn't begrudge you some small entertainment before you settle down.'

The offer was tempting. Besides, what could it possibly matter if Rhys delayed his return a few more days?

Even a few weeks, he admitted. His brother and sister-in-law would probably be glad to have their home restored solely to themselves. If only temporarily.

Which brought up the larger question. The proposed trip to London would only delay the evitable: a return to his brother's estate and his brother's largess.

Rhys would, no doubt, be given things to oversee, which he would, of course, carry out to the best of his ability. And both of them would know, but never admit openly, that those duties could have been done more efficiently by any of the extremely competent people his brother already employed.

'What say you?' Keddinton's thin lips were curved into a smile, his greying brows raised questioningly.

Why not? Rhys thought. Better that than the prospect of what lay ahead.

And far, far better than dwelling on the events of the last two weeks.

'If you're sure it won't inconvenience you.'

Keddinton's smile widened, although it never seemed to

reach his eyes. 'I should be delighted to have you accompany me. Do you a world of good, too, I should think. I'll write Fairmont and tell him of our plans before I go up to bed.'

The days since the raid had been exhausting, but Nadya had welcomed their demands. They helped fill the void she refused to acknowledge, even to herself. Instead she sought ways in which she could help those members of the *kumpania* whose lives had been disrupted by that night's horror. In doing so, she sought to atone for the nagging sense of responsibility she felt about what had happened to them.

After Rhys left, Andrash had come to her to warn her that she should be on her guard. He'd told her that the men who'd beaten him that night had been asking for the *drabarni*. The smith was concerned enough about the possibility they might return that he set up his new tent beside her *vardo*.

While downplaying any threat to herself, Nadya admitted to a sense of relief that he was there. She had no idea why she might have been a target for the raiders' anger, but Andrash's story, added to what the Englishman had said when he found her, argued that might be the case.

As she tried to think of anything she could have done to incur the villagers' ire, her greatest fear was that Rhys's speculation had been correct. That what had happened was in some way connected to her daughter.

Although Stephano had left the day after Rhys, having him in camp, even if for only a few hours, seemed to have set Angel's world back on its axis. Although the little girl still didn't want to let her mother out of her sight, she was at least willing to communicate her fears. And thankfully, her eyes were no longer filled with terrifying memories— both old and new.

In short, life was returning to normal. The move to a new

encampment, although forced and traumatic, had been no real inconvenience, considering the *kumpania's* normal nomadic existence. Most of the possessions that had been damaged or destroyed in the raid had been repaired or replaced. Their injuries were healing, even those of the spirit.

Why then did her life feel so empty?

It wasn't that Nadya didn't know the answer. It was that, in knowing, she had no remedy for it. In all her store of medicines, with her grandmother's legacy of wisdom about healing, there was nothing that could cure the sense of grief and loss she felt.

The loss of a thing that had never belonged to her. And never could.

Once she had foolishly believed she possessed everything she could ever desire. Then fate, that fickle deceiver Magda was always talking about, had mocked her arrogance by showing her something she'd never even dreamed of, before snatching it away to place it forever out of her reach.

The tailor his godfather directed him to was located on Old Bond Street and, Rhys decided from the look of the clothing displayed in the bow window, apt to be costlier than either he or Edward had anticipated. He hated to offend Keddinton, however, by not taking his advice in the matter.

As he stood before the shop, weighing the unaccustomed dilemma, a hand fell heavily on his good shoulder. 'Too rich by far for the likes of you. They're cutting cloth for broken-down half-pay officers a bit farther down the street.'

He turned to find Reginald Estes, late of His Majesty's service, standing behind him. Reggie's round face under its thatch of unruly red hair was wreathed in a smile that left no doubt about his delight in running into a former comrade-in-arms.

'Is that where you got your coat, Reggie? If so, I shall try my luck inside.' Laughing, Rhys slapped the former lieutenant on the back.

The bottle-green creation Estes wore might be the latest fashion for all he knew, but if so, neither Keddinton nor his brother had yet adopted the style. However, the intricately tied cravat at its neck was, Rhys acknowledged, very nearly a work of art, and the cream pantaloons fit his friend without a wrinkle. Reggie's valet must be a talented man to have turned the usually slovenly ex-soldier out so well.

'Oh, no doubt Weston's the best. You won't go wrong here if you're after something your grandfather might wear. 'Course, the bastard's a bit touchy when it comes to paying one's bill. Weston, that is. Not your grandfather. Never met your grandfather that I recall.'

'Since he's been dead for twenty years, you're unlikely to. I will say, however, that he was always well-dressed.'

The good-natured jibing that had been so familiar to Rhys during his days in the Army was welcome after the gloom and doom of the past few months. It seemed a burden that he hadn't been aware he carried had been lifted by Reggie's silliness.

'What are you doing in town, you old cod?' Reggie asked, clapping him on the back in return. 'Besides seeing to your deplorable wardrobe.'

'Spending a few days with my godfather. He suggested this place.'

'Probably ashamed to take you about in your present state. Come on. I'll introduce you. Dressed like that, you'll need someone reputable to vouch for you.'

During the next two hours, Rhys found himself committed to purchasing a vast array of garments he was assured were the absolute minimum any gentleman might require. Even a gentleman, Weston's helper said with a slight sniff, who planned to live quietly in the country.

Rhys couldn't argue with the quality of the fabrics he was shown. Although he avoided the plum superfine Reggie swore was 'all the go,' he was more than pleased with his final selections.

The tailor made no comment about his injury as he expertly pinned the material to hide the slight difference between the height of the damaged left shoulder and the right. Considering the number of ex-combatants returning to England during the last few months, the man had probably seen much worse. Or so Rhys told himself as he was finally permitted to don his own clothing once more.

After the fittings, Reggie had insisted on taking him home for tea. His wife, he assured Rhys, would be more than delighted to make his acquaintance.

'She doesn't believe half the stories I tell her of what we got up to over there. I'll be forever in your debt if you convince her I ain't lying about the rooster and that priest.'

Rhys had almost forgotten the story, but the mere reminder of it had them laughing all the way to the Estes front door. Despite their hilarity on arrival, Reggie's wife Charlotte did seem pleased to meet him.

Once Rhys had been ensconced in the most comfortable chair in the sitting room—the one nearest the fire, of course—she had bustled about, making sure the blaze wasn't too warm or his tea too weak. And in spite of the somewhat delicate nature of the story, Charlotte had covered her mouth with her handkerchief, laughing and blushing prettily when Rhys verified Reggie's version of the affair of the Spanish rooster, leading him to decide that his friend had chosen very wisely indeed.

Actually, the afternoon passed so pleasantly that Rhys had begun to envy Reggie, who'd sold out almost two years earlier due to the untimely death of his father. As heir and now head of a family that included several much-younger brothers and sisters, it had been clear to everyone that Reggie was needed more desperately at home, despite Napoleon's continued perfidy.

It was only after the tea things had been cleared away that Charlotte sent to the nursery for the new baron's daughter. The child, held in the capable arms of her nurse, displayed a head of hair the same unfortunate colour as her father's. Luckily, its texture was like that of her mother's, so that instead of sticking straight up, it formed a halo of adorable copper ringlets around her chubby face. Her eyes, bright blue—also a mirror of her mother's—stared unblinkingly at Rhys.

Suddenly she held out her arms to him. Both her parents and the nurse made appropriate cooing sounds, leaving him no choice but to take her.

The little girl immediately snuggled against him, as if she believed he knew what he was doing. And due to the hours he'd carried Angel, Rhys realized he did.

'I think she likes you,' Reggie said admiringly. 'Of course, Rhys always did have a way with women,' he confided to his wife. 'A regular Don Juan, with those eyes and that hair. The senoritas loved the contrast to their own dark Romeos.'

'Unlike his tale about the rooster, ma'am, that is, I can assure you, the veriest falsehood.'

'I'm certain my husband would never lie to me, Major Morgan. And I promise you, my darling,' she said to Reggie, 'that not every young lady prefers chestnut curls to something more…colourful. And so very interesting,' the young baroness finished with a smile.

'You should get yourself one of those,' Reggie said, bringing Rhys's gaze up from the tiny fingers that were examining his stickpin.

'A wife? If I could find one half as charming as your Charlotte, believe me, I would.'

'I was referring to Isabella. You appear to have cast your spell over my daughter, just as you did all those… ahem…older ladies we encountered.'

Looking down into the wide blue eyes of Reggie's little girl, Rhys felt something shift in his chest. They reminded him too forcibly of those of another child, one who had looked up at him with this same trust. Something the very privileged child he was holding had known from the hour of her birth.

'I must say, Major Morgan, you look as if you've had some experience with children.'

Rhys raised his eyes to meet those of his friend's wife. 'My brother has three—grown or away at school now. And all boys, I'm afraid.'

'Oh, and are you partial to girls?'

'I believe I might be,' Rhys admitted, looking down again into the baby's face.

'Told you,' Reggie said snugly. 'Nothing but a ladies' man, Char. And if you ask me, that's a sad, sad commentary on the current state of our military.'

Chapter Eleven

Since Keddinton was engaged that night, Rhys had no reason to hurry back to his godfather's mansion. Charlotte had been pleased to have him stay for dinner and pleased to leave the two men alone afterwards.

The evening had been spent in laughter and good memories shared between the old friends. Through some unspoken agreement, neither of them had mentioned the other kind of memories.

'So it's back to Balford for you?' Reggie asked finally.

The bottle they shared was almost empty, and the fire in the grate had, by mutual consent, not been fed in the last half hour. Although it was past time for him to leave, Rhys had no desire to return to that splendid and sterile establishment Keddinton maintained in St. James's Square.

'I suppose so. My godfather feels that's the best thing.'

'Not his decision, I should think.' Reggie's speech had begun to slur slightly, but Rhys knew that would be the only sign of his friend's intoxication.

'No, but without his help, what I had hoped to accomplish in London seems impossible. As I understand it, there are too many of us "broken-down, half-pay officers" loitering about, all apparently seeking some position in the government.'

'He's right about that. Town was full of 'em all spring and summer. A shame you weren't up to par then. Most of the Light Horse was here at one time or another.'

Only those who'd survived, Rhys thought. He quickly banished that reminder. It didn't fit with the pleasant mood of the day. Something he was attempting not to lose.

'I wish I could have been here.'

'Next Season. Come up and snatch a rich wife for yourself. Then you won't have to worry about your godfather doing the right thing by you.'

'Is that what you did, Reggie? Scouted for a rich wife?'

'I fell in love with the first blue-eyed beauty who batted her lashes at me. That was such a novelty after those years spent among the doe-eyed senoritas.'

His gaze on the dying fire, Rhys had a brief mental image of another pair of dark eyes. Because of them, he knew that no matter how much time he spent in London during the coming Season, he wouldn't fall prey to a blue-eyed beauty.

'Whatever your method of choosing a bride,' he said aloud, 'marriage seems to agree with you.'

'Char's a good girl. Got her head set on straight. No silly fits of the vapours. And she ain't constantly nagging me to take her to balls and such. We spend most of our evenings at home, just as quietly as this one. And with Bella, that's been even more enjoyable. I highly recommend falling in love, my lad. With the right woman, of course.'

'And what if one falls in love with the wrong woman?' Rhys asked softly.

For a long time there was no sound in the room but the

hiss and pop of the dying fire. Then Reggie bestirred himself to pour the last few drops left in the bottle into his glass.

'Care to tell me about her?'

'What?' Lost in his thoughts, Rhys was almost unaware his friend had taken up his last statement.

'The wrong woman. Is she married?'

'No.'

'Poor as a church mouse, then?'

'Probably.'

'But you don't care.'

He didn't, Rhys realized. For a man without any prospects except his brother's charity, that was a hell of an admission.

'It seems that I don't,' he confessed.

'Then...what's the impediment?'

Rhys's laugh was a breath of sound born out of all the impediments society would very quickly point out if he dared bring Nadya into their midst. Even good friends like Reggie would be appalled.

They would think it strange if he dared to take the Gypsy as his mistress. To even consider making her his wife...

'Can't think of one?' Reggie teased. 'Then decide which pair of your new britches will most readily bend at the knee. Without detriment to their fit, of course.'

Rhys shook his head, lifting his own glass in an effort to break the pall of melancholia that had fallen over his spirits. He hadn't allowed himself to think about Nadya in those terms before. Now, having acknowledged the barriers that loomed around such a notion, he couldn't get it out of his head.

'Shall we broach another bottle?' Reggie asked as he struggled out of the depths of his chair. 'Can't believe I've let a friend's cup run dry.'

'Not for me,' Rhys said. 'It's obvious by the direction this conversation has taken that I've had quite enough.'

'So what *is* the problem?' Reggie stooped to stir the embers. When they flared up, he put his hands before them, his back to Rhys. 'Is she a light skirt? Afraid you'll introduce her to a friend one day only to discover they are already…a little too well acquainted?'

'I don't believe that's a possibility.'

Not for *his* friends. And he realized that the number of men with whom Nadya might be 'well acquainted' was something he couldn't bear to consider.

'Cross-eyed? Buck-toothed?' Reggie asked straightening away from the grate. 'No, you're too accustomed to diamonds of the first water falling all over you to consider any lesser level of pulchritude. You don't care if she's poor, and you don't think she's a whore. What's left?'

Rhys shook his head, lowering his eyes again to his glass.

'You can't bring her up, old boy, and then make a state secret of why she's unacceptable. And I'm far too drunk to think up any more reasonable guesses.'

'If those are your *reasonable* guesses—'

'Reasonable in that they'd keep most of us from proposing marriage. Clearly they aren't your reasons. We've been friends a long time, Rhys. Endured situations together I wouldn't live through again for anything in this world. So if you choose not to tell me why the woman you love is unacceptable…' Reggie shrugged and turned back to the fire.

'She's Romany.'

The word fell into the room like a stone tossed into a still pond. He could sense its effect on his listener, although Reggie didn't move. Not immediately.

When he did turn, his brows were raised. 'A Gypsy?'

Rhys nodded, searching his friend's face for any sign of disgust or disbelief.

'How the hell did you meet a Gypsy?'

'It's a long story. And that really doesn't matter. I only told you so that you'd understand why…' He stopped, realizing the trap he'd fallen into.

Why I can't marry her? Why society wouldn't accept her if I did? Why my family and friends would never speak to me again?

'Never met one myself,' Reggie said. 'A looker?'

Rhys hesitated, unsure how to convey to his friend the beauty he found in Nadya's slightly alien features. Especially in light of Reggie's earlier confession about having fallen in love with Charlotte after only one look at her very conventional English charms.

'Much like the women we met in Spain, I suppose. But…different as well.' Although inadequate, the adjective was accurate.

'You can't marry her,' Reggie said bluntly. 'Not the thing. Not done, you know.'

'Why should it matter? Any more than Harry Smith marrying his Juana.'

'You ain't Smith, Rhys. And this isn't enemy territory. Men do strange things when they're at war.'

'I don't think that had anything to do with Smith's decision.'

'Maybe not. I don't know and I don't care why he did what he did. I'm just telling you that you can't bring a Gypsy into Society. You have to know that. Besides, your family wouldn't stand for it.'

'I know.'

It felt like a betrayal of his feelings for Nadya to admit it, but Edward would be appalled. And furious. Whatever warmth had grown between them in the last few months would be totally and irreparably destroyed.

'Nothing but thieves and liars, the lot of them.'

'That's not true, Reggie. They're no better or worse than the rest of us. The ones I encountered seemed decent enough.'

'Tell that to the Carlows. See what they say to you.'

'The Carlows? Do you mean Hal's family?'

'Damn Gypsies put a curse on them. Years ago, of course, but some of the bastards are still causing them trouble.'

'If Hal told you that, he's having you on.'

'I didn't hear it from Hal. To be honest, I can't remember where I heard it, but my ears pricked up because of who was involved. Something about the family having been tied in with a traitor. He murdered some nobleman, who'd taken a Gypsy mistress. She cursed everyone involved. And their descendents. Can't remember what happened to the families, but the Carlows seem to think there's something to the tale.'

'The Rom I met were interested in nothing but making an honest living. Hardly the stuff of curses.'

'Make fun if you will, but what I'm telling you is the truth. How'd you feel about introducing your Gypsy to Hal's family under the circumstances?'

'I'm not introducing her to anyone. Frankly, I'm sorry I mentioned her. I had thought the two of us could talk about this with some semblance of sanity.'

'About you marrying a Rom? Is that what you call sanity? I doubt your brother will think so. Or the Carlows.'

'I'm sure you're right.' Rhys got to his feet, putting his glass down at the table by his chair. 'Thank you for a pleasant evening, Reggie. Please convey my gratitude as well as my compliments to your wife.'

'Now don't go all stiff-necked on me, Rhys. We've been friends too long for that.'

'Just not long enough to listen to one another with civility.'

'I'll be as civil as you damn well please, but I can't stand by and watch you ruin your life. No one you know would receive her. You'd be an outcast as surely as if you were a traitor. And in a way—' Reggie stopped, his flushed face revealing the depth of his emotions.

'And in a way…?' Rhys prodded softly.

'In a way, you would be. To your family. Your class. You know that as well as I do. You just don't want to admit it.'

There was nothing to say in response to that claim. Rhys did know how they'd react.

'Have her if you want. We've all felt that burn in our blood for someone unsuitable. Be discreet about it, and no one will be the wiser. Lapses in judgement, even of the sexual sort, tend to follow a man, if you know what I mean.' Reggie reached out to touch Rhys's shoulder in much the same way that he had on the street today.

His friend had spoken honestly, his view a reflection of that most of their acquaintances would express, but the sense of camaraderie Rhys had felt earlier was gone. He and Reggie had fought side-by-side on more occasions that he could count. He'd once ridden off the battlefield behind Reggie after his own animal had been shot from beneath him. They had been friends for years. And they would remain friends. Those ties went too deep to be totally severed.

Besides, Reggie had spoken out of love and concern, not vindictiveness. He'd never even met Nadya. With his generosity of his spirit, he would probably treat her with respect if he did. And yet, having acknowledged all those things, Rhys knew he would never again feel about Reggie Estes as he once had.

* * *

Rhys remained in London only a couple of days after the uncomfortable ending to the evening he'd spent with his friend. Seeming preoccupied, Keddinton hadn't prevailed upon him to prolong his visit. His godfather had instead reiterated his advice that Rhys should return to his brother's home and content himself with the life of a country gentleman.

Rhys had said all that was polite, hiding his disappointment about the viscount's refusal to help him. Keddinton had children of his own, as well as several other godchildren, and he was presently involved in the attempt to find a diplomatic solution to the havoc Napoleon had wrought on the map of Europe. Why should he be concerned with the affairs of another 'broken-down half-pay officer,' despite whatever long-ago friendship he'd shared with his father?

Rhys prevailed on Weston to complete one of the coats he'd ordered and then arranged for the rest of his purchases to be sent on to Balford Manor. They seemed too fashionable for the life he should lead there, but given their quality, they would undoubtedly last for years. Perhaps even until country fashions caught up with those of the town.

He considered visiting Reggie again to say goodbye, but couldn't bring himself to do it. His friend might have told him only what anyone else would have if they'd known about his feelings for Nadya, but in Rhys's head those uncomfortable truths would always be associated with his former comrade-in-arms. And after all, Reggie hadn't seen fit to call on him either.

As he looked out of Keddinton's carriage, Rhys's mood matched the bleakness of the rain-washed October landscape they were passing through. He was returning to the comfortable cocoon of his brother's home, an existence he'd left with such high hopes only a fortnight before.

Like a dog with its tail tucked between its legs.

The analogy might be apt, but it also smacked of self-pity, something he had thus far managed to avoid. He'd survived a wound that by all rights should have killed him. He still had the use of an arm the field surgeons had been determined to amputate. And he possessed a family who would welcome his return. What the hell did he have to feel sorry for himself about?

He allowed the curtain to fall over the glazed window and leaned back against the comfortable leather seat. No, he would do exactly what he had always done. Make the best of the situation in which he found himself. Undertake whatever task he was given and do it to the best of his abilities. And be grateful for the many things with which he had been blessed.

Eventually, he would succumb to Abigail's matchmaking and establish his own household. He would have children, and he would raise them to value the same precepts he'd been taught. Courage. Honour. Loyalty. The latter included, of course, loyalty to his family, his friends, and as Reggie had pointed out, even to his class.

And if he occasionally dreamed of something very different from all of those, he would endeavour to keep those dreams—which could become nothing else—to himself.

Chapter Twelve

Rhys spent one night at his godfather's country estate after he left London. As he set out for home the following morning, his brother's bay again seemed almost as eager as he. Their solitary ride along sunken lanes that ran under the cathedral-like branches of the beech trees, their beauty shrouded in the morning mist, epitomized everything he'd missed about England during his long absence on the Continent.

Unfortunately for his peace of mind, it also reminded him of the days he'd spent in the Gypsy encampment. The closer he came to the area where he'd first encountered Angel, the more difficult it became to deny his feelings for her mother. Or the troubling thoughts that had haunted him after the raid.

Nadya had refused to answer his questions about her 'daughter,' but he knew that the fair-haired child did not share her blood. Could the mystery surrounding the little girl's origin be at the root of the hatred he'd seen at work the night of the raid? If so, then they both were still at risk.

It was only as he skirted one of the villages scattered on the downs that he realized he might be able to track down and then question at least one of the participants of that attack. There couldn't be that many Olivers living in these hamlets near the original encampment.

Most of the villages would be small, consisting of fewer than two dozen families. In each, he had no doubt he could find a gossip willing to point out any man of that name.

Once Rhys had seen that man with his own eyes, he would know whether or not he was the one who'd been pummelling Andrash that night. And if so, he thought with a sense of purpose that replaced the one his London sojourn had destroyed, he had some pummelling of his own to do.

No Oliver resided in either the first or second settlement Rhys visited, but in the latter someone had sent him to a nearby village where, they said, a certain Oliver Burke lived. Once there, he received direction to Burke's cottage from the first person he encountered.

The man he'd sought was sitting on a stool outside his thatch-roofed croft, smoking a pipe with a neighbour who leaned indolently against its stone wall. If there had been any doubt in Rhys's mind he'd found the right Oliver, it would have disappeared at the shock in the villager's eyes when he recognized his visitor.

Rhys dismounted in the lane and then, holding the reins of the bay, walked toward the two. He wasn't able to identify the second man as someone who'd been involved in the raid, so he turned his attention to the first, on whose jowl he could see a yellowing bruise. One Rhys was certain he'd inflicted.

Burke had forgotten to draw on the pipe he held as he'd watched Rhys approach. His gape-mouthed stare made it clear the Englishman he'd encountered in the Gypsy camp was the last person he had expected to find on his doorstep.

'Oliver Burke?' Rhys made his inquiry in a tone that had once been reserved for disobedient subordinates.

The man swallowed. His florid face flushed a deeper crimson, but his reply was full of the same kind of bluster he'd displayed during the raid. 'Who'd be asking for him?'

'Major Rhys Morgan. Of His Majesty's 13th Light Dragoons.' Rhys had used his rank deliberately in an attempt to create some perceived authority for his mission. 'I'm seeking information about a recent attack on the Rom encampment in Harpsden Wood.'

The neighbour straightened, seeming to shrink away as if trying to distance himself from such an act. Even if the bully Rhys had encountered that night refused to recognize his right to ask questions, the reaction of the man with whom he'd been sharing an evening smoke indicated that the rest of the villagers would probably acknowledge it.

'Don't know nothing about any raid.'

'I *know* you were there.' Rhys said without a hint of uncertainty. 'I saw you. I heard someone call you by name. That's how I found you.'

'You be mistaken, friend. I haven't been in the Wood in more'n a year.'

'I have no intention of disputing the point. All I want to know is *why* you went there last week.'

'You be mistaken,' he said again. 'Whoever you saw weren't me.' Burke raised his pipe to take a draw. If not for the tremor of his hand, the act might have been effective. As he blew out the cloud of bluish smoke, he shook his head. 'Got nothing to tell you 'cause I know nothing about no raid.'

'I wonder which of us the magistrates will believe.'

The man's mud-coloured eyes went dark with a sudden

fury. Then his face hardened, because he knew the answer to that as well as Rhys.

'They be thieves, the lot of them. Honest folk got a right to protect their property.'

'Is that what you were doing? Protecting your property by burning theirs?'

'You never saw me light no fires. I'll call you liar if you say you did.' Burke shook his pipe to emphasize his point.

'I saw you drive a woman and a child from their home and then pursue them into the forest.'

'What concern be that of yours? The wench your woman? Is that why you were in their camp?'

'I was injured, and she cared for me. I owe her my life.'

Something changed in the beefy face. 'You went to the Rom for healing?'

'How I came to be there isn't under discussion. How you came to be there, on the other hand…'

'I told you. I wasn't.' The man had reverted to his original denial.

For a moment Rhys didn't react. Then, just as a malicious amusement had begun to dawn in the mud-coloured eyes, he hooked his toe under the bar at the front of the stool Burke was sitting on and jerked it from under him. The man fell backward, hitting his head on the stone wall of his own cottage.

The neighbour took the opportunity to bolt. Rhys wondered briefly if he'd gone for help. If so, he had even less time to acquire the information he'd come for.

He reached down with his right hand to pull Burke upright by the sturdy homespun of his shirt. Twisting the cloth more tightly between gloved fingers, Rhys threatened, 'Tell me why you went to the camp that night, or I swear to you, I'll knock your head against that wall again.

And I'll keep knocking until you'll beg me to let you unburden yourself.'

If Burke had expected him to abide by any kind of gentlemanly standards, he would soon realize his mistake. After all, the villager was still a dangerous man. He was strong as an ox and had proven himself to be without scruples. And he was almost twice Rhys's weight.

'Now tell me why you were there.' Rhys tightened his grip in preparation for carrying out his threat.

'A swell paid me,' Burke croaked.

The information wasn't what Rhys had been expecting. For a moment, it caught him off guard.

'Who?' he demanded.

'Never told me his name.'

'What did he tell you?'

'To go to the Rom camp…and make trouble.'

The hesitation before the last indicated he was lying.

'And you took it upon yourself to decide what kind of trouble that would be?' Disgusted, Rhys threw Burke back against the wall.

Hands against the ground, the man pushed himself upright. 'Look here, you,' he began, trying to regain his former bluster.

In response, Rhys picked up the stool he'd overturned and, holding it by one leg, swung it back as if intending to use it. 'I'll crack open your head if you lie to me again.'

For the first time since the confrontation began, the bully visibly cowered.

'Who sent you?' Rhys demanded, pressing his advantage.

'Never told me his name.' When Rhys again threatened with the stool, he lifted his forearm, holding it in front of his face. 'That's the truth. I swear to you.'

'You don't know him, but you were willing to do his bidding. At some risk to yourself and the others.'

'He paid me.'

'How much?'

'Five guineas. And enough for drink to convince the others.'

To put them in the right frame of mind, Rhys thought bitterly. 'And what did he pay you to do? Exactly.'

Burke's eyes considered his face and then the raised stool. 'Find their healer and burn her out.'

Although his instincts had told him there had been some personal animosity involved in the violence he'd witnessed that night, hearing those words chilled Rhys to the bone. All the fears for Nadya's safety that she herself had belittled came flooding back.

'Kill her, you mean?' he demanded sharply.

The man shrugged. 'He just said to burn her tent to the ground.'

That's why so many of them had been set to the torch. And why the two caravans, which should have been their real targets, had remained untouched.

'You didn't bother to ask why?'

'Wasn't none of my concern, now was it?' Burke's cockiness was beginning to return.

'If I wanted to find the man who paid you, where would I look?'

Burke shook his head. 'Never seen him before or since.'

'You saw him then. When he gave you the money. Tell me about him.'

Burke shrugged again. 'Like yourself.'

'What does that mean?'

'Wore a neckcloth. High boots. A beaver. And the way he talked, a' course.'

It made no sense. Why would a gentleman wish to harm Nadya? Unless Rhys's first suspicion had been correct.

'And the child? What did he tell you about the girl?'

Burke shook his head, his puzzlement seeming sincere. 'Never said a word to me about naught but the healer.'

'And the rest of what happened? All cover for the murder you were about?'

'That's not all on me. They were up for it. Abram's cow took sick right after the Gypsies come back to the Wood. Everybody knows they bring bad luck. Animals sicken. Babes, too. Crops fail. No good ever came of letting them close.'

Nadya had been partially right in what she'd said that night. Any accusation, no matter how ridiculous, was enough to set off the kind of rampage Rhys had witnessed. This man might have been paid to instigate that attack, but with enough liquor, his fellows had had no qualms about joining in his mischief.

'I ought to kill you now.' Without his conscious volition, his arm cocked the stool again.

'Here, now,' Burke protested, his forearm poised once more to ward off the expected blow. 'Don't do nothing you'll come to regret. You and me can strike a bargain.'

Rhys laughed. 'What do you have to bargain with? You claim not to know the name of the man who paid you.'

'I don't. I swear it. But mayhap I can find it out.'

'How?'

The man's shoulders rose again in a shrug, but he didn't lower the protecting arm. 'Go back where I met him.'

'And where was that?'

'The Bull and Bear.'

The Bull and Bear was an inn near Wargrave. According to the loquacious innkeeper at Buxton, it had a reputation for bad ale, damp mattresses, and travellers who awoke in the morning with sore heads and empty pockets.

'And what would a "swell" be doing in that rathole?'

'Looking for rats,' Burke said shrewdly.

He was right. Where else should a gentleman go to find someone willing to undertake his dirty work?

'What makes you think he'll come back there?'

'Don't know as he will. What I *do* know is I'm the only one who can sniff him out for you if he does. You give me your direction—'

'And you'll come and tell me if you see him again?' Rhys laughed. 'What kind of fool do you take me for?'

'One who's interested in why someone would want to get rid of a Gypsy. Or have I got that wrong?'

He didn't, of course. That didn't mean Rhys trusted Burke to provide him with any information he might stumble upon.

'I'll give you two days to discover his name.'

'What if he don't show up in that time?'

'Someone at the inn is bound to know him. It will be up to you to discover that person.'

'What's in it for me if I do?'

'More than he paid you.'

'More than five guineas?' The thought created an avaricious gleam in the mud-coloured eyes.

'If your life's worth more than that to you.' Rhys set the stool down. 'Because I promise you that your life is what it will cost if you fail.'

Burke's gaze held on his a long time before he nodded agreement. Rhys had no way of knowing whether he would carry out the mission he'd been given. He might choose to disappear instead, but his property here argued against that.

For some reason he had believed Burke's claim not to know the name of the man who'd sent him. That assessment was based on nothing more solid than having dealt with a great number of men under stressful situations.

Yet those same instincts had served Rhys well during his years in the Army. All he could do was trust to them now.

Chapter Thirteen

$\infty\!\!\!\!\infty\!\!\!\!\infty\!\!\!\!\infty$

In the turmoil of everything that had happened the past weeks, poor Angel had suffered the most. From the days Nadya had spent caring for Rhys to the terror of the raid and through the tribe's forced relocation, the little girl, who had few emotional reserves to begin with, had experienced the kind of disruption that would have proven a disaster only a few short months ago.

Other than her obvious distress on the night of the attack, she had somehow managed to weather those storms, which had shaken even the adults. Nadya knew, however, that the fragile fabric of trust she'd worked so hard to create must, to some extent at least, have been damaged.

With Rhys and Stephano both gone and the injuries the tribe had incurred during the attack now healing, she had directed her full attention to reassuring Angel that nothing had changed about the love that would always be her due. Every sunny afternoon found the two of them in one of the meadows near the clearing where the *kumpania* was encamped.

Today Nadya had spread her shawl over the grass. She sat, the book in her hand forgotten, watching her daughter run in ever-increasing circles around her. Angel was apparently pretending to be a bird, arms spread wide in the autumn sunshine.

Too few fine days like this remained before the rain and the cold would drive them back inside, Nadya thought with a sigh. And there, despite all her attempts at exorcism, the ghost of a tall, fair Englishman still haunted her.

As she had so often during the last week, she tried to change the direction of her thoughts. She turned her head, looking at the nearby beeches whose leaves had begun to shade toward bronze with the drop in temperature.

After a moment, her eyes returned to the field before her. For an instant her heart faltered, until she spotted the small figure she sought. Angel was no longer running in circles. Instead, as straight as an arrow's flight, the child headed toward a solitary horseman who had just appeared on the horizon.

Nadya scrambled to her feet, shading her eyes with her hand as she tried to make out his identity. Not Stephano. The gloss of the horse's hide wasn't midnight black.

By that time she, too, had begun to run, her longer stride eating up the distance between her and her daughter. At some point she realized that the rider had spurred his mount, so that he, too, was racing toward the little girl.

And despite any effort she could make, he would reach her long before Nadya could.

Her every instinct screamed danger. Rhys's questions about Angel echoed in her head as she ran.

The rider pulled up just as it seemed the flashing hooves of his mount would strike the child. He dismounted almost before the bay had stopped, scooping up the laughing child to toss her high into the air.

The afternoon sun glinted off chestnut hair, tousled now

by the small fingers that gripped it. *Not Stephano*, Nadya thought again, although Angel's reception had been as enthusiastic as that normally reserved for her uncle.

Nadya's steps had gradually slowed with each realization. Now she walked, trying to control her breathing as she combed trembling fingers through her own disordered curls.

Not only had Angel's recognition preceded her own, the child's surety about her reception seemed unhampered by doubt or misgivings. Nadya's was not. She had sent Rhys away, knowing in her heart that, in spite of what she felt for him, it was best for both of them.

Now, after she had begun to gain some small measure of peace with that decision, he was back. Looking at her as if he, too, were unsure of his welcome.

As the man and child watched her approach, Nadya fought to remember all the good reasons Stephano had given her for sending the Englishman away. Seeing Angel's arms wrapped confidently around his neck, none of them seemed convincing.

'At least she wasn't running toward an edge this time,' Rhys said as he smiled at her.

'What are you doing here?' Her question sounded almost hostile. Certainly unwelcoming. Nothing that mirrored the emotions clamouring in her breast.

Rhys's smile faded. He set Angel down, and she immediately began circling them, arms once more outstretched as if in flight. He watched a moment before he looked up at Nadya.

She'd almost forgotten the effect he had on her senses. Temporarily as mute as her daughter, she could think of nothing to say that might mitigate the harshness of her question.

Not until he answered it. 'I came to warn you.'

'To warn me? About what?'

'I located the man who led the raid. His name is Oliver Burke.' He looked as if he expected it to mean something to her.

She shook her head, uncertain what response he'd expected.

'You don't know him?' he prodded.

'I don't think so. Should I?'

'He says he was paid to instigate the villagers into attacking the camp.'

'*Paid*? By whom?'

'He claims not to know the man's name. Only that he's a gentleman.'

'But…' She shook her head again. Rhys was acting as if the information should mean something to her, and it didn't.

'He says the man instructed him to burn your tent.'

That tracked with the questions they'd asked of Andrash. Yet none of it made sense.

'But…why? What possible reason…?' The question faltered at what she saw in his face.

'All he was told was that you were to be "burned out." He claims not to have been given a reason.'

Despite the slurs she and her people had suffered through the years, despite the misgivings both Rhys and Andrash had already expressed, for the first time in Nadya's life she was faced with the sure knowledge that someone meant her harm.

'Won't you tell me now about Angel?' Rhys asked softly.

'She's my daughter. That's all you need to know.'

'But not your blood.'

'Is that what makes a child belong to someone? Their blood?' she demanded fiercely. 'If that's what you believe, you know nothing about the love a mother feels for her child.'

'You're right. I don't. But I do know about men's hatred. I'm trying to protect you from whoever planned that assault. I can't do that unless you tell me the truth.'

'I'm not your concern. Neither my safety nor my life.'

'Why not? You saved mine.'

'I absolve you of whatever indebtedness you feel because of it. You owe me nothing. Leave it alone, Rhys. Leave us alone.' She turned, intending to pick up her daughter and carry her back to camp. Where they belonged.

Rhys gripped her elbow, pulling her around to face him. 'Does Angel belong to someone else, Nadya? Did you take her because you wanted a daughter? Is that what you're afraid of?'

'You think I stole her?' Furious, she wrenched free. 'That's what Gypsies do, isn't it? You heard those stories at your nursemaid's knee, didn't you? Along with the other fairy tales she told you.'

'If not that, then what? What's this all about?'

'Nothing. Nothing that's any of your concern.'

'You made it my concern when you asked me to help Andrash. And when you trusted me enough to put Angel into my arms.'

She couldn't argue with that. She had drawn him more deeply into the events of that night. How could she now pretend he didn't have the right to ask these questions?

'Whatever they wanted had nothing to do with Angel, that I promise you.' Even that was a concession she resented having to make. She shouldn't have to deny his accusations. He should know her better than that by now.

'Since you seemed to be their primary target, how can you be so sure that it had nothing to do with her?'

'Because Angel belongs to me.'

His lips tightened. 'Saying she belongs to you doesn't

change the fact that she isn't your daughter. All anyone has to do is look at her to know that. She isn't yours, Nadya. Lying doesn't change that reality.'

'I'm not lying. She's mine, Rhys, because I bought her.'

His silence lasted so long she could hear the sound of Angel's skirts brushing against the tall grass as she circled them. A bird called from the nearby woods. And still he didn't speak.

'You…bought her?' Rhys finally repeated, his eyes full of disbelief. 'You can't buy a child. Not an English one.'

'It would be different, I suppose, if she were a blacka-moor? Or a Rom?'

'But she isn't,' he said, ignoring the question at the heart of her argument. 'She's English. An English child. You can't own her as if she's some…piece of chattel.'

'I can if I outbid everyone else.' Even now she felt the horror she'd experienced as she'd watched that frenzied bidding.

'Are you saying someone put Angel up for auction?'

'Her father. And the other bidders were all men, Rhys.' His face had begun to change, but now that she'd started, she couldn't prevent the flow of words. Or the memories they evoked. 'As he said, what else is she good for? She can't learn a trade. She can't follow instructions. She can't even become someone's servant.'

She watched the realization of what had been about to happen to Angel dawn in Rhys's eyes. His reaction was the same horror that had driven her to outbid them all, spending almost the entire amount the sale of her father's gems and precious metals had brought.

And she had never begrudged a shilling of it.

'So whatever the motives behind the attack,' she finished quietly, 'believe me, it had nothing to do with Angel. I can assure you her father was more than pleased with the bargain he'd struck.'

'Where?'

'What can that matter? It's finished. He isn't sending anyone to search for me. Or for her. If anything, he's looking over his shoulder, afraid I'll be sorry of my bargain and try to return her when I find out she's both deaf and mute.'

His mouth closed, his lips tightening against the emotions those images had evoked. His gaze found the child, still lost in her fantasy world, oblivious to the argument of the two adults she circled.

'Then why?' he asked, his eyes coming back to meet hers. 'Why would someone have sent Burke—'

'I don't know. Maybe…'

'What?' he demanded when she paused.

'Magda's the one who deals with the *gadje*. Maybe someone had us confused.'

'But you're the healer.'

'A *drabarni* can also be one who deals in potions. Maybe…' She shrugged.

'May I talk to her?'

'To Magda?' Despite the seriousness of his expression, she smiled at the idea. 'She won't talk to you. But I can tell you Magda would be flattered to believe someone has a grudge against her.'

'And pleased to hear that because of it, they were out to harm you?'

'No, of course not. I'm not sure she'd believe that, even if I told her. Magda places too much emphasis on the role fate plays in our lives.'

'I don't understand.'

'If you fight against what's supposed to happen, you risk not only your future, but your health and happiness.'

'Surely she wouldn't believe you're fated to come to harm.'

It was difficult to explain to someone like Rhys her grandmother's fatalism. If Magda had an enemy, she would avoid any situation in which that person might take advantage of her or do her injury. But she would also believe that enemy had been put in her life to test her courage or her wits. Or even to cause her to follow a certain path or drive her to a particular action.

'She wouldn't want that, but to Magda, everything happens for a reason. Even bad things.'

'Then ask her if she has any reason to think she's created an enmity strong enough to cause someone to want to harm her.'

'I'll talk to her,' Nadya promised.

She would, if only because she valued Magda's counsel. And also because what Rhys had told her put Angel at risk.

She turned to locate the little girl, realizing for the first time that she was no longer pretending to fly. Instead she was sitting cross-legged on the ground, holding one of the beech leaves up to catch the rays of the sinking sun.

'We have to get back before Magda begins to wonder about us. Are you returning to your godfather's?'

Rhys shook his head. 'Actually, I was on my way home when I realized that I might be able to locate Burke, simply by asking a few questions.'

'Home? To your brother's house?'

'I'll break my journey at Buxton tonight, but yes, I'm returning to Edward's. I'll escort you back to camp first.' He nodded toward the bay, contentedly cropping grass.

'I don't think that's a good idea.'

'Your half-brother's still there?'

'Stephano left shortly after you. It isn't that. It's...

Andrash heard Stephano send you away. If you come back, it will seem as if I'm disobeying him.'

She had ignored Stephano's orders to get rid of the *gaujo* before, but those had been given in private. At the time, she had believed the health of her patient should come before a stricture she couldn't see any reason for. Now, for her own peace of mind, it would be better if Rhys were gone.

'I won't stay. Not if it will make things difficult for you. After what Burke told me, however, I'll feel better if I see you safely back.'

'We've come here every day since you left,' she protested. 'No one's bothered us. Why would today be any different?'

'Maybe they don't know where you're camped. That isn't to say whoever hired Burke doesn't have someone looking.'

If she'd been alone, Nadya would have continued to refuse. But Angel's safety was more important than her feelings about this man she'd already admitted was beyond her reach.

Rhys walked over to where the little girl was still examining the effect of sunlight on the webbed tissue of the fallen leaf. He stooped, balancing in front of her, exactly as Stephano had done.

Angel's reaction was the same as it had been with her uncle. She threw her arms around Rhys's neck, allowing him to pick her up when he rose.

As he walked back to Nadya, carrying the little girl, for the first time she realized that anyone seeing them together might take them for father and daughter. No matter how much she loved Angel, in appearance the child would always belong more to Rhys's world than that of the Rom. It was even possible that, just as Stephano had, she would one day return to that world.

'Do you ride?' Rhys asked as he collected the bay's reins.

'Of course.'

She did, but not like the ladies of his acquaintance. She considered the practice of sitting on the back of a horse as if one were in a drawing room chair absurd. If Rhys found her style of riding peculiar, that would simply be another of many things he'd thought strange about the way she lived.

He led the bay over and then, still holding the reins, put Angel down in order to hand Nadya up. Nadya gathered her skirts and placed her foot in his cupped hands. When he lifted her, she swung her other leg over the gelding's back and settled into the saddle astride.

The bay, disconcerted by her unfamiliar weight or the brush of her skirts, sidestepped. Nadya ran a soothing hand down his neck, bending forward to whisper into his ear the same Romany endearments with which her brother complimented the black.

When she had reassured the horse, she glanced down to read the surprise in Rhys's face. He had the presence of mind to close his mouth—and the wisdom to keep it closed.

'I can take her now.' She managed to keep any hint of self-satisfaction from her tone.

Rhys obediently handed Angel up to her. The little girl, who delighted in riding with Stephano in exactly this way, settled into the saddle in front of her mother. As soon as she had been secured by Nadya's arm around her waist, Rhys began to lead the horse toward the woods.

'I thought you asked if I could ride.'

He looked up at her questioningly. 'Is something wrong?'

'I haven't been led since I was put on my first pony.'

'My apologies.' Those were accompanied by a slight bow. 'Your reins, ma'am.'

Rhys's smile had been teasing, but there was, she would have sworn, admiration in his eyes as well. With her left arm still around Angel's waist, she took the reins in her right and touched her heels lightly to the bay. He began to move, ambling in the direction of the camp.

After a few moments, Nadya looked over her shoulder. Rhys was walking behind them, his eyes focused on the ground. She pulled the bay up, holding him until Rhys came up beside them.

'What's wrong now?'

She would be playing with fire. And she knew it.

She also knew that she had told him goodbye once, had sent him on his way because it was the right thing to do. Stephano had it made very clear to her, if she'd had any doubts, why that had been the right thing.

Now Rhys was back. Because, he said, he was concerned for her safety. She knew the kind of man he was, so she believed that to be his reason. But because she had read what was in his eyes the day she'd been foolish enough to shave him, she also believed he had found it as difficult to say goodbye as she had.

'It will be dark soon. We'll reach camp much quicker if you ride, too.'

'Should I remind you there's only one horse?' Although his expression was serious, his eyes were smiling.

Nadya decided she preferred them that way. 'On the rump, I mean. The Rom do it all the time. Of course, something like that may be beneath your dignity.'

'Whatever dignity I might once have had was lost on the battlefields of Iberia. The last time I rode on the rump of someone else's horse, my own had been shot from under me.'

Perhaps it was a trick of the fading light, but his eyes, which seconds before had been amused, suddenly seemed shadowed, almost distant. Whatever she thought she'd seen there cleared as he smiled up at her.

'Are you certain *your* dignity won't suffer? I would hate

to do anything that might harm the *drabarni's* well-deserved reputation.'

'The Rom are a very practical people, Major Morgan. They would think it strange if we didn't share the animal.'

'Are you sure?' he asked softly, his eyes serious again.

'I'm sure the temperature will drop when the sun sets. And I'm not sure my grandmother won't send out a search party if we aren't home before that.'

She slipped her foot out of the stirrup and tightened her grip around her daughter's waist. Then she held her breath until he moved.

With one fluid motion he swung up behind her. She could feel the heat from his body even before he put his arms around her to take control of the reins.

'Put your foot back in the stirrup,' he ordered.

'Afraid I'll fall off?' she teased as she obeyed.

'If you do, we all do.'

Without waiting for a response, he touched his heels to the bay's side, and the horse broke into a trot.

She was too aware of the movement. Aware, too, of the man behind her, his arms enclosing her as he deftly guided the bay into the trees.

The ride would last only minutes, despite the slower pace they would be forced to maintain once they reached the densest part of the forest. But with something approaching contentment, she acknowledged that at least she would forever have the memory of those.

Chapter Fourteen

Night fell before they reached Magda's caravan. Most of the Rom had already taken shelter against the growing chill in the bender tents scattered around the clearing, so there were few to witness their arrival.

With her half-brother's very public dismissal of the Englishman from camp, that was probably a blessing. Of course, there was no way to prevent her grandmother from sending word to Stephano that Rhys had returned.

Still, Nadya admitted, the old woman had been relatively uncritical of her care of the Englishman and about the length of time he'd remained with them. Maybe her unusual reticence would continue.

If it didn't, and Magda did inform Stephano, Nadya would deal with her half-brother's anger when she was forced to. Tonight...

Tonight she would enjoy having Rhys here. Just as she had relished the feel of his body against hers during the ride to camp.

'Do you want me to go in with you?'

Rhys had leaned forward to ask his question as he

reined in the bay before her grandmother's *vardo*. His mouth was so close she could feel the warmth of his breath against her cheek.

She resisted the urge to turn her head. There had been quite enough temptation.

'To talk to Magda?' As she shook her head, a strand of hair that had escaped her kerchief caught in the late-day stubble on his cheek. She freed it with her fingers. 'Besides, she may not be here. She much prefers sleeping on the ground.'

'To sleeping inside the caravan?'

'After my father purchased his, Magda felt it elevated his status above that of her and her family. She took it as a slight to the position of the Beshaleys. When Stephano took over the leadership of our *kumpania*, at her insistence he commissioned a wagon to be made for her, larger and more ornate than my father's.

'While Magda loved the thought of owning a caravan, she found it hard to forego the old ways. With tonight's cold, however, she may be inside. If so, as soon as I've given Angel something to eat and put her to bed, I'll ask. Whether she'll tell me anything or not…' Nadya shrugged.

'Even if it might keep you safe?'

'Admitting she fears someone gives them power over her.'

After dismounting, he held up his arms for Angel. 'You know that's ridiculous.'

'Perhaps. But it's the way she thinks. To Magda, being Rom means being strong, totally self-sufficient, and bound by nothing except the laws of the *kumpania*. Fear hampers one's freedom, so she'll never admit to being afraid.'

'She sounds remarkably like my grandmother,' Rhys said, setting Angel down on the ground beside him.

The little girl immediately clambered up the steps of

Magda's caravan. He then turned, holding up his hands for Nadya.

Although she was perfectly capable of dismounting on her own, temptation overruled rational response. Even knowing the strain lifting her down would place on his damaged shoulder wasn't a strong enough deterrent to keep her from wanting to be in his arms. Even if only for a few seconds.

She swung her leg over the bay's back and then leaned down to place her palms on Rhys's shoulders. His hands closed around her waist, accepting her weight as she slid off the horse.

Although he had ridden behind her from the meadow, their bodies in constant contact, that was very different from the situation in which she found herself now. So close, her breasts brushed against his chest as he set her on the ground.

Even then Rhys didn't release her. He stood, looking into her eyes, the smooth planes and strong angles of his face illuminated by the campfires.

When he began to bend toward her, there was no thought of turning away. She wanted his kiss. Had wanted it for weeks. No matter the repercussions, she intended to savour this moment.

Her lips opened under the first tentative touch of his, and he responded to her reaction. His hands left her waist to gather her into his arms.

If the brush of her nipples against his chest had been sensuous, the feel of her breasts crushed against its hard wall of muscle was overwhelming. The dams of reason and restraint she had so painstakingly built against falling in love with this man were destroyed by sensations too long denied.

His tongue probed hers, caressing and then retreating.

She strained upward, desperate to increase the contact between them. On tiptoe, she sought his mouth again.

Assured that his embrace was welcome, once more Rhys responded. His hands cupped under her hips, lifting so that despite the barrier of their clothing, she could feel his arousal. Her arms circled his neck, as her yearning body sought to become one with his.

Any thought about the propriety of what they were doing fled before the flood of heat that invaded her body. She had wanted this man from almost the first moment she'd seen him. Now she knew that he had wanted her, too.

Rhys deepened the kiss, his mouth demanding, and she held nothing back. It was too late for pretence or caution. They had at long last acknowledged a need that, unspoken, had simmered between them until it could no longer be denied.

Convention decreed they should not be together, but neither had led a conventional life. Why should they be bound by something they had both so long ignored?

'I now see what has kept you from your dinner, *chavi*.'

Magda's comment dashed their passion as if the old woman had thrown cold water on them. Rhys released her so suddenly Nadya was forced to grasp at his arm to maintain her balance. He stepped back, looking up at the caravan.

Nadya turned to find the old woman standing on its steps, her hand on Angel's shoulder. The child didn't seem bothered to find her mother in Rhys's embrace, but as Nadya tried to formulate some explanation, her grandmother took the initiative.

'Go inside,' she said, directing the little girl with her hand. 'Your mother will be in soon.'

When Angel had disappeared into the *vardo*, Magda looked back at her again. 'Do you want the whole camp as well as your daughter to witness your disgrace?'

'I feel no disgrace, *Mami*.'

'Nor did your mother. And see what good came to her from being so headstrong.'

'I'm not my mother.'

'It seems that in this you are too much like her.'

'Surely I may kiss whoever I please.'

'Of course. But only the foolish believe there are no consequences to doing what they please.'

'The fault is mine—' Rhys attempted to interject.

'Perhaps in the world of the *gadje* only men may choose whom they kiss,' Magda said. 'In our world that is a mutual decision.'

'It *was* mutual.' Nadya's response was almost defiant. Her grandmother was treating her like a girl caught kissing some boy already promised to another.

Still, the bonds of respect were too deep between them for her to reject Magda's correction entirely. Especially in front of an outsider.

And that was the crux of the matter, of course. Her grandmother, with her many romantic liaisons, would have been the last person alive to deny Nadya's right to choose a mate. Indeed, she had encouraged her to find a man within the tribe, someone worthy to marry a woman of her breeding and position.

Magda would have been thrilled to find her kissing Simon or Philippe. But a *gaujo*? Nothing would engender more disdain from the old woman.

'Even if our feelings were mutual,' Rhys said, 'as a guest in your camp, I had no right to pursue them.'

'I gave you that right.' Nadya turned, almost as angry with his defence of her actions as with her grandmother's condemnation of them. 'I'm not a child to be schooled in my behaviour.'

'And will you give *your* child to his English wife, *chavi*, as your mother did? To be discarded as worthless when she has replaced it with children of her own?'

Stephano's rage and bitterness sprang from that betrayal. Her grandmother was warning her to expect no less at the hands of her *gaujo* lover.

Nor could she argue against that counsel. Nadya had never believed Rhys would marry her. How could he? If he took her for his wife, he would become a pariah among his own people. She would never ask that of him.

'It was a kiss, *Mami*,' she said softly, her former defiance defeated by that reality. 'Nothing more, I promise you.'

'I may be an old woman, but I know that kisses lead to other things. Especially kisses like that.' There was a hint of amusement in her grandmother's voice. Or perhaps admiration.

When Magda continued, however, whatever Nadya thought she'd heard there had been replaced by sternness. 'Stephano has said that he doesn't want the Englishman here. Since your reasons for defying your brother no longer exist, why have you brought him back?'

Apparently Magda had tired of playing duenna, a role she was little suited for. But the change in her approach gave Nadya the opportunity to ask her grandmother what she had promised Rhys she would.

Although it seemed far-fetched that anyone might mistake the old woman's reputation for spells and charms and fortunes for her own prowess with medicinal herbs, Nadya could think of no reason anyone would wish harm her. The kinds of dealings Magda had with the *gadje* were far more likely to create enmity.

'Rhys came back to warn me.'

'Is that what I have just witnessed? A strange *gadje* sort of warning then, I think.'

Ignoring Magda's gibe, Nadya doggedly ploughed on. She would ask what she had promised Rhys she would ask, and then he could leave. 'Rhys has learned that the men who attacked the camp that night were paid to do so.'

Magda cocked her head as if considering the idea. 'Paid by whom?'

'Someone their leader described as a gentleman,' Rhys offered.

'A narrow field then,' Magda said, 'if he spoke about the *gadje.*'

'I took it to mean someone of a certain social class.'

'A nobleman you mean.' This time the old woman's voice was openly amused.

'Someone of wealth or standing,' Rhys amended.

'Such as yourself.'

'I can claim neither of those, I'm afraid.'

'Why be "afraid" of who you are? Are you ashamed of it?'

'In my world, someone who allows others to believe him to be of a higher status than he really is would be considered not only dishonest, but dishonourable.'

'Then perhaps the "gentleman" you seek is nothing of the kind. Since you know he paid others to carry out his mischief, you already know he is dishonourable.'

'What does it matter?' Nadya interrupted.

Magda delighted in this kind of circular reasoning, but it was getting them nowhere. Now that Nadya had been forcibly reminded of the obstacles between whatever fulfilment of her relationship with Rhys she'd been imagining only minutes ago, all she wanted was for him to satisfy himself that her grandmother wasn't the answer to the riddle he sought to solve.

'Rhys believes the man who paid for the attack had a grudge against someone in camp. You're the one who most often comes in contact with the *gadje*. Have any of them reason to be angry with something you've sold them?'

'Sold them? Do you think me a peddler, *chavi*, whose wares are defective?'

'A charm that didn't work as promised? A foretelling that went awry? You know what I'm asking. Don't pretend you don't.'

'If you won't pretend that the men who came here were looking for me.'

It took a moment for Nadya to realize the implications of what her grandmother had said. 'You know.'

'That they were hunting for you? I am a fortune-teller, *chavi*.' The old woman was again clearly amused.

'But that isn't how you knew.'

'Andrash told me they were seeking our *drabarni*. He asked me for a charm to protect you. He was even willing to pay for it. I guess he didn't know you already had one.'

In the firelight, Nadya could see the eyes of the old woman move from her face to Rhys. She couldn't tell, however, whether their expression mocked him.

'Did you make the charm he asked for?' Rhys asked.

'Why should someone pay me for a charm to protect my granddaughter? She is always under my protection.'

'And under mine,' Rhys vowed softly.

Nadya waited for Magda's retort. The old woman's wits were as sharp as her tongue. This time she employed neither.

'Your enemies are not ours, *gaujo*. Neither are your friends. Be warned, though: Some of them are not yours either. If you seek to protect Nadya, you are asking questions in the wrong place.'

'Are you telling his fortune, *Mami*?' Nadya interrupted scornfully. 'Should he cross your palm with silver?'

'*You* should see to your daughter. She's tired and cold and hungry, and my stew pot is empty. If there is silver to be expended, perhaps it should be used for that.'

'I'll find something for her to eat,' Rhys volunteered.

Surprised by his offer, they watched as he led the bay in the direction of the smith's tent. When he was out of earshot, Nadya looked up at her grandmother again.

'Am I never to have anything?'

'Do you want your fortune told after all, *chavi*? I thought you didn't believe in such foolishness.'

'Do you know it?'

'Since the hour of your birth.'

'Then perhaps one day when I have silver enough for something besides stew, I'll let you tell it to me.'

'See to your daughter. I'll wait out here for your *gaujo*.'

'He isn't what you and Stephano think.'

'You have no idea what I think, *chavi*. As for Stephano...' Magda hesitated, as if she had changed her mind. 'Let me worry about your brother. You tend to your child.'

It was obvious the old woman intended to speak privately with Rhys. To again warn him away from her? Or to caution him about Stephano's anger if he found him here?

Nadya could, of course, refuse to go inside. She knew from past experience that, in the long run, it would do no good to refuse her grandmother's commands. Magda would have her say, in her presence or not.

In truth, she needed to see about Angel. She needed to wash the little girl's face and hands and get her ready to eat whatever Rhys brought back.

Besides, going inside would keep her from having to

watch him leave once again. After the events of today, she knew that would be even harder to bear than the first time had been.

Nadya wasn't outside when Rhys returned with the soup and bread Andrash had procured for him. Her grandmother stood on the steps of the wagon, her shawl wrapped closely around her thin body.

'Soup, not stew,' he said, handing the pail up to her, 'but I'm assured it's thick with chicken. I brought enough for Nadya, too.'

The old woman took the container, holding it to her nose. 'You may not be able to tell chicken from hedgehog, *gaujo*, but Rose Dendri can. How much did she charge you?'

'A friend gave it to me,' Rhys said, handing up the half loaf Andrash's woman had wrapped in a white cloth.

'It's good to have friends who will feed you,' Magda said.

'Yes, it is.'

'Even better to have friends who will take care of you.'

'I've had my fair share of those as well.'

'Would you present my granddaughter to those friends?'

The remembrance of Reggie's reaction prevented Rhys from answering that question as quickly as he had the others. And when he did, he told her the truth. 'To some of them.'

'Come back to us when you can show her off with pride to all your friends, Major Morgan.'

'It wouldn't be lack of pride that prevented me, ma'am. I told you. I am sworn to protect her.'

'She would need protection from your friends?'

'Not physical protection, but…' Rhys took a breath, knowing how important an ally the old woman could be. 'There are other kinds of injury. You yourself said that some of my friends aren't friends. Will you hold me responsible for their actions?'

'When you ask for someone's most valued possession, they want assurance you'll treasure it.'

'I give you my word—'

'We have learned not to trust the word of the *gadje*. Nadya will tell you that.'

'Then—forgive me—why ask for mine?'

'I didn't. I don't care about your word. I only care about my granddaughter.'

'As do I.'

'So much so that you would make a spectacle of her?'

He had already admitted fault in that too-public kiss. Despite Nadya's reaction to his claim, he still accepted the blame for it, so he said nothing in his defence.

'You and I are not the only ones here who have enemies among the *gadje*, you know.'

Magda's words were so soft that at first Rhys wasn't sure he'd heard correctly. He opened his mouth to ask if she would repeat them, but before he could, she disappeared back inside the caravan.

You and I are not the only ones here who have enemies among the gadje.

She had told him that some of those he had considered his friends were not—a truth he couldn't deny. Now…

Was she suggesting there was someone else in camp who might have been the cause of the attack?

He knew Nadya had been its target. But the old woman had seemed to dismiss the notion that she'd been responsible for it. If she were not, then who was her grandmother talking about?

'It's Magda's way.' Andrash tore the other half of Rose's loaf of bread into two pieces, handing one to Rhys. 'She talks in riddles. That way, if what she tells you today doesn't come true tomorrow, when you're expecting it to, something may happen next week to make you think that's what she meant instead.'

'It didn't seem as if this were meant to be riddle. It felt as if she wanted me to know, but she didn't want to be the one to tell me.'

'I wish I could help you, my friend, but I don't know who here might have enemies among the English. We trade with them. They buy what we make. In exchange, we get tea and sugar and things we can't grow or raise on our own. If we cheat them, they don't come back, so we deal honestly with them. If one of our people is found to be a thief or a liar, we take care of him ourselves because he endangers all our livelihoods.'

'Have you had to deal with someone like that lately?'

The smith shook his head, taking a spoonful of the soup he'd dipped from the pot that hung on the tripod over his campfire. The woman who'd been sitting with him when Rhys came looking for Angel's supper had left.

'Not lately. A year ago, maybe more, we had such a problem. But that wasn't around here. It was in the north. Besides, we made restitution to the *gadje* who'd been cheated.'

'And the Rom?'

'He did what he needed to do to make things right.'

'Then he's still here.'

'Where else would he be?' Andrash said with a shrug. 'He's *familia*.'

There seemed little point after that in pursuing the topic. They ate together in a companionable silence, each lost in his own thoughts.

When they had finished, Andrash got up and took the

metal pan Rhys had eaten from. He placed it in a bucket filled with water outside his tent. When he started to add wood to his fire, Rhys rose, holding out his hand.

'Thank you for the soup. Please convey my compliments to your friend.'

Andrash laughed. 'Rose thought you'd be too fine to eat hedgehog, but they're fattening for the winter this time of the year, and the meat is particularly rich. Baked in clay in the ashes of a fire...' The Rom made a smacking sound.

'Rose would be surprised at what I've eaten through the years. But nothing better than this. Thank you for everything, my friend.'

'You aren't leaving, are you?' Andrash seemed surprised.

'Despite your hospitality and Nadya's, I have been led to believe I'm not welcome here.'

'Ah. Stephano. But Stephano isn't here.'

'I understood that his word carries a great deal of weight among your people.'

'He is the *Rom Baro*. The big man. But *you*... You are my friend. It's late. It's cold. And it's a very long way to any other place you might find accommodation for the night. My home isn't much—' with his hand the Rom gestured at the round tent behind them '—but you are more than welcome to share it.'

'I don't want to cause trouble for you.'

'If trouble comes, it comes. But I think it won't tonight,' the Gypsy added with a conspiratorial grin.

Rhys was tempted. And for more reasons than the cold or the distance to the nearest inn. 'If you're sure...'

'Not so fine as the *drabarni's vardo*, but you'll be out of the wind, and there are plenty of blankets. In the morning, if we're lucky, Rose will bring us a chestnut cake.'

'You're a fortunate man, my friend.'

'Rose is courting me. I am quite the catch, you under-stand. The competition is fierce, but I think Rose's cooking, if it should continue to be good, is going to give her the advantage. At least, I have led her to believe that is so,' the smith added with a wink.

Rhys laughed, clapping him on the shoulder as they made their way inside the tent, which was surprisingly spacious despite the low ceiling. And the blankets were as plentiful as Andrash had promised.

Long after they had settled down to sleep, the smith on one side and he on the other, Rhys lay awake, listening to the soft crackling of the dying fire outside.

The images of the afternoon spun endlessly through his head. Angel running through the sunlit meadow, arms out-stretched. What had been in Nadya's eyes as she'd invited him to ride. Her face when he'd lifted her down from the bay. Her parted lips, reddened by his kiss. Her grandmother, like some avenging angel, issuing her warning and predictions.

You and I are not the only ones here who have enemies among the gadje.

How was he, who knew so little about her people, supposed to figure out who the old woman was talking about? He could ask Nadya, but other than suggesting Magda herself, she had seemed at as much of a loss as Andrash to come up the names of those who might have earned the enmity of the *gadje*.

Sighing, he turned over, attempting to find a more com-fortable position for his aching shoulder. Although he'd slept in more primitive conditions than these, apparently he'd become spoiled by Abigail's well-stuffed mattresses.

'Maybe she meant Stephano.' Andrash's voice seemed to come from a great distance.

'What?' Rhys propped himself up on one elbow, peering through the darkness toward the other side of the tent.

'Magda. Perhaps she was talking about Stephano.'

'You think he's the one who has enemies among the *gadje*.'

The word came as naturally to him now as if he'd used it his entire life. As if he himself wasn't one of those to whom the derogatory term applied.

'He's always spent time in London, but lately he's been there more than here. And he's changed. He's always been…difficult. Now it's as if he's possessed.'

'By what?'

'I don't know. Stephano isn't a man who shares what he thinks or feels. Or, for that matter, what he's doing. I know he's been injured, though. I've seen the scar myself.'

'What kind of scar?'

'The kind a ball makes. If someone shoots a man, wouldn't you say that man has enemies?'

Rhys didn't bother to respond to what had appeared to be a rhetorical question. Besides, he wasn't the one who needed to provide the answer. It seemed to him that was something Stephano's grandmother should be forced to consider.

And this time, he wouldn't let Magda get away with the kind of equivocation she clearly excelled at.

Chapter Fifteen

Her rest broken by troubling dreams she couldn't quite remember, at first light Nadya pulled on the clothes she'd discarded last night and wrapped her shawl around her shoulders. She left Angel to sleep while she took the goatskin to fill with the day's water from the nearby stream.

As she passed Andrash's tent, her eyes widened at the sight of Rhys's bay tethered nearby. Despite all her self-directed recriminations last night, her pulse quickened with the realization that he hadn't yet left.

The blacksmith had offered him shelter and wisely Rhys had accepted. Which meant she would see him again.

She couldn't quite decide how she felt about that. She had spent a large portion of the night rebuilding the defences his kiss had shattered. Defences against her grandmother's mockery. Against her own dreams and physical desires. Against every memory of the hours they'd spent together.

She turned her gaze from the horse, keeping her eyes steadfastly on the path to the stream. She would get the water they needed and then retreat to her caravan.

Rhys would be gone again in a few hours. All she had to do was find something to occupy herself inside until then.

She started down the slope that led to the streambed. Mist hung over the water, giving the scene the quality of a dream. As she neared the bank, she realized belatedly that, despite the hour, she wasn't the only one here.

Rhys stood in the centre of the narrow stream, his back to her. He was lifting handfuls of water in his cupped palm, letting them run down his chest and then over each shoulder.

As she watched, he ran the fingers of the hand he'd been using through his hair, combing it away from his face. The droplets that fell from the chestnut locks clung to his back and broad shoulders.

Almost against her will, her eyes traced downward, following the line of his spine to the narrow waist and then on to the rounded buttocks and strongly muscled horseman's thighs.

For days she had cared for his fever-wracked body, tending its every need. Although she had, of course, acknowledged his masculinity, she had tried to view him then as her patient. Someone in need of her skills.

This was something vastly different. This was a man, completely and totally male, displayed in undeniable virility.

She closed her mouth, swallowing against its dryness. Before she could move, leaving him to finish his bath in the privacy he'd had every right to anticipate at this time of day, Rhys turned.

He froze at the sight of her. Their eyes locked and held. In the eerie stillness of the mist-shrouded dawn, it seemed as if they were the only two people in the entire world.

If only that were true...

It wasn't. Nor could it ever be.

Wherever they went, there would always be those who

believed they had no right to be together. Not the least among them her own family.

She turned, hurrying before she lost her resolve, and stumbled back up the slope. She had thought he would call out to her. Say her name. Say something.

He didn't. And in the silence of the still-sleeping camp Nadya returned to her *vardo* and lay down beside her daughter.

She shivered occasionally, long after the chill from the outside air had been banished by the sweet, soft warmth of the little girl's body.

When Angel woke, she traced the tear stains on her mother's cheeks and made the soothing sign Nadya had taught her. And for the first time since she'd brought her daughter home, Nadya was thankful the little girl couldn't ask what had caused them.

The more Rhys thought about what Andrash had suggested, the more sense it made. It was clear that whatever activities Stephano was engaged in, they had made him enemies. It seemed possible that, having failed in their attempt to kill him, those enemies now sought revenge on his family.

Nadya had convinced him that Angel's heritage was not, as he'd once believed, at the root of the attack. And he could imagine no other reason anyone would want to harm a woman whose life had been devoted to succouring pain rather than causing it.

Even Magda's love charms and fortune-telling seemed flimsy excuses for the level of destruction he'd witnessed the night of the raid. Almost as ridiculous as blaming that kind of violence on a general animosity directed at the Rom because of ailing cattle or failed crops. Those might well provoke malicious acts, but attempted murder?

That seemed more likely to be the result of a very personal hatred. The kind that would cause someone to put a ball into someone else.

Andrash could tell him nothing else about Stephano's affairs. It was probable that Magda could, but improbable that she'd be willing to reveal more than she had last night with her cryptic warning. And since Stephano wasn't around to be questioned, that left only one other source of information.

Which was why, despite the troubling confrontation at dawn, he had come to Nadya's caravan. 'Nadya?'

Although he hadn't seen her or Angel as he'd walked across the encampment, his call elicited no response.

'Nadya, I need to talk to you.'

With his second hail, a few of the Rom working nearby stopped to look at him. Aware of his audience's keen interest in what he was doing, Rhys debated making a third call.

Thankfully, that was unnecessary. Nadya pushed the curtain aside to look out.

Even before she spoke to him, she raised her eyes to survey the surrounding area. Under her gaze, most of those who'd been so interested in Rhys's visit seemed suddenly to discover a renewed fascination with their own pursuits.

'May I come in?' Rhys asked when her eyes returned to him.

'I'm not sure we have anything else to say.'

He had recognized this morning that she, at least, had already come to that conclusion. And whether the attraction that had flared between them would be allowed to grow into something else had always been her prerogative.

Given her grandmother's reaction to their kiss, he could hardly blame Nadya for choosing to distance herself. He'd placed her in the untenable position of being forced to choose between the mores of her culture and her feelings for him.

Still, he had vowed to protect her. If her brother's actions were the cause of the attack on the Gypsy camp, then Stephano must be made aware of the danger in which he'd placed his own people.

Rhys lowered his voice, but refused to give ground. 'It's about your brother.'

'Stephano? Has something happened to him?'

The concern in her voice revealed two things. She loved her brother, which Rhys had known already. And she was frightened for him, which seemed to indicate that she, too, knew about the dangers Andrash had mentioned.

Rhys shook his head. 'Not that I'm aware of. Do you have some reason to think it might?'

Her eyes lifted, once more studying those nearby. Her lips flattened at whatever she saw. She pushed aside the curtain, indicating that Rhys should come inside.

As he entered the caravan, the slightly medicinal smell of its front room carried him back to the days he'd spent here. He ignored those memories, moving past Nadya to sit on the edge of the bed where she'd treated him.

She left the curtain open as she came to stand opposite him. His eyes followed as she glanced into the sleeping partition at the back.

Angel was sitting on the bed playing with the rag doll Magda had made her and his wooden cat. Despite her deafness, the little girl glanced up to smile at them. At a sign from her mother, she went back to what she had been doing.

'What about Stephano?' Judging by her tone, Nadya was determined to keep their conversation off any subject that might provoke last night's intimacy.

'Andrash suggested that whatever he's doing in London has earned him enemies. Dangerous ones.'

For a few seconds, Nadya didn't reply. When she did,

it wasn't to deny what Andrash had told him. 'If that's true, I don't know anything about them.'

'Do you know why he's away from camp so much?'

That she did know was revealed in her eyes and as quickly screened by her lashes. When she lifted them again, all he could read in her face was resolve.

'That's Stephano's business. If he wanted you—or me—to be privy to it, he'd have made us aware. Since he hasn't...' She shrugged.

'And you're comfortable with that? Even if what your brother is doing puts you and Angel at risk?'

'First you think that happened because I stole Angel from the *gadje*. Then you thought it was because Magda told someone a fortune that didn't come true. Now you're decided it's all Stephano's fault. Whose fault will it be tomorrow, Rhys? I told you why they came that night. We're Rom. That's all the reason they've ever needed.'

'Was that the reason they were looking for you?'

She had no answer for that. Nor did she attempt to fabricate one. 'That isn't your concern.'

'*You're* my concern. Do you think that what happened between us—'

The sound of her laughter was almost ugly. 'A kiss? Does that give you the right to pry into the affairs of my family?'

'You know that isn't all—'

'A kiss,' she repeated flatly. 'Nothing more. And nothing less than I've shared with a dozen before you. It didn't bestow upon you the right to question me or protect me. Please don't act like a disappointed schoolgirl who has suddenly discovered that the object of her affections doesn't return them.'

Rhys understood that she was attempting to distract him from the affairs of mysterious brother. Even knowing what she was doing, it still hurt to have her employ that particular weapon.

Or perhaps, he acknowledged wryly, the epithet she'd chosen for him was appropriate.

'Andrash says your brother was recently shot.'

Her eyes widened, but she didn't hesitate in her reply. 'Although I've never known Andrash to tell a lie, I have no reason to think that's true.'

Her grandmother had apparently taught her the art of circular discourse. 'He didn't come to you for treatment?'

'No.'

'What would that tell you? If what Andrash says is true?'

She shook her head. 'That Stephano didn't want me to find out about the wound, I suppose. And if he didn't want me to know, why do you think he would want a stranger to have knowledge of that injury?'

'Magda would know, wouldn't she?'

Her smile was twisted. 'Magda knows everything. Just ask her. Be prepared to pay for her wisdom, of course.'

'I think she's terrified for him.'

'Why would you say that?' Sarcasm had been replaced by concern.

'She told me last night that someone else in camp has enemies. When I told Andrash what she'd said, he suggested she meant your brother.'

She shrugged. 'Then it seems Andrash knows more than I about my brother's business. And his health. Perhaps you should continue this conversation with him.'

'What did Magda mean when she said you're like your mother?' Another of the old woman's cryptic statements that had played through Rhys's head all night. One he wasn't completely sure he wanted an explanation for.

'My mother became the mistress of a *gaujo*.'

And will you give your child to his English wife, chavi, *as your mother did?* With the memory of Magda's words, everything fell into place.

'And that *gaujo* was Stephano's father?'

Nadya referred to him as her half-brother, but until Rhys had this last piece of the puzzle, he'd made the mistaken assumption they were both full-blooded Romany. Now so many things that had vaguely troubled him about Stephano were explained. His speech, which was clearly educated, even upper class. His features, which differed from the other men Rhys had met here.

Nadya's face was as delicately beautiful as the women of the Ton, but there were attributes, like the unusual shape of her eyes, that marked her as foreign. With Stephano, it was more difficult to pinpoint his ethnic origins. Now he knew why.

'The man was handsome and wealthy,' Nadya went on. 'A nobleman. For a time, my mother believed that he loved her.'

'And Stephano?'

'Was acknowledged to be his son.'

'Until he had other children.' That it was a story as old as time didn't make it less painful for those involved.

'Actually, he was acknowledged as his son until Stephano's father died. After that, his wife's family saw to it that the boy he'd welcomed into his home no longer had a place there.'

'So Stephano came back to live with his mother's people?'

'The *gadje* weren't quite so kind. They sent him to a foundling home. A little boy who'd known nothing his entire life but kindness and the height of luxury.'

'Then…how did he come to be here? And in the position he holds?'

'It wasn't until several years after my mother's death that

Stephano found us. He'd escaped the foundling hospital in the aftermath of a fire and had been living by his wits in London. There, by the grace of God—or as Magda would have it, the hand of fate—he encountered my father, who'd gone to sell his work and replenish his supplies. Stephano tried to pick his pocket, but my father was too clever to become his victim.

'When he questioned the boy he'd captured, he realized who he must be and knew that the story my mother had been told about what had happened to her son was no truer than any of the other lies the *gadje* had told her. He brought Stephano home with him and treated him as if he were his own son. Of course, Magda welcomed her lost grandson with open arms. After all, Stephano was all she had left of her beloved daughter.'

'She had you,' he reminded her.

'I was too much like my father. Too practical. Too grounded in reality. Magda always thought that my other grandmother had had too much influence on the way I was raised. When she was given the opportunity to teach Stephano the ways of the Rom, she was overjoyed. She made sure he was versed in all the things she had once taught our mother.'

There was an undercurrent of Nadya's story Rhys wasn't sure he understood. She loved her brother. Did she also resent the elevated position he'd achieved within the tribe?

'Fortune-telling and the love potions?' he suggested. It was difficult, somehow, to imagine that the man he'd met that day was superstitious.

'The importance of family. The need for vengeance against those who wrong you. Her fatalism. Stephano lapped it all up. Maybe it helped to explain why his life, once so promising, had turned out as it has.'

'Did she encourage him to seek vengeance on those responsible for that?'

'Wouldn't you want revenge if your father had been murdered?'

'Is that what happened?'

She nodded. 'A man, a friend of his father's, was hanged for the crime, but Stephano doesn't believe that's justice enough.'

'What more does he want?'

Nadya shook her head. 'You'll have to ask Stephano.'

'Is that why he spends so much time in London? Pursuing justice for his father?'

'He has a business there.'

'What kind of business?'

She shook her head again. 'I've told you what you asked. I don't know if Stephano has enemies. I only know that he sees himself as the enemy of those he holds to be responsible for his father's death.'

'If Stephano has been shot, as Andrash said, then obviously there have been confrontations between those people and your brother. Maybe they now share his thirst for revenge. What better way to achieve that than to harm his family?'

He could tell she was thinking about it. In the end, it seemed she was unwilling to admit that what had happened that night could have been her brother's fault.

'Then why wouldn't they target Magda? They're much closer than Stephano and I have ever been.'

'Maybe they did. You've admitted there's sometimes confusion over the title. But it seems to me…' He hesitated, knowing how difficult it would be for her to accept what he was about to suggest. 'What about Angel?'

'Angel?' she repeated, her eyes again finding her daughter. 'There appeared to be a great deal of affection between her and Stephano. The men who came that night had been paid to burn your home, Nadya. Angel would have been the least likely to have escaped if they'd been more efficient in carrying out their assignment.'

'Angel wasn't in my home that night, Rhys. You were. Who's to say you weren't their target?'

'I left my enemies in Spain. And believe me, none of them knew I was in your camp that night.'

'Then I think it will be difficult for you to find a solution to the mystery you profess to see in those events. I think that you'd better go.'

He had pushed her as far as he could. At least she would be on her guard. As were Andrash and her grandmother. As for her brother and his enemies…

'Of course.' He stood as if he intended to carry out her request. 'By the way, what's the name of Stephano's business? Perhaps I can throw some custom his way.'

'He never mentioned it.'

'And his father's name?'

'I don't believe he told me that either. Or if he did, I've forgotten it. After all, that part of his life is a world away from this.'

'Perhaps not so far as you wish,' he warned.

'I'm afraid you really must excuse me,' she said coldly. 'I have work to do.'

'Forgive me for keeping you from it.'

It was as if they were strangers. And in every way that mattered, he realized, they were.

'May I say goodbye to Angel?'

He turned to look into the other room. This time the child seemed oblivious to them, intent on her play.

'It might be easier if she doesn't know you're leaving,' Nadya said, her eyes on her daughter.

As the little girl's mother, she had every right to refuse. Still, he was forced to swallow against an unexpected thickness in his throat at the thought he might never see Angel again.

Or Nadya.

She'd made her choice, it seemed, and like her decision regarding her daughter, he couldn't argue against it. Reggie's reaction had reiterated the barriers that he'd already been aware of. Last night, Magda had done the same for Nadya.

'Take care. Of you and of her.'

She turned to meet his eyes. Hers were as cold as her voice had been. 'We're among our own people, who will defend either of us to the death. Thank you, though, for your kind concern.'

She didn't offer him her hand as other women of his acquaintance might have done. Instead, her eyes held on his, their dark gaze calm and unafraid.

He nodded, since there was nothing else left to say.

As he began to turn toward the curtained opening, Nadya added softly, '*Ashen Devlesa*, Rhys Morgan. Go with God.'

Chapter Sixteen

Despite Nadya's rejection of both his concern and his presence in their lives, Rhys had one more promise to keep before he returned to his brother's home. And he was determined that whatever role he would eventually assume under Edward's direction, he would no longer be treated as an invalid. He had proven to himself, if to no one else, that he was capable of more than anyone had been willing to assign to him.

As for Abigail…

The contrast between his sister-in-law's coddling and Nadya's treatment of him tread too close to things he couldn't afford to think about. Instead, he set the bay into a trot that lasted to the outskirts of the village where Oliver Burke's small stone croft stood.

Allowing his mount to slow as he approached the cottage, he studied its environs. Isolated from its neighbours on the side by the open green, the house was backed by a thickly wooded slope leading down to a narrow stream. Since the lane that led from the main road into the village ran within a few hundred yards of the house, he had deliberately waited until twilight so that it would, in all likelihood, remain free of traffic.

Rhys pulled the gelding up behind a stand of oaks and dismounted. As he looped his reins around the limb of a sapling, his eyes continued to survey the scene before him.

A few sheep grazed on the common, but they were unsupervised. Beyond them, scattered lights were beginning to illuminate windows in the peaceful hamlet. Trails of white smoke rose from chimneys to fade against the grey sky.

Neither sign of occupation was apparent at Burke's cottage. Nor was he outside with his evening pipe, as he had been when Rhys had come calling two days ago.

Lips tilting slightly in memory, Rhys ran a hand down his horse's nose as he stepped around it to begin the short journey to the small stone house. The stillness seemed strangely absolute. So much so that the hair on the back of his neck began to lift.

Although he was unsure what his well-honed instincts were trying to tell him, he was experienced enough not to discount their warning. He slowed, taking care to avoid any deadfall in his path that might give away his presence.

When he reached the side of the croft, he leaned against the wall next to its shuttered window, listening for any sound that might indicate the owner was in residence. There was none.

He eased around the front corner, his back pressed against the cool stones, and stopped beside the door. Again, he heard nothing from inside.

Perhaps Burke had not yet returned from his trip to the Bull and Bear. Or perhaps, as Rhys had earlier speculated he might, the man had simply packed up his belongings and taken them to another, less threatening part of the country.

Or maybe he's spent the last two days sitting in the dark, a bludgeon in hand, waiting for my return.

Despite that possibility, Rhys hesitated only briefly before he reached out to lift the latch. He was surprised to find the door unbarred. He took a deep breath, every nerve alert, before he pushed it open.

There was enough daylight left to reveal that the one-room cottage was empty. Since he'd been primed for a very different revelation, Rhys again hesitated, waiting for some reaction to the opened door.

When there was none, he advanced another step, stopping this time within its frame. His eyes searched the darkened corners he'd been unable to see from outside and then made a more thorough examination of the rest.

The bedclothes were tumbled, and the fire in the grate had been allowed to die. The remains of a meal, which included a broken loaf of bread on a wooden board and two plates with some indistinguishable contents, stood on a table near the hearth.

It appeared that Burke had been expecting a guest. Or that his entertainment of one had been interrupted. If so…

Warily, Rhys stepped inside. The room smelled of mould and dirt and something else he couldn't quite place. He lifted his nose, drawing in some of the stale air in an attempt to identify that elusively familiar scent.

Unsuccessful, he took another step forward, making sure no one hid in the remaining corner the door had, until now, blocked from view. The prickling of unease he'd felt outside had not, then, presaged an ambush.

Oliver Burke was not, in fact, waiting to bludgeon him. He wasn't here at all.

Rhys walked across to the fireplace. He stooped to hold

his palm out to the grate and then, feeling no heat, touched the ash with his fingers.

Cold as stone. Like the rest of the cottage.

As he straightened, his eyes fell again on the table setting. The fat in the juices that had pooled around the stew was white and congealed, but more than half of what had been dipped into the plates from the pot that hung over the fire remained uneaten.

He turned, considering the rest. Other than the table and two chairs, the only other furnishings were a small chest, like a seaman's locker, and the tumbled bed.

He crossed the room and bending, threw back the lid of the former to reveal a jumble of clothing. The slouch hat Burke had worn the night of the raid hung on a peg beside the bed.

If the man he sought had left, it seemed he'd taken few of his belongings with him. Rhys released his frustration in a long, pent-up breath.

As he turned away, he realized that whatever he'd smelled before was stronger on this side of the room. And in that same instant, he knew exactly what the familiar scent he'd been unable to identify was.

Two steps carried him to the bed with its disordered linens. Steeling himself, he grasped the top edge of the greyed and fraying coverlet, haphazardly thrown across the bare mattress, and pulled it down.

The body of Oliver Burke lay on its back, glassy eyes staring upward. His throat had been cut from ear to ear. Judging by the amount of blood that had soaked onto the bedding, he'd been murdered in this position.

The lack of disarray in the room argued against a struggle. Taken in conjunction with the table set for two,

Burke had probably been the victim of an attack by someone he'd considered a friend.

The man who'd sent him to the Rom encampment that night? Or, more likely, some other mercenary bastard Burke's 'gentleman' had paid to put an end to what had become an unfortunate association?

It hardly mattered. The man was dead, and with him had died any opportunity to find out who'd targeted Nadya.

Infuriated by the outcome of a plan whose odds had been from the start very long, Rhys drew the coverlet over the dead man's face. His only option now was to visit the tavern Burke had mentioned. It was possible that in asking questions he might attract the attention of Burke's 'gentleman' employer to himself.

His mind occupied with figuring out his next move, Rhys started back toward the open door. Something— perhaps that same primordial intuition that had troubled him before he'd entered the cottage—alerted him now.

His gaze lifted to find a shadow across the entryway. One that hadn't been there before and didn't belong now.

In the split second it took him to recognize the anomaly, hard-earned skills came into play. He threw himself to one side as a shot rang out, echoing too loudly in the close confines of the stone house.

The ball struck the wall behind him, sending splinters of rock throughout the room. Before that noise had faded, it was followed by another.

Rhys had taken shelter behind the only object that had offered any. Now he pushed the chair aside to peer out between the legs of the table.

The smell of black powder lay thick in the air. As it began to clear, he was able to identify the last sound he'd heard.

A man was sprawled face downward across the threshold. The pistol that fired the shot that had missed Rhys's head by inches lay in his slackened fingers. And the hilt of the knife buried deep in his back still quivered from the force with which it had been thrown.

Stunned by the sudden eruption of violence, Rhys waited for any indication his attacker might still pose a threat. Eyes straining against the fading light, he saw the shadow that had warned him earlier again fall across the threshold.

The man who cast it this time immediately appeared in the opening. His gaze swept the scene before it found and held on Rhys, still crouched behind the table.

His smile mocking, Nadya's half-brother bowed to him, the sweeping gesture almost theatrical. Then he stepped into the room, looking down contemptuously at his victim.

He put his booted foot against the man's back and bending, drew out his knife. He wiped its blade with two quick strokes, front and back, on the dead man's clothes.

'He'd been waiting for you outside,' Stephano explained as he opened his coat to place the dagger back into a scabbard under his left arm.

Feeling at a distinct disadvantage, Rhys got to his feet. He had no idea why the Rom would have been watching Burke's cottage. All he was sure of was that Stephano had saved his life. And he couldn't think of a single reason why he would want to.

'As were you?' Rhys suggested.

'I have very good sources of information.' Stephano's smile had widened. 'But I'm not prescient. I came to talk to Burke.'

'So did I. I'm sorry to inform you we were both destined for failure.' He tilted his head toward the bed.

Stephano's brows lifted. He stepped over the body of the man he'd killed to walk across the room.

Unlike Rhys, he didn't hesitate before he pulled the coverings off the body. He stood a moment looking down at the dead man and then threw them over his face again.

When he turned, there was no trace of mockery in his dark eyes. 'My only regret is that someone beat me to it.'

'You knew—'

'That he led the raid? I imagine you and I had the same sources for that information.'

'I talked to Burke two days ago. He claimed someone paid him to instigate the villagers to attack.'

Stephano laughed. 'You didn't expect him to admit that villainy was his own idea.'

'They were looking for Nadya,' Rhys said. 'They beat Andrash to try and force him to reveal where the *drabarni* lived.'

'And then you gallantly rescued Andrash and my sister, and all was once more right with the world.' The mockery was back with a vengeance.

'I overheard one of them use Burke's name and tracked him here,' Rhys continued doggedly. 'Whoever paid him—'

'Planned to ambush you?' As if copying Rhys's earlier gesture, the Rom tilted his head in the direction of the man he'd knifed. 'If that *was* the case, they are now both dead.'

'Burke told me he was a gentleman. As you can see—' Rhys looked pointedly at the man on the floor.

'Ah, yes. Burke. That fount of veracity. That pillar of virtue.'

'Why would he lie?'

'Because he represents the dregs of your society. Violent, ignorant, greedy. But assuming any part of what he told you was true, then when he went back to his patron to tell him you were sniffing around, together they arranged this ambush. The man took the opportunity to get rid of you and Burke at the same time. And now he is dead.' Stephano shrugged. 'It's over.'

'You can't be sure of that. Besides, the central question has yet to be answered. Why would anyone target Nadya?'

'Why indeed,' Stephano said pleasantly. 'It makes no sense.'

'And you're willing to let this go? Nadya's your sister, for God's sake.'

'While I admire your tenacity, might I remind you that what happened that night is none of your concern?'

Rhys felt his temper flare. He couldn't be sure if that was the sole result of the Gypsy's sarcasm or because her brother's words had echoed Nadya's rejection closely enough to represent an unwanted reminder of its finality.

'And might I remind you that someone just tried to kill me. That seems reason enough to make it my concern.'

'Then go home, soldier boy,' Stephano suggested. 'You should be safe there.'

Wrapped tightly in cotton wool.

Although the last phrase had found voice only inside Rhys's head, Stephano's comment had again come too near his own thoughts not to be coloured by them. The anger that had begun in response to the Rom's mockery threatened his control.

'I haven't been called *boy* in a very long time.' The softness of his words would have been warning enough to anyone who'd served under his command. 'But then it's been a very long time since I've been one.'

The eyes of Nadya's brother considered him a moment before the Gypsy's well-shaped lips lifted in a smile. 'I have offended you. My deepest apologies. How may I make amends?'

Although the tone of his comment had lacked the Rom's customary sarcasm, Rhys didn't feel inclined to forgive the slight. He hadn't liked the man in their previous encounters. Knowing Stephano's tragic story hadn't lessened that animosity.

Perhaps the fact he just saved your life should.

'By not discounting my concerns for Nadya's safety.'

The Gypsy's smile faded. 'I am always concerned for the safety of my family.'

'I'm sure you know better than anyone why you should be.'

For a few seconds there was no response but the tilt of a brow. 'Indeed? And how did you arrive at that conclusion?'

'Your grandmother suggested you've made dangerous enemies in the course of your…endeavours. If they want to strike back at you, what better way than to injure those you hold dear?'

The contours of the Rom's handsome face hardened. 'Why would you listen to the gossip of a superstitious old woman?'

'Because she knows you better than anyone else. If Magda believes what you're doing is dangerous, who am I to doubt it?'

'Magda should stick to her Tarot cards and her palm readings. Has she read yours?'

Rhys shook his head. 'Should I ask her to?'

'Only if you want to know what the future holds. Few of us do.' He looked down at the dead man at his feet. 'Would he have come here tonight if he'd known what fate had in store?'

'I don't believe in fate,' Rhys said.

It was not the absolute truth, but he'd seen too many men become reckless in the belief that if it were their time to die, they would, and there was nothing they could do about it. He'd stayed alive through years of the most brutal combat by believing his fate rested in his own hands, controlled by his intellect and courage rather than by something that had been written in his stars. Or in his palm.

'Then you're a lucky man. Or a foolish one.' Stephano took the two steps that would carry him to the door. When he reached it, he looked back over his shoulder. 'The villagers have finally roused themselves to investigate. With your background and position, I'm sure they could never believe you to be at fault in this. I hope you'll understand if I, on the other hand, decline to await their judgment regarding my part in it. I bid you goodnight, Major Morgan. And farewell. Have a safe and uneventful journey home.'

With that, the Rom slipped out of the cottage as soundlessly as he had entered. Faintly in the distance, Rhys could hear the murmur of voices that had alerted Stephano to the arrival of Burke's fellow citizens.

The Gypsy had probably been correct in his supposition that Rhys would eventually and without penalty be able to explain his presence in a house that also contained two dead men. That might, however, prove to be a time-consuming process, one in which he would be forced to call upon the influence of his brother. Or even his godfather. Neither possibility appealed to him.

After a quick look around to make sure there was nothing here to identify either himself or Beshaley as Burke's guests, Rhys crossed to open the shutter and, putting one leg over the low sill, climbed out.

He had untied the bay and was in the process of mounting before the villagers' voices grew loud enough for him to distinguish what they were shouting. Leaning forward over the neck of his horse, he sent the gelding thundering down the lane toward the main road.

Long before he reached it, he knew there was no pursuit. Nor would there be.

The constable would be called, but despite Rhys's earlier visit to the cottage, there would be no way for anyone to connect him with tonight's events. Or to Burke's death.

It was possible that some of the men Burke had persuaded to accompany him on the raid of the Gypsy encampment might consider his death to be payback by the Rom. Whether or not they would act on that idea…

Is none of your concern. Both Nadya and her half-brother had gone out of their way to make that clear.

Go home, soldier boy. You should be safe there.

The temptation to do exactly that was stronger than it had ever been before. The attraction involved with fighting windmills had always escaped him.

Go home. And he would, if only because Nadya had given him no other option.

Just not yet…

Chapter Seventeen

If Nadya had been expecting either praise or sympathy from her grandmother for sending Rhys away, she would have been disappointed. When she told the old woman that her former patient had gone home, Magda had acted as if she'd lost her mind. Now, three days after Rhys's departure, Nadya was beginning to believe her grandmother had been correct.

She knew that if she had pursued their relationship, Stephano would no doubt have disowned her, perhaps even sent her into exile. Compared to what she had given up to stay in his good graces, she was no longer sure she cared.

And what about Rhys? logic demanded. *Do you care about him? What kind of reception would he have had if he'd returned to his family with a Gypsy in tow?*

Of course, it was possible that Rhys had never intended to take her home. Maybe he had planned to provide her with a cottage nearby, a place he could visit when his physical desires for her drove him away from whatever marriage his family would eventually arrange.

Which would leave her in the same situation as her

mother. A *gaujo's* whore. A woman who had no rights under English law, not even to the disposition of her children.

Regret and reason circled endlessly in her mind, and now, three days removed from Rhys's departure, she was no closer to resolving the debate than she'd been when she had told him goodbye. Except she hadn't even done that, she admitted. Or allowed Angel to. And like her mother, the child had grieved that he was gone.

Despite the chill of the early October afternoon, today she had left her daughter with her grandmother in camp and walked alone to the meadow where the two of them had spent so many happy hours. She wanted time to think without the distraction of watching over Angel.

Once there, she had again spread her shawl and sat down in the heart of a countryside where always before she'd found peace. She was determined to reclaim her life—one that had given her joy and a deep sense of satisfaction.

To do that, she must dispel this pall of doubt that continued to depress her spirits. She had made her choice, one she knew was correct by any standard she might apply. Now she had to let go of all the 'what ifs' that plagued her every waking hour.

She had no idea how long she'd sat there, the weak afternoon sun on her back, before a movement in her peripheral vision warned her she was no longer alone. She turned her head to see Rhys standing at the edge of the trees. And despite all her arguments that it was better he had gone, she couldn't prevent the involuntary increase in her heart rate at his return.

'Is Angel with you?' His eyes searched for the child before they returned to her.

She shook her head, not trusting her voice. She had just realized that, for almost the first time since he'd regained consciousness, they were truly alone.

The same thought seemed to occur to Rhys. He stepped through the trees and began to walk toward her.

She rose before he reached her. 'What are you doing here?'

He took a breath, deep enough that it moved his shoulders. 'I still believe you're in danger.'

She should be flattered, she supposed, that he was obsessed with her safety. But of all the things he might have said to her, that was the last she wanted to hear.

'The target of some nefarious plot to deprive my people of their *drabarni*. How could I possibly have forgotten?'

'Oliver Burke was murdered. Someone had cut his throat before I could talk to him again.'

If her half-brother had also discovered the name of the man who'd led that raid, he might well have enacted his own form of justice. One that would prevent further harm to his people.

'And you believe Stephano had something to do with that?'

'*Stephano*? Why would you think that?'

Rhys's surprise seemed genuine, making Nadya wish she hadn't mentioned her half-brother's name in conjunction with the murder. After all, there was no way he could know her brother's weapon of choice had always been the knife. Learning Burke's throat had been cut had instantly led her to wonder if he'd had a hand in the man's death.

'Because you're here,' she lied. 'I thought you'd come to confront him.'

'Actually…' He seemed disinclined to finish the thought.

'No?' she prodded.

'Stephano was there. At Burke's cottage. But I don't believe he had anything to do with his death.'

This time Nadya was wise enough to hold her tongue. She thought it strange Rhys didn't suspect her brother, even though that had been her first thought. Of course, he wasn't as familiar with Stephano's thirst for vengeance on those who'd wronged him as she was.

'So Stephano knew about Burke?' she asked.

'Andrash gave him his name. Stephano had been able to trace him, just as I had.'

Then it seemed even stranger that Rhys didn't think her brother had anything to do with the man's death. That wasn't an idea she wanted him to dwell on, of course. She suspected Rhys's code of honour would force him to go to the authorities if he thought Stephano was involved.

'Then perhaps he was also able to determine why Burke incited the villagers.'

'I'm afraid any trail that might lead us beyond Burke has ended. I've spent the last few days at the inn where he told me his employer approached him, but no one there seemed to know Burke. And if any gentlemen frequent that establishment, no one was aware of that either.'

'Then…forgive me, but why have you come back?'

A muscle in his jaw tightened and then relaxed. 'Unfinished business, I suppose.'

'I don't understand.'

'Nor do I. Every time I leave you I think…'

'What?'

'That it's the right thing to do. The honourable thing. And then…then I find myself drawn back again, once more searching for words that will make sense of what I feel.'

Her heart had begun to pound, but they'd been down this same path too many times to allow false hope. They both knew nothing could come of what was between them.

Nothing except what might happen here…

'And have you found those words?'

He shook his head. 'Only ones that tell me I shouldn't be here. Not with you. Not alone.'

'We both know all the arguments against it.'

'And seem to have rejected them,' he said softly. 'So that we're back to this.'

'And what is *this*?'

'I don't know. All I know is that I've never felt about another woman the way I feel about you.'

At one time hearing him make that confession would have meant everything to her. Now she wondered if it were enough.

And even if she decided it was enough for now, would it be enough when he was gone? When she'd been deserted like her mother so that he could marry the oh-so-respectable *gadje* wife his family would choose for him?

'What do you want from me, Rhys?' The words were an expression of her frustration. So much so that she didn't expect an answer.

He gave her one. 'Whatever you're willing to give.'

And that was her dilemma. What was she willing to give of who and what she was? A woman respected within her tribe. Valued for who she was, as well as for what she knew. One whose position had been secured from the moment of her birth.

All of that would be at risk if she gave herself to this man. This *gaujo*.

She had no doubt what Stephano would do if he found out she'd disobeyed one of the strongest taboos of her people. Not only was he her brother, he was also the leader of their people.

And the unfortunate product of a misalliance exactly like this one would be.

That was the term the *gadje* used to describe a highly unsuitable match, and exactly what their pairing would be to her people. As well as to his.

'There's too much at stake,' she said finally. 'For both of us. You know that.'

Rhys nodded, but took another step forward. Close enough now that she could have reached out and touched him.

'You shouldn't have come back,' she said instead.

'Is that what you wanted? Never to see me again?'

That was a lie she couldn't bring herself to give voice to. Not even to protect him.

With her silence, he took the last step. As near to her as he had been when he lifted her down from his horse that night. The night they had kissed.

Even the memory of Magda's scolding wasn't enough to prevent her from doing what she had wanted to do since he'd walked out of the trees. She stepped into his arms, which closed around her as if they, too, knew she belonged there. As if none of the things that should have kept them apart mattered.

Her face lifted for his kiss. This time there was no hesitation. His mouth met hers, claiming it, branding it as if he intended that they should never be separated again.

His touch ravaged her senses. All her logical arguments for why this couldn't be dissolved in the intensity of what he could make her feel.

After a long time, he lifted his head, looking down into her eyes. They had opened slowly, reluctant to return to even this much reality.

He smiled at her, his thumb tracing across the moisture his lips had left on hers. She opened her mouth to capture it, suckling while her gaze held his.

He bent his knees to lift her, carrying her into the denseness of the forest. When he finally set her on her feet, her knees trembled so that she was forced to put her hand on his shoulder for balance.

He stripped off his coat and waistcoat and laid them on the ground. His fingers struggled with the intricacies of his cravat until hers replaced them, untying its knot and letting the cloth drift down to the blackened leaves that formed a carpet around them.

As soon as he pulled his shirt off over his head, she was there, pressing her body against the strength of his. She put her hands on his shoulders and, standing on tiptoe, reached for his mouth. He responded by pulling her closer, her breasts once more crushed against its muscled wall.

When he broke his kiss this time, it was to trail the heat of his lips down the line of her throat and into the valley between her breasts, exposed to his touch by the low neck of the blouse she wore.

She drew a shuddering breath, as the warmth of his tongue moved over her skin. The scent of his body was in her nostrils. Clean. Sweet. Dearly familiar.

She moved her hands down his chest, and then lower, her thumbs trailing down the line of dark hair that centred his stomach. With the tips of her fingers she traced along rib and muscle until she reached the barrier of his pantaloons. She slipped her fingers inside them, brushing over his hipbone.

When he eased the neck of her blouse down, so that his lips caressed the swell of her breast, something released deep inside her body, sending heat scalding through her veins. And still her body begged for more.

She wanted the masculine abrasiveness of his chest, which she'd felt beneath her palms, against her breasts. The only way to accomplish that...

She took a step back, reaching down to strip her blouse off over her head. Before it reached the ground where his clothing lay, she was back in his arms, the warmth of his body replacing the chill of the air against her dampened skin.

Flesh to flesh.

This was what she had craved. What she'd dreamed of. Yet even as she gloried in his nearness, it was not enough. It could not be. Not now. Not when she had tasted the reality of things she'd only imagined before.

As his mouth closed over hers once more, his kiss was different somehow because of this new intimacy. And, although she tried to prevent the desertion of his lips, she made no protest when he knelt, drawing her down to the scattered clothing he'd arranged to form a makeshift bed.

It was not a marriage bed—that could never be hers—but it was theirs. One the two of them would share.

And when they had, she would deal with the consequences of this decision. One she made not only with her heart, but with her head.

Rhys lay down beside her. For a long time, he didn't touch her, content to look down into her face.

His eyes traced her features as if he'd never seen them before. Or if he were trying to memorize them.

In preparation for the time when they would no longer be together?

What did that matter? They would at least have this. This here and now. And as for what would come when it was over...

Rhys lifted his torso, propping on one elbow to smile at her. With one finger he followed the line of her lips, which opened under his touch. He dragged their slight moisture down the curve of her chin and then into the small hollow at the base of her throat. He lowered his head, pressing a kiss against its pulse.

His fingers cupped around the fullness of her breast,

cradling it to meet his mouth's descent. As his lips closed around her nipple, already hardened with the afternoon's chill, molten heat ran through her body.

And then the release she'd felt before was suddenly there again. Her mouth opened involuntarily, her sigh of pleasure audible.

Rhys's practiced caress didn't falter. Instead, he seemed to delight in discovering new ways to create that reaction.

His patience unlimited, with his teeth, lips and tongue, he taught her the ancient art of approach and withdrawal. Of pleasure so intense it was almost pain. Of anticipation and release.

It wasn't enough. Nothing could be. Not until he had taken her. Not until he had made love to her in every way that had been devised by the imagination of man since the beginning of time. Only then, perhaps, would the need she felt finally be satisfied.

And so he began that final lesson, employing again all the pleasures he'd introduced her to. He loosened the tie that held her skirt at the waist—the long fingers that had seemed unable to deal with the intricacies of his own clothing having no problem with hers—until she lay completely naked. Completely exposed to his gaze.

As he had studied her face, his eyes examined her body. She wondered if the darkness of her skin, so different from the fairness of the women he'd known, would repulse him.

And then, as his gaze returned to her face, he whispered, 'You are so beautiful.'

Before her brain could formulate a reply to that unexpected compliment, he bent his head. With his tongue and lips, he followed the course her thumbs had traced over his body. He took time to thoroughly examine her navel before his mouth moved lower, stopping her breath with anticipation.

Her fingers involuntarily locked into his hair. Even she was unsure if that was done in protest. If so, it had no effect on what Rhys was doing.

With his lips and his tongue, he repeated all he had taught her before. Advance and withdrawal. Pleasure so intense it verged on the edge of pain.

Again and again he brought her to the edge of release, only to leave her shivering there until her body unwillingly retreated from what it now so desperately sought. A fulfilment she had never experienced before.

Then at last, when it seemed as if the master had misjudged the limits of the instrument he so skilfully played, his mouth returned to hers. As it did, he began to push into her body.

She felt him hesitate when he encountered the barrier she'd given him no reason to expect. He raised his head, looking down into her eyes.

She smiled at him, granting him permission to take what was already his. When he did, the pain was sharp, far more intense than she'd thought it would be, but his kiss eased both her fear and uncertainty.

There was neither in his movements. With as much assurance as he'd displayed from the beginning, he carried her past both, bringing her with him to their final destination.

When the tremors began inside her body she clung to him, riding out the storm that washed over her in waves of pleasure that were so much more intense than the pain that had preceded them. Until at last they lay together, spent and sated. Still joined in every way that mattered, body and soul.

After what seemed an eternity, he raised his head again.

Opening pleasure-drugged eyes, she found him once more looking down on her.

'Tell me again about those dozen men.'

Still captive of the web he'd woven over her senses, for a moment she couldn't think what he meant. And then she remembered the lie she'd told.

Wordlessly she shook her head before she pushed upward, straining toward his lips to stop the questions. He evaded her by leaning back, taking them out of reach.

'I haven't asked you about the women in your past,' she protested.

When she lay down again on his coat, her submission was rewarded by the slow movement of his thumb against the tip of her breast. Back and forth it teased across nerve endings that had first been aroused by this same relentless movement of his tongue.

'I can't remember any,' he said, smiling into her eyes.

'Liar.' Despite the harshness of the word she'd used, her lips curved into an answering smile.

'Not at the moment.' He lowered his head to drop a kiss on her nose.

'Were there many?' There must have been, given the skill which could make her body sing so readily to the tune he'd set for it.

'None who were important.'

'No unrequited first love?'

'But of course. She was a kitchen girl who saved me the cream. I was five.'

'And since then? When you weren't five.'

'A girl about to embark on her first Season. I was madly in love with her, and I believed my affections were returned. Perhaps they were. Until her father discovered I was not only a younger son, but a younger son with no prospects. My heart was broken. A few dark-eyed senoritas I met in Iberia managed to put the pieces back together, but it had been irreparably damaged. Or so I thought.'

His mouth lowered again, so that the last was whispered against her ear. His tongue explored its contours, trailing moisture.

'Until now.' His words were a breath that stirred against the dampness.

'And now?'

'I met the *drabarni*.' He raised his head to see her face. 'I'm simply another in the long line of people she has healed.'

'I didn't know soldiers could wax poetic.'

She had discovered that she loved looking at him. The slant of the afternoon sun turned the chestnut hair as golden as the beech leaves. His eyes, clear and filled with light, were almost translucent.

'And I didn't know Gypsy girls—' His eyes changed, darkening suddenly as the sentence he'd begun trailed.

'What is it?'

He shook his head, but the spell they'd been under had shattered. A cloud moved across the face of the sun, obscuring it.

'It's late. You should go back before your grandmother sends someone to look for you.'

And found them together.

Into the idyllic fantasy of the last few hours, reality intruded. His words evoked a sense that what they had shared was something to be ashamed of.

Responding to his urgency, she sat up, searching for her blouse among the garments scattered around them. Rhys located it before she could.

He held it out to her, and she took it, pressing its cool

dampness against her breasts. For the first time she felt that she should hide their nakedness.

They had not talked about what would happen next. Perhaps nothing. After all, Rhys had made no promises. And she had expected none.

He had been in the process of pulling on his shirt. When his head emerged through the opening, he must have realized she hadn't even begun to dress.

'What's wrong?'

She shook her head and with trembling fingers began to put on her own clothing. It all seemed to be happening so quickly, as if he were in a hurry to be gone.

A thought made more bitter by the remembrance of his unhurried lovemaking.

When she looked up from straightening her crumpled blouse, Rhys was holding out her skirt. After she had taken it, he offered his hand to help her up. Ignoring the gesture, she awkwardly got to her feet, turning her back on him to finish dressing.

When her garments had finally been arranged in some semblance of order, she couldn't stop the shivers that occasionally racked her body. They were not caused by the cold, but by the enormity of what she had done.

Despite what had happened between them, Rhys seemed intent on returning her to the encampment as quickly as possible. Would he then be on his way back to his home and family? Would there be another goodbye? This one—finally—the last.

'Ready?' His voice held none of the uncertainty she was dealing with.

Nor could she explain why she felt as she did. She had made the decision to give herself to this man. He'd taken nothing from her that she had not willingly given.

She nodded without meeting his eyes and then, head down, walked past him toward the opening in the trees. As she stepped through it, her heart stopped.

A small form hurtled toward her across the meadow. When she arrived, Angel buried her face against her mother's shirt. Nadya had automatically put her hand on the child's head, but her eyes were riveted by the man who followed the little girl.

Her brother's face had broken into a smile when he'd spotted her. One that quickly disappeared when Rhys stepped out of the trees behind her.

Chapter Eighteen

It was clear from the anger darkening Stephano's features that he knew exactly what had happened between them. Nadya's dishevelled clothing and disordered hair would have been enough to condemn her without the guilt her face must surely reveal.

'I warned you.'

Nadya thought those words, ground out between clenched teeth as Stephano rushed forward, were directed at her. Then her half-brother pushed her aside in order to reach Rhys.

Employing skills learned as a street urchin in London, Stephano hooked his booted foot behind Rhys's knee, so that the ex-soldier's leg buckled. As he stumbled forward, her half-brother's perfectly timed upper cut sent him crashing back into the tree behind him.

'Stop it.' Dragging her daughter with her, Nadya grabbed Stephano's arm, trying to prevent him from finishing what he'd begun.

Her vehemence startled him enough to slow his attack. As she held him, his furious eyes searched her face.

At whatever he saw there, his lips tightened. 'You beg for his life? You know the law.'

'I have the right to choose.'

'Not if I forbid you that choice.'

'The wrong was mine, Stephano, not his.'

'And you'll pay. But so will he, *jel'enedra*. So will he. It is our way.'

'*Our* way? What do you know of *our* way? My father loved our mother. And he didn't ask who she had loved before. It didn't matter to him.'

'What has that to do with this?'

'Our way isn't always black or white. Sometimes it's finding forgiveness in your heart for those who've sinned.'

'My father loved my mother. What was her sin in that?'

'Then what is my sin in this?'

His eyes widened, but he had no answer. After a moment he jerked his arm from her grip, almost stumbling over Angel as he did. The child was watching them, her eyes moving from one to the other.

'Take her back to camp,' Stephano ordered.

'So you can kill him without destroying what she feels for you?'

'You want your daughter to watch the *gaujo* die?'

'Why should he die, Stephano? He did nothing I didn't ask him to do.'

'He made you his whore.'

'As your father made your mother his?'

'You have no right to speak of my father.'

Her laugh mocked his denial, but she knew she was treading a dangerous path. As the leader of their *kumpania*, Stephano had the right to exile her for what she'd done. And there would be few among the Rom who would oppose any punishment Stephano decreed for the *gaujo*, and none brave enough to do so openly.

'This isn't about your father,' Rhys said. 'Or your mother. Or whatever else is between the two of you.'

In their fury at one another, they had almost forgotten him. He stood there defiantly, the mark of Stephano's fist on his chin.

'You're right.' Stephano began to move toward the Englishman again. 'It's about you making my sister your whore.'

Almost faster than the eye could follow, Rhys's right fist caught the Rom under the chin, rocking him back. The shock on Stephano's face quickly gave way to rage. He rushed forward again, only to be met by Nadya, who stepped between them.

'Rhys didn't make me anything I didn't want to be. If you must blame someone, blame me.'

'Oh, I do. Believe me.'

'Let him go, Stephano. Let this go. If you don't, you'll make trouble for our people. You're the one who told me about his connections.'

Stephano's laugh was bitter. 'When he leaves you to bear his bastard alone, Nadya, will you give that child to Lord Keddinton to rear?'

'Why? Did the *gadje* do so well with your upbringing that you feel I should?'

With the back of his hand, her half-brother struck her. It was the first time in her life Stephano had hit her, and the violence of it shocked them both, so that for a moment they simply looked at each other.

Angel reacted first. She flew at her beloved uncle, small fists flailing at his legs. Her high-pitched keening as she hit him over and over again was the sound of grief rather than rage.

Distraught, Nadya rushed to pick up daughter. She tried

to reassure her, but the little girl resisted all her efforts at comfort. The terrible noise she made continued unabated.

Stephano endured it as long as he could. When he removed the child from Nadya's arms, Angel twisted and turned in his hold, but he was strong enough to control her.

'Take your whore with you when you leave,' he said to Rhys. And then to Nadya, 'Angel isn't going to end up in some foundling home when the *gadje* tire of her.'

As stunned by Stephano's pronouncement as she'd been by the blow to her face, Nadya tried to wrench her daughter away from him. Ignoring her protests, he carried the struggling child across the meadow toward the Rom encampment.

Nadya had to run to keep pace with his long, angry stride. Nothing she said slowed his advance. Finally, he pushed her away with his left arm, easily maintaining his hold on the now-hysterical child as he did.

He had shoved her hard enough that, off balance, she stumbled and fell. On hands and knees, she turned to look beseechingly at Rhys, who followed them.

He bent to help her to her feet. 'We'll get her back.'

'You don't know him.'

'Will he hurt her?'

'Of course not. How could you think that? He loves her. More than his own life. That's why he's taken her. He's terrified he's going to lose the only person who's ever loved him totally and without qualification.'

Rhys didn't argue with her assessment. He put his arm around her instead, offering Nadya the comfort her daughter had been denied.

As they entered the Gypsy camp, Rhys had no idea what lay ahead. All he knew was that he was responsible for what had just happened. Nadya had warned him that any relationship between them would damage her standing in the tribe. Knowing that, he'd been unable to leave her alone.

Today had been the final betrayal of all that he felt for her. And of his own concept of honour.

Even while accepting the blame, he couldn't believe Nadya's brother would be vengeful enough to separate her from her daughter. The cruelties Stephano had endured as a child had scarred him, but it was hard to fathom that a man who professed to love his sister could do what he had threatened.

And if he did...

There was no way he was going to allow that arrogant bastard to take Angel. Being separated from Nadya would destroy her fragile sense of security. And it would kill Nadya.

As Stephano carried the struggling child through camp, the Rom who'd been working outside stopped what they were doing to watch. Hearing the terrible noise Angel still made, people also emerged from the bender tents, the women with sewing in hand or infants balanced on their hips.

Their *Rom Baro* strode to the central campfire. It was obviously a pre-arranged signal, for the members of the tribe began moving toward that location. One of the women reached out in an attempt to take the girl from his arms, but he refused to give her up.

When most of the Rom had gathered around him, Stephano began to speak, raising his voice to be heard over the child's hysteria. 'The *gaujo* my sister sheltered has abused her hospitality.'

As her brother spoke, Nadya straightened away from Rhys's support to stand beside him, her head held high. She'd made no attempt to smooth the disorder of her curls, and her lips were still reddened from his kisses. To Rhys she had never been more beautiful, more regal or more distant.

Whatever the outcome of this, she was the one who stood to lose the most—not only her place in the tribe, but also her daughter. Rhys vowed that he wouldn't let that happen. Not if he had to fight every man here to prevent it.

'He has defiled my sister by making her his whore,' Stephano went on. 'As the head of her family I claim what is my right according to our laws.'

The low murmur his words provoked from the assembly contained an element of shock. Rhys couldn't be sure if that was because of the term by which the Gypsy had referred to Nadya or by his last assertion.

He glanced at the woman beside him, seeking guidance about what was taking place, but her attention was locked on Stephano. She didn't seem afraid, which reassured Rhys that whatever right her half-brother had just claimed, it apparently didn't involve a physical punishment of some kind for her.

'Are we not to hear from your sister, Stephano?' Magda said from the steps of her caravan, a position of command that was enhanced by both her age and rank among the Rom.

It took a few seconds for Rhys to realize why the silence that had fallen after the old woman's question seemed so complete. Angel had stopped crying and was looking over Stephano's shoulder at her great-grandmother.

'My sister has no authority to speak here.'

'Of course she does. Ask Cora about the authority of the *drabarni*.' With Magda's words, one of the women, heavily pregnant, put a protective hand over the bulge of her belly. 'Or Sunar, whose arm Nadya set last month. Or Andrash, who she tended after the raid. It is for them to say what place Nadya has in our *kumpania*.'

'No longer. The *drabarni* is unclean.' Stephano's face was cold even as the murmur of shock or concern followed his words.

'Your own mother took a *gadje* lover and bore him a son,' Magda said. 'When she had done that, she returned to us and married a good man who loved her despite her disgrace.'

'If there is such a man here, someone who wishes to marry this *gaujo's* whore, then I will give my sister to him. Is that what you want from me, *chivani*?' Stephano asked.

'Do you not care what I want, Stephano?' Nadya voice held no hint of embarrassment or apology for what she'd done. 'Should I not have some say in my future?'

'You chose it when you became the Englishman's whore.'

'I chose to give my body to a man. As my mother did before me. And her mother before her. As every woman here has done.'

'And by our laws you are free to go with that man,' Stephano said. 'If he still wants you.'

'What if I choose not to go with him?'

Was that what Nadya wanted? To stay here rather than be with him? Was her standing among her own people more important to her than the future they might have together?

If so, that, too, was her prerogative, Rhys acknowledged regretfully. One he had no right to oppose. Although she had given herself to him, she had promised him nothing.

'Then I declare you outcast,' Stephano decreed flatly.

The murmur began again, but the tenor of it was different. This time there was a distinct feel of protest and disagreement in the sound.

'That's a decision for the *kriss* to make,' Nadya protested.

'This is your *kriss*. I am its judge.'

'And you judge me because I gave my body to a man? Or because that man was not Rom?'

'You know the law.'

'Who here brings charges against me?' Nadya held her hands out, palms up, as if in supplication to her people.

'I do.' Stephano's words drew another disapproving response from the crowd, but he continued to speak over it. 'You have dishonoured your family and the *kumpania*.'

'As our mother did. Did her family bring her to trial?' As she asked that question, Nadya seemed to appeal to her grandmother who, after her initial comments, had watched without taking part in the proceedings.

'As head of the *kumpania*, Stephano has the right to censure your behaviour,' Magda said.

Nadya's body stiffened, reacting to what must seem another betrayal, but her chin lifted. 'Does he also have the right to take my daughter from me, *chivani*?'

'Angeline isn't your daughter,' Stephano said before the old woman could answer. 'She's chattel. Something you purchased. As property, she falls under the jurisdiction of this court. To be disposed of when her owner is exiled.'

Another blow. Another almost invisible reaction from the slight, proud figure standing beside him. One more than he could bear.

'You aren't taking Angel away from her,' Rhys said into the heavy silence. No matter Nadya's instructions that he should hold his tongue, he was tired of her brother's assumption that he could do whatever he wanted.

'Who will stop me, *gaujo*? Will it be you?' Stephano's well-shaped lips curved into a smile, but his eyes were as hard as the obsidian they resembled.

'If no one else will.'

'And how do you propose to do that?'

'By taking Angel from you.'

The Rom's smile widened so that the whiteness of his teeth gleamed like those of a wolf closing in for the kill.

'You think you will do that in front of my people?' It was more taunt than question.

'I don't believe your people agree with what you're doing.'

'It doesn't matter whether they agree with it. They have sworn an oath of allegiance to me.'

'What value is an oath given to a blackguard and a scoundrel?'

'Isn't that the definition of the Rom among your kind?' The wolfish grin widened, and the crowd's response, although muted, was once more in Stephano's favour.

Nadya had been right. This wasn't a society he had any chance of understanding. Or influencing. A place where English law had no jurisdiction and garnered no respect.

'Rhys doesn't speak for me,' Nadya interrupted, 'but you know Angel isn't chattel, Stephano. You're using some arcane law to punish me for what happened between the *gaujo* and me.'

'You made your choice. If the Englishman wants to take his whore with him when he goes, I have no objection. The girl stays with her people.'

'That's absurd. Angel's my daughter. You've acknowledged she's mine.'

'Of course she is yours. You bought her, and so you owned her. An ownership you forfeited when you broke our laws.'

'I have always defended you, Stephano.' Nadya's voice was quiet, but passionate. 'Whatever you did, I made excuses for it. You of all people understand what it means for a child to be taken from the ones who love her.'

'I know what it means to be taken from everything and

everyone you've ever known. By uprooting her from the *kumpania*, that's what you would do to Angel.'

'I don't want to uproot her. I told you. I want to stay here. I want to be what I have always been to our people. Their *drabarni*.'

'And the *gaujo*?'

Nadya didn't look at Rhys. It seemed as if she had erected a wall between them since they'd left the meadow.

'He will go back to his people. To his life.'

'Without you?'

'I would be less welcome there than he is here.'

'Yet you chose him over your own people.'

'Don't do this, Stephano. What happened between us is over. We accept that. We have no choice but to accept it.'

'And you, *gaujo*? What do you say?'

'Nadya?' Rhys asked softly.

She turned to look at him then. Her eyes pled with him to say to her brother what he wanted to hear, but Rhys couldn't bring himself to do that. No matter what happened, he was at least going to tell the Rom the truth.

'I love your sister. What happened wasn't something either of us had planned. This afternoon…' Unconsciously Rhys shook his head, unsure whether what he was about to say next would make this more difficult for Nadya, and yet unable not to say it. 'I want to marry your sister.'

Rhys had no idea how to interpret the resulting rustle of movement among the assemblage. There was no doubt, however, about the interpretation of Stephano's shout of laughter.

'And you will then take her into the bosom of your family, I suppose?'

'Yes.'

'That I should like to see, Major Morgan. That I should like to see very much indeed.'

Stephano *would* probably enjoy seeing Abigail's reception of Nadya. It would almost certainly prove his point.

'I want my daughter, Stephano. Tell me what must I do to get her back?'

Nadya's words ignored the proposal Rhys had just made in an attempt to cut through her half-brother's games. Even as Rhys dealt with his disappointment at her lack of reaction to it, he understood that retrieving Angel must be her first priority.

Stephano enjoyed manipulating their emotions too much to give up that pleasure without a fight. 'Your paramour says he will take her from me. That's something else I should like to see, *jel'enedra*. Wouldn't you?'

'What do you want?' Nadya asked again.

'I want him to fight me for the girl.'

The reaction from the Gypsies this time wasn't sound or movement. Nor was it a simple silence. It was as if they had collectively drawn breath and were holding it.

By now what was underway had become clear, even to Rhys. Stephano wanted blood because his sister had been defiled. Angel was simply the tool he had used to bring that about.

'All right.' Even as Rhys agreed to the Rom's demand, he knew he might well be defeated. But if facing this bastard in combat was his only hope of making the Rom return Angel to her mother, Rhys was more than willing to fight him.

'You don't understand.' Finally Nadya had turned to look at him again, her words low and intense.

'I understand that this is what he's wanted from the beginning,' Rhys said. 'He won't be satisfied until it's done.'

'I will marry the *drabarni*.'

Intent on their own conversation, they turned, almost in unison, to see who had made that surprising offer. Andrash was making his way to the front of the group as he continued to address Stephano.

'I will marry her and take care of the child, *Rom Baro*. Neither will trouble you again.'

'Are you sure you wish to take the *gaujo*'s whore into your bed, my friend?' Stephano's smile was mocking.

'I would be greatly honoured if our *drabarni* would agree to be my wife.'

For a moment it seemed Nadya's half-brother was at a loss. The smith's offer had apparently spoiled his plan. As Stephano's own mother had again gained acceptance in the tribe through her marriage to Thom Argentari, as Andrash's wife, Nadya could not be forced into exile for her sin of lying with a *gaujo*.

As quickly as that small hope formed, it was destroyed. And by someone Rhys had not thought to be Stephano's ally.

'The *gaujo* is Andrash's friend.' Magda's voice was again pitched to carry over the clearing. 'He credits the Englishman with saving his life on the night of the raid. He would make any sacrifice to save Major Morgan's life.'

'Marrying the *drabarni* would be no sacrifice, *chivani*,' the smith protested. 'Not to me.'

'You do me a great honour, Andrash,' Nadya said. 'And an even greater kindness. But I won't marry you. I can't. You love someone else.'

'If you marry me, *drabarni*, your daughter will become my daughter as well,' Andrash argued earnestly. 'Just as Stephano became your father's son in everything but blood.'

'No matter what you promise here, Andrash, in the end Stephano won't allow this. It isn't what he wants.'

'Your lover has bragged that he will take your daughter from me. If he does, it will be up to them—' Stephano gestured toward the crowd '—whether or not you are allowed to stay. And if he doesn't succeed, you know what will happen.'

'Angel loves you,' Nadya said. 'And you love her. Why would you do this?'

'Here, among our people, I know she is safe. And will be for the rest of her life. Out there…I have reason to know too well—as does Angel—what happens to children in his world.'

'All right,' Nadya said.

Rhys wasn't sure what she'd just agreed to. Surely she wouldn't give up her daughter so easily.

'There are things in my *vardo*—' she began.

'Which now belong to the *kumpania*.'

'She isn't leaving,' Rhys said. 'Not without Angel.'

'The fight he proposes is to the death.' Finally Nadya had looked at him again, her eyes anguished. 'He wants you dead.'

That's what she'd meant when she told him he didn't understand. And yet, despite that threat, for the first time since they'd left the clearing Rhys felt a ray of hope. If Nadya were willing to give up Angel in order to protect him from her brother, it was obvious she cared for him. Far more than she had admitted before her people.

'He isn't the first to want that.' He smiled in an attempt to reassure her, but her eyes glazed with tears instead.

Nadya had seen him at his most vulnerable. Injured and ill. In comparison to her robust brother, Rhys must always have appeared at a disadvantage.

And in truth, he had little cause to be optimistic. As he'd discovered earlier this afternoon, Stephano's checkered past had given him certain skills Rhys's more conventional training hadn't provided.

Of course, the men he'd faced on dozens of battlefields through the years had not adhered to the standards of gentlemanly conduct. The Rom wasn't the only one who'd learned to fight in a hard school.

Bolstered by that knowledge as well as by the unexpected evidence of Nadya's love, he turned to address the man who was so eager to bring about his death. The ploy he was about to try was worth chancing. After all, according to Nadya, all Stephano really cared about was punishing him.

'No matter what happens between us, Angel stays with her mother.'

'Why would I take that condition from you, *gaujo*? If you lose, so does your whore.'

'I find I'm growing very tired of hearing you say that word.' Rhys began to strip off his coat. Despite the disadvantages he'd acknowledged, he was more than ready to match skills with the Gypsy.

'Don't do this,' Nadya begged, taking his arm. 'You're simply playing into his hands. He *wants* to kill you.'

'He can try.' Rhys pulled his arm from her grasp and began the long walk to where her half-brother waited.

Chapter Nineteen

The crowd parted before Rhys until only Andrash stood in his way. As he approached the smith, he could read sadness in the man's dark eyes.

He smiled at his new friend, reaching out to grasp his shoulder. 'Will you keep this for me?' He held out his coat. 'If he wins—' he indicated Stephano with a lift of his chin '—it's yours.'

'He'll show no mercy,' Andrash warned softly as he took the garment. 'And he carries a second knife in his boot.'

Rhys briefly tightened the grip of his fingers to express his thanks before he nodded. When he looked up, he realized Stephano had taken the opportunity to walk over to his grandmother's caravan. He was lifting the little girl up onto the steps where the old woman stood.

'Take her inside. And keep her there.' Due to the waiting stillness that had fallen over the crowd, Stephano's command was clearly audible.

'There are others more deserving of your enmity than this man,' Magda warned as she reached out to take the child's hand. 'What of those under your mother's curse, Stephano?'

'I'll take care of them in time.'

'Nadya is your sister. Your own blood.'

'And I am about to kill the *gaujo* who dishonoured her.'

Magda shook her head, her hand on the little girl's back. Although Angel clung to her grandmother's skirts, her wide blue eyes remained on her mother.

'She loves him.'

She didn't mean Angel, Rhys realized, his heart literally leaping in his chest. Magda was talking about Nadya. And him.

If he'd needed any more incentive for the coming battle, the old woman's words would have provided it. Knowing how close Nadya was to her grandmother, he believed that Magda had just reinforced the realization that Nadya would never have agreed to give up her daughter unless she truly loved him.

'She shouldn't have.' The curtness of Stephano's reply indicated he was as eager as Rhys to get on with this.

'We don't choose who we love. Something you'll discover soon enough, *chaveske chav*.'

Stephano's laugh was brittle. '"The fault is in our stars" I suppose.'

Despite their disagreement over what he was doing, the Rom reached up to touch the old woman's hand. Her gnarled fingers closed tightly around his, holding them as if she were afraid to let him go.

'In hers and in yours,' she said.

'Then perhaps fate will let him win. Would you like that, *Mami*? No, I didn't think so.' Stephano's voice, which had softened as he'd addressed his grandmother, grew hard once more. 'Take Angel inside. She loves him, too.'

For a long moment, the old woman stood looking down at her beloved grandson. Then her eyes lifted, seeking those of her other grandchild, who still stood on the out-skirts of the crowd.

Rhys's gaze followed. The wind, more chill as the sun began to sink, lifted a few strands of hair to curl around Nadya's face. As if she sensed that Rhys was looking at her, she turned toward him, her eyes filled with despair.

All my fault, Rhys acknowledged bitterly. Nadya had known what would happen if they broke the taboos of her tribe. And she had known how ruthless her brother could be. Now, because he hadn't been able to control himself—

'This way, Major.'

Andrash stood at his side, indicating a new area of activity. One of the Rom drew a large circle in the well-trodden dirt at the centre of the encampment. Another was sharpening a long, broad-bladed knife on a whetstone. A matching weapon lay on a table nearby.

Despite Andrash's warning that Stephano had 'another knife,' only now, seeing the pair of these, did Rhys realize the type of duel he'd agreed to. The art of the *navaja* was well known throughout Iberia. Although these deadly folding knives, with their cunning lock mechanism, were used every-where there, they were virtually unknown in England.

That might provide an advantage for Rhys that the Gypsy couldn't be aware of. Fascinated by the skills dis-played in a *navaja* he had witnessed, Rhys had been in-structed in their use by one of the Spaniards his regiment employed as a scout. Other than the Rom, Rhys was one of the few people in this country remotely familiar with the ritual combat Stephano proposed.

The fault is in our stars…

Maybe there was more to Magda's ability than either he—or Nadya—had given her credit for.

He blew out a slow breath, trying to remember everything

he'd been taught that long-ago afternoon. At the same time, he attempted to block from his mind the images of the wounds both combatants had suffered during that *navaja*.

Ultimately, someone had decided the carnage had gone on long enough and put a stop it. That wouldn't happen here. Andrash was right about that. After what had taken place between Rhys and his sister, Stephano would show him no mercy.

'Have you ever fought with knives?' the smith whispered as they watched the weapons being brought to a fine edge.

'Bayonet drills.' Rhys's joke fell flat, so he told the truth. 'I have some rudimentary skills. Nothing to compare to Stephano's, I'm sure.'

If possible, the smith's expression became even more grim. 'He's very quick. And he can use a knife with either hand.'

An ambidextrous opponent. What other handicap could be heaped upon his head? Rhys wondered.

'Any other tendencies I should know about?'

As his adversary was doing, Rhys began to turn up the sleeves of his shirt. The Gypsy hadn't removed the colourful vest he wore, so Rhys left his waistcoat in place as well. It would at least provide another layer of fabric between the sharpness of the blade and his skin.

As if that might make a difference.

'He studied fencing under an Italian master when he was with the *gadje*,' Andrash added. 'Forgive me, my friend. I mean to say while he was with his English family. I don't remember the man's name, but he was reputed to be an excellent teacher. Stephano's father was, after all, a nobleman who could afford the best for his son.'

Rhys looked again at the man sharpening the *navajas*. 'Those aren't rapiers, Andrash.'

'No, no, I know. But Stephano learned to fence before

he learned this. Some of his moves may come from that early instruction.'

Rhys couldn't see how that was possible. The art of fencing was like a dance. This…this was more apt to resemble a slaughter.

Very possibly mine.

'Ready?' Stephano asked.

Rhys had opened his mouth to answer before he realized Nadya's half-brother was addressing the man preparing the weapons. Before he'd become aware of his mistake, his heart rate had accelerated in preparation for what was about to occur.

Time seemed to slow. The sights and sounds and even the smells around him became amplified by his heightened senses, just as they always had been before the charge was sounded. He turned his head, trying to locate Nadya.

She was no longer where she'd been as this unfolded. His eyes searched the compound, finding her at the foot of the steps leading up to Magda's caravan. She was talking with her grandmother. And contrary to Stephano's instructions, the old woman had not yet taken Angel inside.

'You have first choice.'

Andrash's comment jerked Rhys's attention back to the duel. He hadn't understood what the smith meant by 'first choice' until he saw that the man with the weapons was advancing toward them, holding the knives he'd honed by their curving bone handles, one in each hand.

'Does it matter?' Rhys asked under his breath.

'I can choose for you, if you wish. There's probably little difference, but…' Andrash shrugged fatalistically.

'Thank you.' That settled, Rhys's gaze returned to the slender woman at the steps of the *vardo*.

Nadya had apparently given up trying to reason with her

grandmother. She now approached her brother, who refused to look at her, even when she placed her hand beseechingly on his arm. When Stephano shook it off, turning his back on her, she stepped in front of him, still pleading for his attention.

After a moment, Stephano signalled to someone in the crowd. The man came forward to take Nadya by the arm and draw her away. Although the Gypsy treated her with respect, it was clear he'd been ordered to get her out of the way.

The primary emotion Rhys felt as he watched was relief. He knew what he was fighting for. Nadya's presence wouldn't make any difference in how hard he fought. It might, however, prove to be a distraction. And he could afford none of those.

'This one,' Andrash said decisively.

Rhys glanced down at the weapon the smith held out to him. As he wrapped his fingers around the hilt, he realized it was longer and heavier than the one he'd handled in Spain. His lips lifted at the memory of Andrash's suggestion that this might in any way resemble a duel with rapiers.

'You find our customs amusing, *gaujo*?' Stephano had come over to take the remaining blade.

'I'm never amused when asked to kill a man. Or to let him kill me.'

'Dying is a serious undertaking.'

'And usually an unpleasant one.'

'We are agreed on that, at least. Perhaps it is time we began this particular unpleasantness.'

The Gypsy's hand thrust forward, the tip of the big knife it held grazing the material of Rhys's waistcoat. That it had not cut more deeply was only because he'd jumped back, arching his spine to remove his vital organs from its path.

The Rom held his weapon loosely, but with confidence. After his failed first feint, he had begun circling Rhys, looking for another opening. Keeping both his hands in front of him, Rhys mirrored his opponent's moves, so that always they faced one another.

The crowd had re-formed around the circle in the dirt. Rather than cheering on their favourite, as the London mob did with their pugilists, the Gypsies were silent, as watchful as the combatants themselves.

Stephano's next attempt to get under his guard was a sweeping slash of his knife. Rhys countered it with his own, so that for the first time metal clashed against metal. As the Gypsy's blade slid harmlessly off, Nadya's brother stepped away, playing to the watchers by bowing slightly.

Seizing the opportunity, Rhys used a fencer's lunge to draw first blood. The wound in Stephano's shoulder was superficial, because Andrash had been correct in his assessment. The Rom was as agile as a dancer. He had seemed to sense Rhys's move even before he'd begun it. Despite that quickness, Stephano, the more experienced fighter, had not escaped unscathed, which gave Rhys's confidence a needed boost.

The collective gasp from the assembly at his success was a reminder of its one-sided allegiance. Rhys blocked that and every other consideration from his mind, concentrating instead on the next opening his adversary might offer.

Instead of providing one, Nadya's half-brother began a series of attacks. Knife held low, he jabbed and slashed, driving Rhys backward while forcing him to use his own weapon as a shield to ward off the other's blade.

Stephano's knife came at him again and again, its movements dizzying in their virtuosity. Thrust and jab and parry over and over again until they were both panting and drenched with sweat.

As suddenly as he'd begun them, Stephano stopped

the attacks. Exhausted but wary, Rhys watched as the Rom moved to the other side of the ring, never turning his back to him.

The Gypsy's shirt clung to his skin as Rhys's did. The sleeve on Stephano's wounded arm was now pink from the mingling of sweat and the blood he'd lost. The moisture in his hair had intensified its tendency to curl. His face was flushed with exertion, his mouth open as he pulled deep draughts of air into his starving lungs.

After a moment, the Rom raised the arm not holding his knife in order to wipe his eyes. Rhys mimicked the gesture, his own breath ratcheting in and out in the stillness.

He couldn't understand why Stephano had retreated from a strategy that would eventually have proved successful. He could only be grateful he'd been given this respite, however brief.

Stephano wiped at his eyes again before he closed them tightly once and then twice. With his free hand he pinched the bridge of his nose, holding it between his thumb and forefinger as if attempting to stop a nosebleed.

Although the Rom still appeared coiled to strike, Rhys knew he should take advantage of his opponent's momentary inattention. Despite that acknowledgement, he was unable to command his exhausted body to move. After all, the fight would, he knew, resume soon enough.

The Gypsy peered across the ring, eyes narrowed as if he were having a hard time seeing in the twilight gloom. He seemed in no great hurry to get back to the duel.

'Torches,' the knife sharpener shouted. 'Bring the torches.'

'No.'

Stephano's denial had been sharp and decisive. The men who'd started to obey the first directive halted in their tracks, the confusion on their faces matching that Rhys felt.

Then he had no time to think about anything other than the man who now launched himself across the circle, his blade moving with a power and intensity that seemed impossible, given the long minutes they'd already fought. All Rhys could do was try to defend himself, which he did with growing desperation.

Both of them bled from minor cuts. None of those was serious in and of itself, but the combined loss of blood would eventually begin to sap strength neither could afford to lose.

Rhys found it harder and harder to fuel his lungs with the air needed to sustain the relentless pace the Gypsy had set. If he didn't put an end to this soon, he knew that, after all he'd endured to survive the massive wounds he'd sustained at Orthez, he would die in this place. Figuratively as far from his home and family as if he were still in Iberia.

Suddenly, with a speed that left him no time to think, it happened. The Rom's blade slid in under his guard, searching for his heart. Rhys turned, so that what could have been a fatal thrust became instead a gash along his side.

Then, acting on instinct alone, he clamped his elbow down as hard as he could over the Gypsy's still extended arm. He would only be able to hold it there for a matter of seconds, but those allowed him time to twist his torso so as to bring his body behind that of his enemy. Once there, he laid the edge of his blade against Stephano's exposed throat.

'Move and you die,' he gasped into the Rom's ear.

Frozen in place, they stood joined, front to back. For an eternity, it seemed that their harsh breathing, almost in unison now, was the only sound in the clearing.

'Drop your knife,' Rhys commanded.

'To the death,' Stephano reminded him. His voice was strained from the angle at which he held his head to keep Rhys's knife from cutting his skin. 'Kill me. Or we fight on.'

'Do you acknowledge that your life rests in my hands?' Rhys increased the careful pressure he'd been exerting against Stephano's windpipe.

He didn't want to kill Nadya's brother, but he knew he was physically incapable of resuming their duel. Whether or not Stephano would accept his life at Rhys's hands was something only the Gypsy could decide.

The Rom swallowed against the increased bite of the blade. If Rhys had judged it correctly, Stephano should now be able to feel a trickle of blood down his throat.

'Your decision,' he urged. 'Do you want to punish Nadya enough to die? Or do you want to keep your life to pursue whatever it is Magda thinks is your destiny? And,' he added, determined to force this concession from Stephano, 'allow your sister to pursue hers?'

'You believe *you're* her destiny?' Despite his predicament, the Gypsy's disdain was clear.

'Yes.'

The surety in that voice brought Rhys's eyes up to find the speaker. Magda once more stood on the steps of her caravan looking down on the combatants.

'No,' Stephano ground out.

'You are blinded by pain because your heart knows you're wrong. I have told you, Stephano. This is not your destiny. Give him your word and seek those things that are.'

The Rom said nothing for a long time. Then Rhys felt the tension drain from the lithe body he held against his own.

Despite his acquiescence, the Rom couldn't resist a final warning, his words loud enough so that only Rhys would hear them. 'Betray my sister, and I swear I'll hunt you down and skin you like a wolf.'

'Fair enough.' Rhys took his knife from the Gypsy's throat and stepped back.

He was prepared for the man to whirl and come at him again. Instead the Rom straightened away and then turned to face him while letting his own blade fall to his side.

'It seems the stars are on your side, Major Morgan.'

'According to Magda, at least.'

The Rom's mobile mouth ticked up a reluctant fraction. He lifted his knife slightly, one dark brow raised questioningly.

Rhys nodded permission and watched as Stephano closed the blade and slipped the weapon into the waistband of the loose trousers he wore. He then removed the kerchief with which he'd tied back his hair to dab at the blood that was still trickling from the cut in his throat and into the open neck of his shirt.

Finally, with a glance over his shoulder, he gave an order in his own tongue. As two of the Rom hurried to obey, Rhys had time to wonder if Stephano intended to keep his promise or if he now planned to throw other impediments in their path.

Only when he saw one of the two who'd left lead Nadya toward the circle did he begin to believe this might really all be over. Of course, other than Magda's encouraging words and Nadya's concern for his life, he had little cause to believe she would leave with him, even now that her brother had agreed to let her go.

Because he had been watching her face, Rhys knew the instant she became aware they were both still alive. Her eyes had touched on Stephano first, and then, seeing Rhys standing beside him, they widened. When she began to run toward him, he understood that she had expected to emerge from the tent where they'd confined her to find his lifeless body sprawled in the centre of the ring.

Her steps slowed as she approached. Her eyes moved

from him to her half-brother, clearly seeking an answer as to why they should both still be standing, but it was to Stephano that she spoke. 'I don't understand.'

'Your *gaujo* chose to let me live, *jel'enedra*. It seems he feels we should both fulfil our destinies.'

'Our destinies?' Her eyes again had found Rhys.

They examined him from head to foot, looking for injuries. With her experience, it must have been obvious those he'd suffered were not life threatening.

'I leave it to Magda to inform you what yours might be,' Stephano said. 'She has already set me on mine.'

'That wasn't Magda,' Nadya said. 'You chose your path of blood and vengeance.'

'Forgive me if I decline to debate you right now as to its merits. Or the impetus for it.'

'And Angel?'

'She was part of our bargain. She's yours. Whatever you decide to do.'

'Whatever I decide?' Nadya's gaze returned to Rhys, once more searching his face.

'I have asked your brother for your hand in marriage.' That was not the literal truth, of course. He had imposed his will on him at knifepoint instead, but the object was the same.

'And…he agreed?'

'Willingly.' Rhys managed to keep any trace of satisfaction or irony out of the word.

The Rom made some sound, causing Nadya to glance at him. When her eyes returned to Rhys, her expression was troubled.

'You know what marrying me would mean to you. And to your family.'

'To me, it would mean the woman I love has agreed to share her life with me. To my family…' He hesitated, knowing all too well what might happen on his return to Balford Manor. 'I love my family, Nadya, but I can live content if I never see them again. I cannot live without you.'

With his words, her eyes filled with tears she refused to let to fall. After a moment, she looked up to where her grandmother stood. 'Nothing will ever be the same.'

'I have known that from your birth. The lines in your palm do not lie. Do not fight against your fate, *chaveske chei*. Nothing but grief can come of that.'

'How can this be my fate? *To leave my people.* To leave everything and everyone I've ever known. To go to a place where I shall be forever alien. Forever an outcast.'

'That isn't how it will be, Nadya. I swear to you.' Rhys held his hand out to her, almost in supplication.

Still she hesitated, and then she turned again to her grandmother. 'And Angel? What of her destiny?'

'It has always been with her kind. Even you, who mock the hand of fate, knew that. She, too, will find what you are offered. If you're brave enough to accept he who offers it.'

This was, and always had been, Nadya's decision. Her brother's hatred had required Rhys prove his willingness to die for her and Angel, but nothing had changed the divide that lay between their worlds. He wasn't convinced anything could.

'Are you sure?' As she turned back to him, for the first time Nadya's eyes dared to hope.

'Marry me,' Rhys said again.

She hesitated a heartbeat longer before, reaching out, she clasped his fingers. Her hand trembled, but its hold was strong and sure.

He used it to pull her to him. He put his arm around her shoulders, looking down into her eyes. Despite, or perhaps because of, the people who were gathered around them, he kissed her, savouring the receptive softness of her mouth only briefly before he raised his head to smile at her again.

Her lips, slightly parted from his kiss, didn't respond. After a moment, she turned to face her people.

'This is my choice. I make it with the permission of our *Rom Baro*. May God keep you all.'

Andrash's was the first voice to repeat that blessing. Then slowly others among the throng began to wish them well.

Curious as to how Stephano was dealing with the loss of his sister, Rhys looked where the Rom had been standing when Nadya had accepted his hand. He was no longer there.

Nor could Rhys find him among the crowd. The Gypsy had been defeated, but it seemed he'd been unwilling to watch the victor claim his spoils.

'Your daughter, *gaujo*.' Unnoticed in the commotion, Magda had descended the steps of her caravan with the child. Now she held out the little girl's hand, not to Nadya, but to him. 'I give her into your care.'

He nodded, accepting Angel's hand as her mother had taken his. The child smiled at him, her beloved rag doll clutched to her chest. In the same hand, she held the wooden cat he'd made for her.

Nadya touched her daughter's hair before she wrapped her arms around her grandmother. The words she said to the fortune-teller were in Romany. Even if they hadn't been, they were so softly spoken Rhys wouldn't have known what she said.

'Go with God, *chavi*,' Magda answered. 'You will find your place.'

'I have already,' Nadya said.

The old woman nodded, her eyes suspiciously bright. 'Now go, before he changes his mind.'

Magda wasn't talking about him, Rhys realized, but

about her grandson. From what he knew of Nadya's half-brother, he was perfectly capable of going back on his word to try and stop them.

With the old woman's warning, things seemed to happen very quickly. A brief conversation between the two women, and Magda began to issue commands that were obeyed with the same alacrity Stephano's had been.

His brother's bay was harnessed between the traces of Nadya's wagon, which was then pulled up before them. While Rhys helped Angel up its steps, Nadya kissed her grandmother before she turned back to the watching Gypsies.

She said nothing, but her gaze rested briefly on each individual. Those she had cured. Those she had delivered into this world. Those with whom she had watched loved ones leave it. Her face twisted briefly with emotion, but she quickly followed Angel up onto the high seat of the caravan.

At last, Rhys and the old woman stood alone in the dirt where he had fought her grandson. Her dark eyes met his assessingly before she touched his forehead with her right thumb. 'May your sons bring you honour and may your daughters bear you many strong grandchildren, who will care for you in your old age.'

Rhys controlled his urge to smile at the triteness of her blessing. He wondered if she would expect him to cross her palm with silver in response to its nonsense.

'Thank you,' he said instead.

As he leaned forward to kiss her on the brow, he realized how small and frail she was. The force of her will was powerful enough to make one forget both her age and her size.

'As you, Rhys Morgan, shall do as well,' she added for his ears alone.

He stepped back, unsure of her meaning. She had turned away before he could ask, clearly done with her fortune-telling. Apparently it would be up to him to puzzle out what that last cryptic addition to her blessing had meant.

He took his place beside Nadya, who held Angel on her lap. Andrash handed up the reins, smiling at him.

'I'll never forget you, my friend,' Rhys said to him.

'Nor I you, Rhys Morgan. I owe you my life.'

Rhys shook his head. 'You owe me nothing, but…'

'Yes?'

'Look after her.' Rhys nodded in the direction of the old woman who was slowly mounting the steps of her own caravan.

Andrash nodded. 'With my life. That I promise you. Go with God, *drabarni*.'

'Thank you, Andrash,' Nadya said. 'For everything.'

When Rhys set the bay in motion, the woman beside him did not look back at the world in which she had spent her entire life. Her eyes remained focused stoically forward instead, her arms wrapped tightly around the little girl who would always be, if not a daughter of her blood, the child of her heart.

Chapter Twenty

The inn yard at Buxton, when they reached it, was crowded with the conveyances of travellers seeking haven from the cold October rain, which had begun to fall shortly after they left the encampment.

The weather wasn't, however, why Rhys drove the bay past the hostel's welcoming lights, with their promise of food and warmth. He wasn't ready, not tonight at any rate, for the stares their presence there would occasion.

Besides, they had shelter of their own. And a blessed privacy available within it.

When it became too dark to safely navigate the deepening mud of the road, he found an opening in the trees and drove the *vardo* through it and into a small clearing partially concealed by the surrounding woods. If anyone still looked to do harm to Nadya, they would be less conspicuous here than on display to curious eyes in a busy public house.

Nadya disappeared inside the caravan as he tethered the bay behind it. He fed and watered the animal from the provisions stored in covered barrels carried on the back of the wagon for that purpose.

Although the rain had now slackened, he was soaked to the skin by the time he climbed the steps of the caravan and pushed aside its curtain. Snug against the wind and rain, the interior seemed as warm as any room at the inn. And far more welcoming.

Angel was again sitting on the bed in the sleeping partition, playing with her toys. Her damp clothing had already been replaced by her nightgown.

Nadya was slicing bread and cheese onto plates she'd taken from the shelves across from the patient bed. She turned to smile at him, but considering the conditions of their first night together, he wondered if she might not be sorry of her bargain already.

'The storm appears to be lessening. Tomorrow should be a better day for travel.' The weather seemed, as always, a safe topic in awkward situations.

'And if not, we can stay here.'

Rhys could detect no strain in her voice, but this was hardly an auspicious start for their journey together. More troubling, he couldn't guarantee things would improve when they reached Balford tomorrow.

'What's wrong?'

Nadya's question brought his head up. She still held the cheese and the knife she'd used to cut it, but her eyes were on him.

'I'm sorry.' It seemed there was so much more he should say. A promise that things would soon be better. Reassurance that she hadn't made the greatest mistake of her life in choosing to come with him rather than stay with her people.

'For the rain? I didn't realize it was in your control.'

He shook his head. 'I wanted to give you so much more.'

With the hand that held the knife, she gestured at their

surroundings. 'This is all I've ever known, Rhys. All I'd ever wanted. Until I met you,' she added softly.

'Not sorry of your bargain?'

She shook her head, smiling at him. 'Not yet, at least.'

'Good. Things *will* get better, I promise you.' It was a vow he had no right to make, considering the reception that he suspected would await them tomorrow.

'After you've eaten, I want to look at those cuts. I'm brewing a cup of tea made from the bark I told you about. An attack of recurring fever can be brought on by so many things.'

'Like knife fights?'

She glanced up in time to catch his grin, but ignored it to concentrate on her preparations for dinner. 'Why don't you take your wet things off?'

'Because I have nothing to put on in their place.' As he said it, he looked to the back of the caravan where Angel played.

'There are plenty of blankets.'

Unable to argue against the wisdom of her suggestion, he began to remove his coat, followed by his waistcoat. Soaked with rain, bloodstained, sliced in a half dozen places by Stephano's blade, it was fit for nothing but discarding. His shirt, stuck to his skin in several places by dried and clotted blood, was in equally bad shape, but the lawn could be washed and repaired, while the brocade was beyond hope.

In the process of undressing, he discovered that, not only did he have several painful mementoes of Stephano's knife, the muscles in his arms and shoulders ached from the strain of that combat. He thought longingly of the deep slipper tub and unlimited hot water his brother's house would have offered. When Nadya came up behind him to wrap a blanket around his shoulders, the loss of those amenities went out of his head.

She pressed a kiss on the side of his neck. 'Eat. Everything looks better when viewed from the perspective of a full belly.'

'That sounds like something Magda might say.' He turned to take the food she'd prepared.

'She probably did say it. For all her fortune-telling mumbo-jumbo, no one ever accused my grandmother of not being practical.'

'As well as romantic, apparently?'

Nadya's brows lifted questioningly. 'Romantic?'

'She seemed to feel that…' He shrugged before he finished. '…that you and I were destined to be together.'

'My destiny,' Nadya repeated with a smile. 'Magda tends to cloak her desires in terms of what fate has decreed.'

'Her desires? You think she wanted you to marry me?'

Nadya shrugged. 'To her, you're a rich *gaujo*. How better to assure the future of two people she loves?'

'I'm not rich, Nadya.'

The anxiety that had gnawed at the pit of his stomach since they'd left camp increased at the thought of how far from the reality her description was. The bread and cheese that had seconds ago been so appetizing seemed repellent now.

'I said that was Magda's view.'

'And I have no idea about our reception tomorrow—'

'I think that you do, Rhys. But believe me, it doesn't matter. I'm not expecting your family to welcome me.'

'My brother isn't…' He shook his head, unsure even of what he could say about Edward's reaction. 'My sister-in-law has a very rigid view of Society and of her place in it. Anything she sees as threatening to that would upset her.'

'Is she the one who took such good care of you when you returned from Spain?'

He nodded. With all Abigail's peculiarities, he could not fault her kindness or her concern for his recovery.

'Then I shall cherish her as my sister. No matter how she feels about me.'

Nadya's calm in the face of the storm they faced tomorrow, which was likely to be far more severe than the one they had endured today, should have given Rhys hope. Instead it made him wonder if she could have any idea about the kind of approbation she was likely to encounter among the Ton.

'It may take her a while to become accustomed to the idea of our marriage. I believe my sister-in-law had already selected a wife for me from the local gentry.'

'Poor girl.' Nadya's eyes were alight with amusement.

'In truth, Nadya,' he tried again to warn her, 'tomorrow may be…difficult.'

'Today I believed my brother was going to kill you because I could not resist the temptation you offered. What could tomorrow bring that could be worse than that?

'Eat your supper, Rhys. Whatever happens, my love, I promise you we'll deal with it together.

'This probably needs stitching,' Nadya said as she examined the long gash along Rhys's side.

Ignoring his objections, she had cleaned and anointed the other injuries her brother had inflicted with salve made from a recipe passed down from her paternal grandmother. This one, however, was deeper than the rest.

'Just bind it.' His right arm held shoulder high, Rhys had watched her probe the cut.

'It will be more apt to leave a scar if I do.'

His laughter brought her eyes up. 'Are you telling me you object to another scar?' he asked.

She leaned forward to touch her lips to the scars that marred his shoulder. 'Of course not. But I reserve the right to object any time you've been hurt.'

'Thank you. Now bind it up.'

If she changed the dressing every day, it would heal almost as well as if she sewed it. And in all honesty, she would rather not cause him more pain.

'Once it's clean,' she conceded.

With the same care she'd employed on all the other cuts, she made sure no thread or bit of fabric had become embedded in this one. Then, using her fingers, she rubbed salve into the raw flesh.

True to her grandmother's training, while she worked, Nadya's concentration was on the wound rather than the wounded. Her eyes came up again at Rhys's sudden intake of breath.

'This is where the knife penetrated the deepest,' she explained. 'That means it's more prone to suppuration.'

'I'm familiar with the process,' he said flatly.

He would be, of course. Although she'd never actually watched an English surgeon at work, she had treated on more than one occasion patients who'd suffered at their hands.

'I know you are, my love. I intend to prevent your further exposure to it.'

When she was satisfied that every part of the cut was cleansed of debris and covered by her grandmother's concoction, she placed a clean piece of lint over the gash and then began winding the narrow strip of cloth she'd prepared for the purpose around Rhys's waist.

As she tied the ends of it together, she said, 'I believe you'll survive. In spite of everything my brother could do.'

'Thank you, milady.'

'You're very welcome, my lord.'

'Life *would* be easier.'

'If you possessed a title? It was my understanding that a fair share of those who do have little else.'

'Most have a roof over their heads, at least.'

'As do we,' she reminded him.

'Thanks to your father.'

'To give the devil his due, thanks to Stephano as well. He would have been within his rights to claim my *vardo* as property that belonged to the *kumpania*.'

'I think Magda was more responsible for seeing to it that you left with what's yours than your brother was.'

'My grandmother's always been a powerful force among our people. She knew it was only fair my inheritance went with us.'

'Fair perhaps, but I didn't expect her to give her blessing to your going with me.'

'To my people, Rhys, we are already married. We were from the moment I accepted your hand. I thought you knew.'

He shook his head. 'I should have. Handclasp marriage. I've heard the term, of course, but, forgive me, I hadn't realized the significance of what you did this afternoon.'

'If you're having second thoughts, I'm sure such a primitive custom isn't binding on the *gadje*,' she teased.

'It is on this one. Besides, I've already accepted your dowry.' He glanced at the roof of the caravan, against which the rain continued to beat.

'And paid for it with your blood.' She touched the swath of white she'd wrapped around his body.

He put his hand over hers, looking down into her eyes. They stood without speaking for a long time.

'I need to put Angel to bed,' she said finally. 'It's been a hard day for her as well.'

'I'd like to say goodnight.'

'Then come with me. That's another of Magda's favourites. 'Begin as you intend to go on.' I hope you'll say goodnight to our daughter every night.'

'She's going to have quite an adjustment to make.'

'Learning to live like the English?'

'Learning to sleep by herself.' When her eyes widened, he added with a smile, 'Luckily, that particular battle needn't be fought tonight. Actually, as much as I love you, I don't believe it would even be possible tonight.'

Considering the duel, the blood loss, and everything else he'd been through today, she hadn't expected him to make love to her. But Rhys was right about the other.

His role in their lives was something else Angel would have to adjust to. Still, having Rhys with them would make up for the loss of her beloved uncle.

Rhys would help to fill that void in her own life. As well as so many others.

Angel was not the only one who faced adjustments. And for Nadya, no matter how well Rhys's people treated her, the loss of her own family would always weigh heaviest on her heart.

Nadya had made him stop a few miles from his brother's estate so she could bathe and change. While she did, Rhys had entertained Angel, who in Nadya's skilful hands had—miraculously—already been transformed into some approximation of a proper English child.

When Nadya finally emerged from the partition in the back, Rhys's heart sank. Although he'd had no doubt the fabrics used in the full skirt, the lace-edged blouse, and the embroidered shawl she wore were as rich as any he'd ever seen, her appearance could only be described as exotic.

The combs he'd noticed once before again held her curls off her face. Along with them a gold necklace set with what appeared to be rubies gleamed at her throat, its matching earrings in her ears.

'I know my clothing isn't what the English—'

'It's beautiful,' Rhys interrupted. 'As are you.'

He could tell from her smile that he'd struck the right note. And given what he suspected they would face, Nadya would need every bit of confidence he could provide.

She touched the necklace she wore. 'This set was my father's wedding gift to my mother. I realized as I fastened it, these are the only things I have left that he made.'

Because she had traded the rest for a little girl who was about to be sold into the most terrible form of slavery.

'It's magnificent.'

'Thank you. They're my real dowry, Major Morgan. The gems themselves are fine enough, but the workmanship is unsurpassed by anything you could buy in London.'

'I'm sure it is.' Rhys *was* sure, but in the back of his mind was the thought of Abigail's probable reaction to her new sister-in-law's ensemble.

When the butler answered the door at his brother's home, Rhys was provided with a foretaste of the disaster this visit was destined to become. The servant's fascinated eyes had remained locked on Nadya and Angel even as he'd made Rhys welcome.

'Thank you, Evans. Is my brother in his study?'

'You'll find him in the drawing room, I believe. He and Lady Sutton are about to have tea. Will you join them?'

'Thank you, yes.'

When Evans started to lead the way, Rhys turned to smile encouragingly at the two of them. Nadya's hands were firmly on her daughter's shoulders, as if she were unsure what the child might do. And as they followed the butler, the little girl's eyes widened in an attempt to take in every aspect of her unfamiliar surroundings.

'Rhys!' Edward jumped to his feet as they entered the room to rush toward him.

His brother's face, which had been filled with joy, changed when he saw Nadya and Angel behind him. His forward progress checked so abruptly it appeared he had literally run up against some physical barrier.

'Edward.' Rhys tried to ease the awkwardness by stepping forward to enfold his brother in his arms.

'And what have we here?' Edward asked with a false jollity as their brief embrace ended.

'May I introduce Nadya Argentari and her daughter Angeline. Nadya, this is my brother Edward Morgan, Lord Sutton.'

'How do you do?' His brother's tone was perfectly cordial, but his eyes darted between Rhys's and Nadya's face.

Rhys decided to delay the rest of the pertinent information that should have been included in that introduction. His family deserved a chance to recover from the immediate shock of their unusual visitors.

He could tell by Nadya's brief hesitation before responding to Edward's greeting that she had expected him to announce their marriage. When he didn't, she held out her hand to his brother.

'I'm very pleased to meet you, Lord Sutton. Rhys has told me how important you and your wife were to his recovery.'

Edward's eyes found Rhys, demanding an explanation. 'Indeed. Well, we are highly gratified he has done so well under our care.'

A brief but awkward silence fell after that, but Rhys's brother finally rose to the occasion. 'Won't you join us? My wife was about to pour.'

'Thank you.'

The regal inclination of Nadya's head would have done

generations of Argentaris and Beshaleys proud, Rhys thought. Propelling a still-fascinated Angel ahead of her, she swept forward, leaving Rhys and his brother to trail in her wake.

Abigail, seated behind the tea table, was as round-eyed as Evans had been when he'd opened the door. Brows raised, she looked to her husband and then to Rhys for some clue as to how she should deal with this intrusion. And more importantly, with the intruder.

Edward offered none. 'Rhys has brought guests, my dear.'

'How pleasant. Won't you introduce us?' Despite the politeness of those conventional words, Abigail's smile was as frozen as her tone.

'Abigail, may I present to you Nadya Argentari and her daughter Angel. My sister-in-law, Lady Sutton,' Rhys added as he turned to Nadya.

'How do you do, Lady Sutton?'

'Very well, thank you, my dear.' Her eyes again sought her husband's, the question in them more desperate. 'Won't you both be seated?'

'I'll ask Evans to bring more cups,' Sutton said.

His wife's beseeching gaze followed as her husband exited through the doorway where their butler had disappeared only seconds before. With his departure, their hostess was forced to gather her faltering composure.

'What a lovely child.'

'Thank you,' Nadya said as she settled on the brocade sofa Abigail had indicated.

She had released Angel's shoulders, obviously expecting the little girl to sit down beside her. Angel instead made straight for the tea tray and proceeded to snatch one of the delicate cakes from its china plate. As she shoved the morsel into her mouth, she watched Lady Sutton as if expecting that she would try and take it back.

'Angel!' Rhys's remonstrance had been automatic.

'My daughter neither hears nor speaks.' Nadya added a quick smile to her explanation as she rose to remove the child from temptation. 'She does, as you can see, love sweets.'

It was clear from Abigail's expression that she didn't see. Certainly not why she should be expected to entertain a Gypsy and her thieving child.

'Here we are.' Edward's tone was still jovial as he ushered the butler back into the room.

The man waited as Abigail poured out with shaking hands and then carried the tea around. At least Evans's expression was once more imperviously correct.

'Do you…live around here, Mrs Argentari?' As soon as he asked, Edward seemed to realize the inappropriateness of addressing that question to a Rom. He hid his embarrassment by taking a sip of tea.

'No.' Nadya's reply was followed by the same ritual.

'Perhaps you should tell us the purpose of this visit, Rhys.'

Abigail's thinly veiled demand represented a step in the right direction, Rhys decided. It was past time for him to explain. No matter how that explanation might be received.

'I've asked Nadya to marry me.' Abigail's gasp was audible, but Rhys ignored it to plough on. 'Actually, according to the customs of her people, we *are* married. Of course, we hope those vows can be sanctioned by the church and English law. With Nadya's…' He hesitated, but quickly recovered. 'Given her heritage, we'll need a special license. I had hoped you'd help me acquire one, Edward. And that you would both wish us happy, of course.' He finished by smiling at his sister-in-law.

Edward's cup had frozen midway to his mouth. Abigail's lips were parted, her lace-trimmed handkerchief pressed against her throat, as if she were choking. For what seemed an eternity, neither responded.

'You're joking, I assume,' Edward managed finally.

'I assure you that I am not.' Even as he made that disclaimer, Rhys raised his chin challengingly.

The men he had served with would have known the meaning of that gesture. It was perhaps telling that his brother did not.

'That's absurd, Rhys. You can't marry a—'

'Rom,' Nadya supplied calmly when Edward's description sputtered to a halt.

'I've already married her,' Rhys said softly. 'All I'm asking is your help in finalizing the vows we made before her people.'

'Ask and be damned.'

In spite of how badly this had gone so far, Rhys was shocked by the vehemence of his brother's words. Colour stained Edward's cheekbones, and his lips were clenched so tightly that a muscle jumped at one corner of them.

'After all we've done for you, Rhys.' Abigail's handkerchief was now against lips that trembled with emotion.

It was Nadya who spoke into the stunned silence that followed, addressing Abigail directly. 'Thank you for your very kind care of Rhys, Lady Sutton. Without it, he might not have survived injuries of the severity of his.'

'Perhaps it would have been better had he not.'

The gloves were off with a vengeance. After Reggie's reaction, Rhys had known this would not be easy, but he was shocked by his family's hostility.

'You must forgive me if I disagree.' Nadya's voice was perfectly calm as she rose. 'Thank you so much for the tea.'

She turned, attempting to direct her daughter toward the door to the hall. Angel, it seemed, had other ideas.

Escaping her mother's control, she darted back to the tea tray to scoop up two more of the still untouched cakes. The quick curtsy she made to Rhys's sister-in-law left Abigail once more open-mouthed.

As Nadya passed Rhys on her way out, Angel once more firmly in her control, she said, 'We'll wait for you outside. I assume you won't be long.'

As she walked out through the huge front door, their departure made under the butler's supervision—probably to insure she didn't steal anything before she left—Nadya found herself wondering whether Rhys would join them. After all, she knew from personal experience how difficult it was to say goodbye to everyone you've ever loved.

When the door had closed firmly behind them, Angel tugged on her skirt. Eyes misted with tears, Nadya looked down to find the little girl holding out one of the pilfered cakes.

Despite the pain of the last few moments, Nadya laughed. She shook her head in refusal and then stooped to draw the child close. As her arms closed around her, Angel popped the treat into her own mouth.

At least we didn't leave empty-handed.

She had lifted the child up onto the first step of the caravan and was about to start her own ascent when the front door slammed again. She turned to see Rhys, standing alone in front of his brother's house. The depth of the breath he took was visible, even from the drive.

When he looked up and realized she was watching him, he smiled at her. If she'd had any remaining doubts about whether he loved her, that smile alone would have destroyed them.

He hurried down the front steps. 'My apologies. I didn't expect it to go quite so badly.'

'Perhaps if Angel hadn't taken *all* the cakes…' Her smile invited him to share her sense of how ridiculous this had been.

Despite her best effort, Rhys's eyes were bleak. 'We may need those cakes before this is done.'

'You forget that I've lived alongside Magda for years. I can always read palms.'

'Is that profitable?' Clearly he was willing to be drawn out of his despair.

'It always was for her. Besides, we have other, more tangible assets.' She touched her father's wedding gift to her mother, knowing how difficult it would be to give that up. 'If it comes to that.'

'It won't,' Rhys promised grimly. 'I still have my pension, which is enough to insure that you and Angel will never be hungry. Unless—' Something changed in his face.

'Unless what? What's wrong?'

'Until we're married—a marriage that is recognized under English law—if anything happened to me, you'd have no rights to that money.'

'Nothing's going to happen to you, Rhys.'

His words were enough to tighten Nadya's chest. Not from fear that she wouldn't be able to provide for her daughter—after all, they could return to the Rom, where they would always find welcome. It was the thought of losing Rhys, perhaps from the very suppuration of his wounds she'd tried so hard to guard against, that terrified her.

'No one can be certain of that, Nadya. You understand the fragility of life better than most. It's my responsibility to guarantee that if something did happen to me—'

'Don't,' she commanded, unwilling to entertain the possibility.

'You would both be provided for,' he ignored her protest to finish the unpleasant thought. 'And I believe I know how to bring that about. I told you about my grandmother. That she is like Magda in that she fears nothing.'

'I remember.'

'She's the dowager baroness, Nadya. She can help us procure the special license we'll need to marry under English law. In that, she has the same influence as my brother.'

'And undoubtedly she'll have the same reaction.'

'Perhaps,' Rhys conceded, 'but she isn't conventional like my sister-in-law. She never has been. She's…' He hesitated, seeming uncertain how to describe the dowager Lady Sutton. 'At least she won't turn us out into the cold. I'd stake my life on that.'

'We aren't *in the cold*. We have a roof over our heads—'

'Provided by your father.'

'What can it possibly matter who provided it?'

'It matters to me. You're my wife. Angel's my daughter. And I intend to take care of both of you.'

She didn't object again, stopped by the determination in his eyes.

'I can't guarantee that my grandmother will help us,' he went on, 'but…she's the only person I can think of who might. I have to try.'

The dowager house was smaller than that belonging to the current Lord and Lady Sutton, but to Nadya's country-bred sensibilities, with its sprawling gardens and ancient oaks, it was far lovelier. To her, its ivy-covered stones spoke welcome, as did the cross-hatched windows which threw a cheerful light into the deepening twilight.

Exactly the kind of home she might have chosen if she'd been given the choice.

She wouldn't be, of course. Rhys's grandmother might love him, but just as his brother had, she would surely draw the line at condoning a ruinous marriage to someone who would never be accepted by Society. And Nadya wasn't sure she could endure watching as his heart was broken again.

Angel had fallen asleep in her arms, lulled by the familiar rhythm of the *vardo*'s wheels. The child would undoubtedly be cranky at being awakened. This afternoon's theft might seem inconsequential compared to her misbehaviour tonight.

'Perhaps it would be better if we waited out here.' Nadya looked down at her sleeping daughter to bolster her suggestion.

'Nonsense,' Rhys said as he climbed down. 'I'll carry her inside.'

'It isn't that—' Nadya began and then realized he was no longer listening.

Before she could come up with a more compelling argument, Rhys reached up to take Angel, who woke during the transfer. She laid her head on Rhys's shoulder, content to be in his arms.

As she followed them up the walk, Nadya tried to brush the wrinkles out of her skirt. Deciding that was an exercise in futility, she pulled the thin silk shawl she'd put on with such hope this afternoon more closely about her shoulders.

The man who opened the door in response to Rhys's knock was much older than the disapproving Evans and genuinely delighted when he recognized the caller. 'Master Rhys! We had heard you were home, but never dreamed you were well enough to be up and about. Her ladyship will be beside herself. Come in, my dear boy. Come in.'

Rhys reached behind him to pull Nadya into the light.

'This is my wife, Pembley. Would you ask Grandmama *if* she'll receive us?'

'*If* she'll receive you? Well, of course she will. Beside herself is what she'll be.' The old man held the door open wide as Rhys pushed Nadya forward into the house's welcoming warmth.

The butler closed the door behind them and, still chatting happily to Rhys, led the way down the hall. In no hurry to repeat this afternoon's fiasco, Nadya took time to examine her surroundings, which seemed nearly as opulent as the interior of that other residence.

'This way,' the butler directed with a smile, ushering her toward the room into which Rhys had already disappeared.

As she entered, Nadya saw Rhys bending over to kiss the cheek of an old lady ensconced in a chair near the fire. Her feet were propped on a Turkish ottoman and a light blanket covered her legs.

Nadya's first thought was that Rhys's grandmother was an invalid. As she advanced into the room, however, the dowager rose from her chair and came toward her, hands outstretched.

'What a lovely surprise. Welcome, child. Now let me look at you.'

Nadya had automatically taken the hands the old woman offered. She waited as the dowager made her appraisal.

'What a lovely shawl. You must give me the name of your mantua-maker. It's almost as beautiful as its wearer,' she added, turning to Rhys. 'Why didn't you tell me? Why must the aged be kept in the dark about the most delicious news?'

'Because it *is* news,' Rhys said. 'More current than you can imagine.'

'But I would have come to your wedding,' the dowager

said, her twinkling blue eyes returning to Nadya. 'I can't promise to have danced at it, but I promise you I should have tried.'

'You'll get your chance, Grandmama.'

The old woman's questioning gaze travelled from one to the other. Since she was still holding the dowager's hands, Nadya felt an obligation to explain.

'What Rhys means is that we haven't yet been married. Not by English tradition.'

'I see. By what "tradition" have you been wed, my dear?'

'Nadya—' Rhys began, only to be interrupted.

'Rhys offered his hand in front of my people. When I accepted it, by Romany law we were married.'

'Marriage is, after all, simply a vow between a man and a woman, is it not? However…' Lady Sutton turned back to her grandson, brows raised.

'We had hoped you would help us with the "however."'

'But of course. What can I do?'

'Convince your cleric to send for a special license.'

'Since the poor man owes me his living, I'm sure I could bend him to my will, but…' she turned to Nadya. 'Is that what you want, my dear? Or has this impetuous boy swept you off your feet, so that you haven't had time to decide if you really want to plight your troth to him?'

When his grandmother turned to look at Rhys again, Nadya's eyes followed. Travel stained. Exhausted. His face reflected not only the rigors of the duel he'd fought, but his bitter disappointment in his brother's response to their marriage.

He still held Angel, who seemed totally confident of his love. As was she, Nadya realized. With all the doubts attendant on her decision to marry this man, she had never once doubted Rhys loved her.

'I already have,' she answered softly. 'And I will do so again before any clerk or cleric you wish.'

'No second thoughts, my dear?' His grandmother's blue eyes came back to examine her face, as if searching it for the truth.

'Only those concerning my acceptance in his world. That doesn't matter to me, but I know eventually it will to him.'

'That's not true,' Rhys denied. 'You're all that matters to me. You and Angel.' He smiled down at the child who had touched his lips with one small finger as they moved.

'If we are to live in your world—'

'Then we must decide how best to present you there,' Lady Sutton said decisively. 'It's all in the presentation.'

'It's not that I'm ungrateful for what you're trying to do. Believe me. But there is, I'm afraid, no hiding what I am.'

'Who would want to? You're a Romany princess, descended from a very long line of blue bloods. Forgive me, dear, but do the Rom have blue bloods? No matter,' the old woman went on. 'A very long and distinguished line of ancestors.'

'Nadya is descended from two very powerful families,' Rhys said. 'Her half-brother is the leader of her tribe.'

'Oh, my dear! Your brother is King of the Gypsies. How romantic that sounds. Do you suppose you could convince him to attend the ceremony?'

'You don't understand—'

'No matter. Just the idea that he might show up will be enough to set the tongues of local Society aflap.'

'The Rom don't actually have a king, Lady Sutton. That's a misunderstanding the *gadje*—'

'And the design of your dress must play up these magnificent stones.' The dowager baroness touched the necklace Thom had made. 'I've never seen a more beautiful parure.'

Despite her misgivings about the old woman's plans, Nadya was charmed enough by her admiration of Thom's handiwork to offer an explanation. 'My father made them as a wedding gift for my mother.'

'Your father? But how marvellous! And now you will wear them on your wedding day.' The old woman folded her hands together and held them over her heart. 'The local ladies shall enjoy that bit of romance.'

'You may make it as romantic as you will, Lady Sutton, but I'm afraid the prejudice against my people will overcome any gloss you try to put on our marriage.'

'Some will come out of curiosity, no doubt. Others to have something new to gossip about. But rest assured, my dear, they *will* come. And they *will* be impressed by what they see. You leave that to me. You have quite an air about you, you know. Don't you think so, Rhys?'

'From the first time I saw her.' He smiled at Nadya.

In spite of wishing very much to believe all the objections to their marriage could be overcome by some romantic folderol, Nadya was too much the realist to think even Rhys's grandmother could pull off that particular sleight-of-hand.

'It's not that I don't appreciate your intentions. Please believe that. I just don't want you—either of you,' she amended, 'to be under the illusion that who I am won't really matter as long as we pretend it doesn't.'

'Oh, my dear, how very mistaken you are. Pretence is the key to being accepted in our world. A man may be unable to pay his tailor, but as long as the garments he wears are all the rage, no one gives a fig. Ladies may have as many lovers as they wish, as long as the husbands they've cuckolded include their bastards in the households. It's all a magic lantern show. And that, I fear, may be the most difficult thing for you to accept about your new situation.'

'Believe me, Lady Sutton, I've lived too long knowing how the English feel about the Rom to think that anything, including illusion, can make their intolerance go away.'

'You leave that to me, my dear. I can think of nothing I'd rather do than present you to Society. Now, Pembley, I believe this little one may need a light supper and a warming pan for her bed. Do you wish to share her room, my dear?' The old woman dismissed Nadya's objections as unimportant in the face of such a compelling domestic quandary. 'Perhaps just for tonight. Until she gets used to her great-grandmama's strange house.'

'That might be best.' Even as she agreed, Nadya looked to Rhys for guidance. She felt almost helpless in the face of Lady Sutton's grandiose plans.

'I think we could all use something to eat,' Rhys said. 'Why don't you join us, Grandmama?'

'I have far too much to see to, darling boy, to waste time eating. Pembley will take very good care of you. You have only to tell him what you need, and he'll procure it. I'll see you both in the morning. Now, sleep well, my dear.' The dowager baroness leaned forward to touch her lips to Nadya's cheek. 'I'm so glad you've come to me. If you'd left it to that silly chit poor Edward has married, she would have made a botch of the whole thing.'

'But—'

'Off you go. Pembley will see to all.'

There was nothing to do but let the Lady Sutton enjoy her fantasy while she could, Nadya decided. The truth of their situation, which she had always known, would be brought home to Rhys's grandmother soon enough.

Although Angel was dreaming almost as soon as her head touched the pillow, Nadya found sleep more elusive.

The events of the day circled through her brain until she could no longer abide thinking about them.

She slipped out of the cocoon of a feather mattress topped by fat quilts, being careful not to wake her daughter. Wrapping one of the blankets the housekeeper had placed at the foot of the bed around her, she walked across to the wide windows and pushed aside one of the heavy draperies.

Below her stretched a vast garden, threaded with paths that wandered aimlessly amidst the lush vegetation. A folly, built beside a stream like a ribbon of glass in the moonlight, seemed to beckon to her.

After a quick check to make sure Angel was still sleeping, she eased open the heavy door and stepped out. The carefully banked fire had kept the bedroom warm, but the hall was both dark and chill.

Although she desperately needed Rhys's comfort, even if she had known where to find him, she would have felt that visiting him would be a betrayal of the dowager's trust. Instead, she pulled the blanket more tightly around herself and tiptoed toward the stairs.

She had reached the first landing when she realized someone was approaching it from the bottom of the stairs. Nadya had already begun a retreat, when the voice of Rhys's grandmother stopped her.

'For goodness sakes, child, don't run away. It's only me.'

Feeling as if she'd been caught stealing sweets from the tea tray, Nadya stopped, turning to watch the old woman slowly climb the steps to where she stood.

Once there, Lady Sutton raised her candlestick so that its light illuminated Nadya's face. 'Trouble getting to sleep? Some warm milk, perhaps?'

'I don't believe milk will help.'

'Too many things to think about, I suppose. A wedding.

A handsome new bridegroom. A strange house. No wonder you're excited.'

'It's not excitement that keeps me awake, Lady Sutton.'

'Then what, my dear? Surely you're not worrying about your reception as Rhys's bride.'

'You can't possibly understand the gap that exists between our two worlds.'

'Can I not?' the dowager said with a smile. 'You might be surprised at what I know about gaps.'

Taken aback by the old woman's amused surety, Nadya shook her head. 'I would do anything to protect him.'

'As would I,' Rhys's grandmother confided, putting her arm around Nadya's shoulders. 'He is very special to me. As you will be.'

'But don't you see—'

'I see the woman my grandson wishes to marry. I assure you I shall do everything within my considerable powers to bring that about. And without anyone being hurt. Oh, I can't promise someone won't occasionally say something impolite, but I shall teach you the look I use to freeze naysayers into silence. Nothing succeeds in our world like a haughty stare.'

Nadya's face must have reflected her frustration at that misplaced confidence. Lady Sutton took her chin between her thumb and forefinger, lifting it further into the candle's glow.

'I shall have to tell you my secret, I see. Something even Rhys doesn't know. And if it's all the same to you, my dear, something I had just as soon he never does.'

'Your secret?'

'The reason I know about gaps.'

'I don't understand.'

'Come with me to my room, and I'll show you. Far better than trying to explain here in the cold and the dark.'

* * *

Lady Sutton's bedroom smelled of lavender and powder, a mixture as warm and welcoming as the old lady herself. Her servants were apparently accustomed to her late hours, since the fire had been freshly fed and a multitude of candles bathed every corner with a soft glow.

'Now you sit there.' Rhys's grandmother indicated one of two chairs situated before the fire. She took the opposite, putting her feet on a worn footstool. 'Now, where shall I begin? With my father, I suppose, who was not a gentleman by anyone's standards. As a boy, he was dispatched to London to be apprenticed to a merchant. Which he did. And rather successfully by all accounts.

'He was frugal and hardworking and smart, and eventually, while he was still a young man, he was able to open his own shop. He had discovered that there was then, as now, a great demand for good wine in the city. So he began importing it. He also bought tobacco off ships coming from the colonies and found a thriving market for it in Russia. With all that importing and exporting, he became a very wealthy man, but he was still a merchant. Gentlemen might buy wine from him. They might even borrow money from him, but they would never introduce him to their wives or their daughters. In short, despite his prosperity, despite the fact that he might have bought and sold several times over the noblemen who traded with him, he could never become one of them.'

'Forgive me, Lady Sutton. While being in trade is certainly a barrier to social acceptance,' Nadya said kindly, 'it is quite different from being a Rom.'

'I'm sure you're right, my dear. And Society at that time was not so rigid as it pretends to be now. Ah, there is that word again,' the old woman said with a knowing smile.

'My father, who, like the Americans, believed he was as good as any duke or earl, determined that his daughter…' she inclined her head to Nadya as if they had just been introduced '…that his only and very beloved daughter should achieve what he had not—acceptance in the upper echelons of the class that denied him admittance.'

'And did she?' Nadya asked obediently, although she was already certain of the outcome.

'He bought her a husband. Someone who had both a title and entrée to that elite circle. His name was William Morgan, the fifth Baron Sutton. He didn't have two pence to rub together, mind you, but his blood was bluer than the ocean. As were his eyes.' The old woman's face softened with memory, the wrinkles that marred its beauty almost lost in the candlelight.

'Did you love him?'

'At first…at first, I was dazzled by him. He was so beautiful. Poor Edward, the sixth Baron Sutton, took after my father, as does the current holder of the title. Rhys, however…' She paused, her eyes looking into the past. 'Rhys is very much like my William. Kinder, of course. Less…glittering.'

Nadya laughed, unable to imagine the adjective being applied to her husband, no matter how enamoured she was of him. 'And later?' she probed.

'I decided two could play at that game. I set out to out-glitter my beautiful husband. I spent my father's money like a drunken sailor. On clothes from the most fashionable dressmakers in Paris. On entertainments more lavish than those at Montagu House. On blood mares and splendid high carriages and exotic furniture in whatever style was *au courant*.

'Oh, I heard them whispering behind their fans. They

called me a rich Cit, but they copied my gowns and head-
dresses all the same. And they begged for invitations to my
balls where I danced on the arm of my beautiful, glittering husband. Finally, long after I, or he, had ceased to care
what those fools whispered, they only called me Lady
Sutton. And had forgotten that my father had once sold
them wine.'

Lost in the remembered magic of those days, the old
woman stared into the fire. She didn't seem to remember
anyone else was there. Nadya waited in the perfumed
warmth of the room, content merely to be accepted by
someone who loved Rhys as dearly as she.

After a long time a log fell, creating a shower of sparks.
At the sound, Rhys's grandmother looked up to smile at
her. 'You are a Gypsy princess, descended from the
Pharaohs, the blood of your ancestors older, richer by far
than theirs.'

Nadya had begun to shake her head, unwilling to give her
approval to the fables the romantic old woman was weaving.

'I know you don't care what they think, my dear. And
why should you?' Lady Sutton leaned forward a little in
her chair. 'But you very much fear *he* will.'

'Yes.' Nadya's agreement was a whisper of sound.

'What does it matter that we deceive them? Theirs is a
world of deceit, built on pretence and pretension. Beat
them at their own game, my love. Or if you will not, let
me. Let me give him this. And then, when you retire to your
boudoir, you can laugh together at the sycophants who
fawn at your feet.'

'Do you believe that's really what he wants? To
deceive them?'

'I believe he wants you. And Angel, of course. And,
eventually, other children. No matter what he says now,

Rhys would not like it if his daughters had to wonder what was being whispered about them behind those fans.'

'Even if we manage to fool the local Society…'

'You believe Rhys will want to take you to London and present you to the Ton? If so, my dear, you have much to learn about my grandson.'

'You think he'd be too ashamed of his Romany wife to do that?'

'I think his honour would require him to call out the first man who dared to slight you. He couldn't, however, challenge the ladies to a duel. Rhys is certainly wise enough to know that. No, I think he'll be more than content to live here quietly with you and your children.'

'Here?' She wasn't sure if the old lady was inviting them to stay in the dower house indefinitely or simply to remain in the vicinity after she'd convinced her neighbours of their acceptability.

'It's to be his, you know. Or didn't you?' Lady Sutton questioned softly. And then, reading the surprise in Nadya's eyes, she explained, 'My father didn't buy me only a husband, my dear. He was more far-sighted than that. This house, the land, and everything on it, are not entailed. They belong to me, to be disposed of as I see fit. It shall be my wedding gift to you both. I always intended the estate for Rhys, who was the only one who loved it as I did. So you see, it is simply a matter of deceiving a few country folk who will, I promise you, be delighted to be introduced to Gypsy royalty.'

This time it was Nadya who stared into the fire. After a long time, she lifted her eyes to the old woman's face, uncaring that the candlelight would pick out the track of the tears that stained her cheeks. 'I shall ask my brother to come to the wedding. Whether or not he will wear his crown, I cannot say.'

Lady Sutton smiled at her as if she were a pupil who had mastered a difficult lesson. 'A small sacrifice, I should think, for such a great reward. Your children will forever be grateful to you.'

'"And bear you many strong grandchildren, who will care for you in your old age,"' Nadya echoed the blessing Magda had given Rhys on the day they left the encampment. 'As will yours, dearest Grandmama.'

Lady Sutton smiled at her again. 'Do you think you could sleep now if I take you back to your room?'

Nadya nodded, and when the old woman held out her hand, she put hers into it with the same unshakeable trust with which she had once given her hand to Rhys.

Epilogue

'**W**ilt thou, Nadya, have this man to thy wedded husband, to live together after God's ordinance in the holy estate of matrimony? Wilt thou obey him, and serve him, love, honour, and keep him in sickness and in health, and, forsaking all others, keep thee only unto him, so long as ye both shall live?'

'I will.'

Nadya's voice was not, perhaps, as strong as Rhys's had been when he'd answered that same question. For some reason, a flood of emotion, totally unexpected in response to these unfamiliar vows, thickened her throat. She held to the very different promise in Rhys's eyes as she made this final commitment to become forever a part of his world.

'Who giveth this woman to be married to this man?'

The silence in the small chapel after that question seemed almost oppressive. As she had promised Rhys's grandmother she would, Nadya had written to Stephano, but had, of course, received no reply.

There was no one here of her blood. No one who had the right to speak on their behalf. Lady Sutton had, therefore, instructed her cleric to hesitate only a few seconds before moving on to the rest of the ceremony.

Before he could, however, into that waiting stillness came the sound of boot heels echoing over the ancient stone floors of the chapel. Unable to stop herself, Nadya turned her head to look down its dim central aisle.

Her half-brother stood in the very centre of the church, impeccably garbed in the clothing of an English gentleman. Seeing the grimness of his expression, Nadya wondered whether he had arrived too late to respond to the minister's previously unanswered question.

...if any man do allege and declare an impediment, why they may not be coupled together in matrimony...

The clergyman, too, seemed uncertain of the new guest's intentions. So much so that he repeated the question he had just asked. 'Who giveth this woman to be married to this man?'

His eyes locked on hers, Stephano said, in a voice much stronger than that with which she had made her vow, 'I, her brother, give Nadya Argentari to this man, who has sworn with his blood to keep her safe.'

Stephano's dark eyes touched on Rhys's face, as if in warning. Then he turned on his heel and went out through the heavy chapel door, letting it bang closed behind him.

The shocked silence that followed his departure was far deeper than the anticipating one had been. After a moment, the unsteady voice of Lady Sutton's cleric took up the interrupted vows, completing them and the exchange of rings at a speed indicating he was hoping to finish this before the man who'd spoken of blood payments could return.

Through it all, Rhys had held her hand, his eyes steadying, loving, reassuring, until her unexpectedly fragile composure had once more been restored.

***

Nadya searched for Stephano in the aftermath of the ceremony, but it was not until they were about to climb back into the carriage that she finally saw him. Her brother stood on a slight rise overlooking the church grounds, the reins of the black stallion in his gloved hand.

The King of the Gypsies…

She touched Rhys's arm, drawing his attention away from the effusive congratulations of one of the local gentry. She tilted her chin in Stephano's direction. Her husband's gaze followed, and then quickly returned to her face.

'I won't be long, I promise.' She smiled at him and then stretched on tiptoe to press her lips against his.

Turning, she handed the bouquet of wildflowers she carried to Lady Sutton, who took them with raised brows. 'I warned you that he might not wear his crown,' Nadya whispered, pressing another kiss on her wrinkled cheek.

Then smiling, she made her way through the crowd of villagers who had gathered in front of the church, accepting their good wishes with as much patience as she could. When she reached the fringe of the throng, she picked up her skirt to run to where her half-brother waited.

There was a moment of awkwardness when she reached him, which she quickly destroyed by kissing him on the cheek as well. 'I'm so glad you came.'

'You asked me to come.'

'I know. But I wasn't sure you would.'

His dark eyes left her face to touch on the throng below. 'Is that what you want, *jel'enedra*?'

'*He's* what I want,' she corrected softly. 'Everything I have ever wanted.'

'Then I wish you joy.' His gaze had not returned to her.

'Who and what I am has not changed, Stephano.'

He looked at her then, mocking her words. 'You are wed in a *gadje* church by *gadje* clergy wearing a *gadje* dress.'

'And our mother's necklace.' She touched its centre stone, which had lain cool and comforting against her skin throughout the strangeness of the English ceremony.

'Can you so easily deny your blood?'

'No more easily than I could deny my heart. He is my husband. But you will always be my brother.'

His gaze touched on her bridegroom. 'He could have killed me. I don't know why he didn't. I would have killed him.'

'He knew that if he did, I would never forgive him.'

'Would you have forgiven me?'

'No.'

'Yet you still call me brother.'

'No matter what, we are always linked by our mother's blood.'

His laugh was bitter. 'I have an English sister.'

She shook her head. 'I'm not English, Stephano. Despite the pretence of this…' She touched her gown. 'I'll always be Rom.'

'I didn't mean you, *jel'enedra*. My father had a daughter by the woman who threw me out of his home when he was murdered.'

'You have…another sister?' She wondered if Magda had known. And then wondered why Stephano, who never did anything without a reason, had chosen to tell her this today.

'Someone with whom I share my English blood, as you and I share that of our mother.'

'Do you see her?' Was that where he had disappeared to so often these last months? To visit his other sister?

'Why would I wish to be reminded of what once was and is no more and can never be again?'

'Because she, too, is your blood. As much a part of your father as you are.'

'Do you think she'll help me bring him justice, *jel'enedra*?'

'The English courts did that. Nothing you do can ever change what happened.'

'Our mother cursed the seed of those guilty of his murder.'

'And in her grief threw away the love of a good man.' *And abandoned a daughter who loved her.* 'Don't let Jaelle's madness ensnare you, too, Stephano. Your father would not have wanted that.'

'I think my father wants revenge on those who betrayed him. Then he and Jaelle can both—finally—rest in peace.'

'The dead are beyond vengeance and remorse. It's time to stop chasing ghosts. The living need you more. Although she'd never admit it, Magda's growing old. You have a sister you've never met. And another—' she hesitated, her eyes on his face '—another who loves you very much and who cannot imagine never seeing you again.'

'Shall I come and take tea with Lady Sutton?'

'I think she would like that very much. I know that I should. Angel will steal a cake for you.'

At the mention of her daughter, Stephano's face relaxed into the expression that only Angel could coax those stern features to assume. '*Steal* a cake?'

'I'll tell you about it if you'll come to tea. Come now.' She took his hand, attempting to draw him toward the churchyard.

She could feel him slipping away from her. If something happened to Stephano…

'I don't belong there.' He pulled his hand from hers so roughly that she gasped a little with the pain of it. His brow furrowed in regret, and he lifted her fingers to his lips. 'I didn't mean to hurt you.' The words were whispered against the back of her hand before he released it to touch the cheek he'd struck on the day of the duel. 'I never meant to hurt you. Sometimes…'

'I know.'

Jaelle's madness. She had warned him it could destroy him. She turned her head to put her lips against the long, dark fingers that caressed her face.

'Be happy, *jel'enedra*,' Stephano said. 'Be happy for all of us.'

Before she could reply, he had mounted the black. He touched his heels to the stallion, thundering away without a backward glance.

'Are you all right?'

She turned to find Rhys beside her. 'Of course. Stephano would never hurt me.'

He didn't comment on that assertion. Instead he took her hand, bringing it to his lips as her brother had done.

'He wished us happy,' she said, smiling up at him.

'Then I believe Stephano has inherited Magda's gift, my love. Because that's one Gypsy blessing I can guarantee you *will* come true.'

* * * * *

COMING NEXT MONTH FROM

HARLEQUIN®
HISTORICAL

Available September 28, 2010

- **WESTERN WINTER WEDDING BELLS**
  by **Cheryl St.John, Jenna Kernan, Charlene Sands**
  (Western)

- **THE VISCOUNT AND THE VIRGIN**
  by **Annie Burrows**
  (Regency)
  Book 5 in the *Silk & Scandal* miniseries

- **A RAKE BY MIDNIGHT**
  by **Gail Ranstrom**
  (Regency)

- **BUTTERFLY SWORDS**
  by **Jeannie Lin**
  (Chinese Tang Dynasty)

HHCNM0910

REQUEST YOUR FREE BOOKS!

 HARLEQUIN® HISTORICAL:
Where love is timeless

2 FREE NOVELS PLUS 2 **FREE GIFTS!**

YES! Please send me 2 FREE Harlequin® Historical novels and my 2 FREE gifts (gifts are worth about $10). After receiving them, if I don't wish to receive any more books, I can return the shipping statement marked "cancel." If I don't cancel, I will receive 6 brand-new novels every month and be billed just $4.94 per book in the U.S. or $5.49 per book in Canada. That's a saving of 20% off the cover price! It's quite a bargain! Shipping and handling is just 50¢ per book.* I understand that accepting the 2 free books and gifts places me under no obligation to buy anything. I can always return a shipment and cancel at any time. Even if I never buy another book from Harlequin, the two free books and gifts are mine to keep forever.

246/349 HDN E5L4

Name	(PLEASE PRINT)
Address	Apt. #
City	State/Prov. Zip/Postal Code

Signature (if under 18, a parent or guardian must sign)

Mail to the Harlequin Reader Service:
IN U.S.A.: P.O. Box 1867, Buffalo, NY 14240-1867
IN CANADA: P.O. Box 609, Fort Erie, Ontario L2A 5X3

Not valid for current subscribers to Harlequin Historical books.

Want to try two free books from another line?
Call 1-800-873-8635 or visit www.morefreebooks.com.

* Terms and prices subject to change without notice. Prices do not include applicable taxes. N.Y. residents add applicable sales tax. Canadian residents will be charged applicable provincial taxes and GST. Offer not valid in Quebec. This offer is limited to one order per household. All orders subject to approval. Credit or debit balances in a customer's account(s) may be offset by any other outstanding balance owed by or to the customer. Please allow 4 to 6 weeks for delivery. Offer available while quantities last.

Your Privacy: Harlequin Books is committed to protecting your privacy. Our Privacy Policy is available online at www.eHarlequin.com or upon request from the Reader Service. From time to time we make our lists of customers available to reputable third parties who may have a product or service of interest to you. If you would prefer we not share your name and address, please check here. ☐

Help us get it right—We strive for accurate, respectful and relevant communications. To clarify or modify your communication preferences, visit us at www.ReaderService.com/consumerchoice.

HH10R

*See below for a sneak peek at
our inspirational line, Love Inspired®.
Introducing HIS HOLIDAY BRIDE
by bestselling author Jillian Hart*

Autumn Granger gave her horse rein to slide toward the town's new sheriff.

"Hey, there." The man in a brand-new Stetson, black T-shirt, jeans and riding boots held up a hand in greeting. He stepped away from his four-wheel drive with "Sheriff" in black on the doors and waded through the grasses. "I'm new around here."

"I'm Autumn Granger."

"Nice to meet you, Miss Granger. I'm Ford Sherman, from Chicago." He knuckled back his hat, revealing the most handsome face she'd ever seen. Big blue eyes contrasted with his sun-tanned complexion.

"I'm guessing you haven't seen much open land. Out here, you've got to keep an eye on cows or they're going to tear your vehicle apart."

"What?" He whipped around. Sure enough, mammoth black-and-white creatures had started to gnaw on his four-wheel drive. They clustered like a mob, mouths and tongues and teeth bent on destruction. One cow tried to pry the wiper off the windshield, another chewed on the side mirror. Several leaned through the open window, licking the seats.

"Move along, little dogie." He didn't know the first thing about cattle.

The entire herd swiveled their heads to study him curiously. Not a single hoof shifted. The animals soon returned to chewing, licking, digging through his possessions.

Autumn laughed, a warm and wonderful sound. "Thanks,

SHLIEXP1010

I needed that." She then pulled a bag from behind her saddle and waved it at the cows. "Look what I have, guys. Cookies."

Cows swung in her direction, and dozens of liquid brown eyes brightened with cookie hopes. As she circled the car, the cattle bounded after her. The earth shook with the force of their powerful hooves.

"Next time, you're on your own, city boy." She tipped her hat. The cowgirl stayed on his mind, the sweetest thing he had ever seen.

Will Ford be able to stick it out in the country
to find out more about Autumn?
Find out in HIS HOLIDAY BRIDE
by bestselling author Jillian Hart,
available in October 2010
only from Love Inspired®.

SHLIEXP1010